D0839265

The First Time I Fell

JO MACGREGOR

VIP Readers' Group: If you would like to receive my author's newsletter, with tips on great books, a behind-the-scenes look at my writing and publishing processes, and notice of new books, giveaways and special offers, then sign up at my website, www.joannemacgregor.com.

First published in 2019 by Jo Macgregor
ISBN: 978-0-6398109-6-6 (paperback)
ISBN: 978-0-6398109-7-3 (eBook)

Copyright 2019 Jo Macgregor

The right of Joanne Macgregor, writing as Jo Macgregor, to be identified as the author of this work has been asserted by her in accordance with sections 77 and 78 of the Copyright, Designs and Patents Act, 1988.

All rights reserved. No parts of this book may be reproduced or transmitted in any form or by any means, mechanical or electronic, including photocopying and recording, or be stored in any information storage or retrieval system, without the prior written permission of the author.

Disclaimer: This is a work of fiction. All the characters, institutions and events described in it are fictional and the products of the author's imagination.

Cover design by Jenny Zemanek at Seedlings Design Studio.
Formatting by Polgarus Studio

"Birth in the physical is death in the spiritual. Death in the physical is birth in the spiritual."

— Edgar Cayce (1877 – 1945)

– 1 –

Saturday, March 10

There's a first time for everything, they say. My first time at breaking into a house was not going well.

It wasn't surprising, given that I wasn't a professional burglar. My six years of studying psychology had equipped me to breach the defensive walls of the human mind, but for the door in front of me, I needed a key.

I checked under the mat on the top step — which greeted me with a cheerful *Welcome to the nut house!* — but found only a flattened, desiccated spider. Peering under the ceramic pots of blue spruce on either side of the front door and searching the small front yard for a false rock also yielded nothing. Perhaps I'd missed an obvious trick — this was, after all, a gated community in a small town deep in the heart of rural Vermont, where folks weren't too worried about security. I tested the door.

It didn't budge.

I stole around to the rear of the property, keeping an ear open for the sound of dogs, but heard only the crunch of snow under my new Doc Martens. The back door was also locked, but a small square window on the far side of the house was open an inch. Spotting a wrought iron bench under a nearby tree, I dragged it over, placed it directly beneath the window and climbed onto it. Then, groaning with the effort it cost my upper arms, I hoisted myself up.

Lifting the window outward and holding it up with one arm, I slid underneath and pushed forward. The latch dug painfully into my stomach, and when I let go of the pane, it dropped down onto my back, wedging me between the window and the sill, with my torso inside and my legs outside, wriggling like a trapped bug. Pushing the window back open with an elbow, I squirmed through the opening, but as the balance of my weight shifted, I toppled headfirst onto the toilet, breaking my fall with one arm plunged into the bowl before tumbling onto the tiled floor.

Crap. This was *so* not the way I'd wanted to start.

I scrubbed my hands and rinsed my arm at the basin and then dried off on a pink hand towel before heading downstairs to the front door. The interior of the house was almost obsessively neat — I'd ruin that soon enough — and decorated in a frou-frou style that set my teeth on edge. Lladró figurines of shepherdesses, harlequins and kittens were crowded onto shelves, embroidered cushions held court on old-style sofas upholstered in floral linen with ruffled skirts, and potted plants clustered in corners like church gossips. Lace doilies defended the polished surfaces of side tables as well as the hall dresser, where mail addressed to Mr. and Mrs. Andersen stood at attention in a letter rack.

2

I jumped as the doorbell chimed. Dogs barked furiously on the other side of the front door. Someone had noticed my arrival.

I twisted the latch on the lock and opened the door. A slim man stood on the front step, holding the leashes of two beagles that leapt, yelping and yapping, around his feet. He had brown hair and eyes, a thin nose, looked to be in his early forties, and was not unattractive, although the combination of bowtie and thick cardigan was a little prissy. He'd fit right into the Andersen house, though.

He gave me a friendly smile. "You must be the house-sitter. I saw you drive up."

His gaze darted back and forth between my eyes in the way I'd grown used to in the last few months. After I'd died and been resuscitated back before Christmas, the iris of my left eye had gradually turned from blue to brown, and it looked like the change was permanent.

"I'm Ned Lipton. Lipton like the tea, although I'm not related to the family, more's the pity! I'm your neighbor." He gestured to the house on the other side of the picket fence that bordered the Andersen property. "You have no neighbor on the other side," he added, unnecessarily. "Unless you count the hazelnuts."

A small copse of trees, their twiggy branches like black claws frosted with snow, stood on the other side of the Andersen house. That would account for the nutty crack on the doormat.

"Welcome to the neighborhood," he said.

It was a swankier neighborhood than I was used to. Back in Boston, I lived in a small apartment with little furniture, noisy neighbors and a view of a parking lot. Though normally wedded to the bustling anonymity of the city, that morning I'd packed my laptop, a box of academic texts and journal articles, and a suitcase of clothes and toiletries into the trunk of my Honda and driven back to my old hometown. For the month of March, while the elderly Andersens enjoyed a "Sizzling Seniors" ocean cruise to destinations exponentially more exotic than New England, I'd be looking after their house in the Beaumont Golf Estate, taking care of their dogs, and trying my damnedest to finish my master's thesis.

When I'd told my supervisor, Professor Perry, that I no longer intended to be a psychologist and wouldn't be doing a doctorate, he'd been unsurprised, but he'd urged me to complete and submit my thesis anyway.

"That way, at least you'll get your master's degree and have some letters behind your name. Maybe sometime, somewhere, that'll count for something," he'd said, sounding doubtful.

My mother and father, who still lived in Pitchford and were in the same gardening club as the Andersens, had set up the house-sitting gig.

Dad had called to let me know of the offer. "It'll be an ideal opportunity for you to work in a quiet environment with no interruptions."

"And we'll get to see you every day!" Mom had added.

I'd been tempted more by his sales pitch than hers, but I'd vacillated over the decision, having no real desire to return to Pitchford so soon. Or ever. There were many in Pitchford who would not be thrilled by my return, but at least these beagles and Ned Lipton seemed pleased to meet me.

THE FIRST TIME I FELL

I shook my new neighbor's hand. "I'm Garnet McGee. Are these the Andersens' dogs?"

"Yup. The female, this one with the mostly white face, is Lizzie. And this boy" — he indicated the dog with a black patch over its eye — "is Darcy."

"Cute," I said, crouching down to pat the dogs.

Darcy licked my face and Lizzie sniffed my damp sleeve, no doubt wondering why I smelled like toilet water. Ned unwound the leashes from his legs and handed them to me, along with a bag containing a pooper scoop and a box of disposable bags.

"Nancy — Mrs. Andersen — has probably left a long list of instructions for you, but I'll just emphasize that you do need to pick up every single doggy-doo if you don't want to fall foul of the homeowners' association busybodies. And, trust me, you don't."

"Thanks for the heads up."

"If you need a tour around the estate, or a cup of sugar, or for me to keep an eye on the dogs when you go out, just let me know. And, uh" — he straightened his bow tie nervously — "maybe you'd like to come over for drinks or supper sometime? Or we could do some stargazing? The Hephaestus meteor shower peaks this weekend, and I have a great telescope."

"I'm kind of in a relationship already," I lied, trying to let him down gently.

Ned flushed and said, "Of course. Pretty young lady like you is bound to be. Well, I'll be on my way." He turned to go.

"Wait!" I said. "The Andersens didn't happen to leave their keys with you, did they?"

5

"You don't have the keys?"

"I was supposed to get here earlier for the handover."

My neighbor had been called in for an emergency shift at work, and I'd offered to look after her six-month-old baby until the sitter arrived. It was the first time I'd been alone with such a tiny, helpless being, and it had panicked me a little — the scrunched, purple prune of a face howling unintelligibly, the gag-inducing smell from the diaper, the terrifying responsibility. I seriously hoped the Andersens' dogs would be easier to care for.

"They probably left the keys with the guard at the gatehouse for you," Ned said.

"Of course. I should've thought of that."

He nodded, said, "See you around," and was halfway down the path when he turned to ask the question I'd hoped he wouldn't. "So, how did you get inside without keys?"

"I– There was an open window."

He raised his eyebrows at that, but he also smiled and walked off humming a cheerful tune, so I figured he wouldn't be reporting me to the Homeowners' Association for criminal behavior.

− 2 −

I set the door latch so it wouldn't lock me out, closed the door behind me and set off for the guardhouse, with one leash in each hand and the poop emergency bag slung over my shoulder.

The Beaumont Golf Estate was a high-end gated community built just outside the small town of Pitchford, in Windsor County, Vermont. Two- and three-story custom houses with their own swimming pools, tennis courts and patios out back, dotted a gently sloping hill crowned by a dense wood of trees and hemmed by an eighteen-hole golf course perched above the Kent River. From the Andersen house, located near the top of the estate, there was a glorious view of the rolling foothills which stretched all the way across to the snowy ridges of the Green Mountains. Some residents of the town grumbled that gated developments didn't belong in Vermont, that they ruined the sense of space, openness and freedom. They may have been right, but I still wouldn't have said no to owning one of the Beaumont Estate's fine houses.

Both Darcy and Lizzie strained to go faster, dragging me

into the nearby play park that was set like a gem in its surrounding square of luxury houses. At one end of the park, a couple of children played on swings, a teeter-totter and a jungle-gym tastefully constructed from stained pine logs and sisal ropes, while parents looked on indulgently. As we neared the other end, where a few ducks waddled about near a small pond, the beagles went bananas, barking like the hounds of hell and lunging forward. The ducks clustered together and squawked back loudly. Clearly, this was a long-standing feud between the species.

Aware of disapproving looks shot my way, I sternly instructed Lizzie and Darcy to stop their barking and behave. They ignored me. I wasn't even sure they'd heard me, given the racket coming from both the canine and avian factions. I dragged the dogs away from the park, and pausing at most of the trees along the way so the dogs could sniff and anoint trunks, we made our way through the chill afternoon air down the hill in the direction of the gatehouse.

I paused outside the old Beaumont house. Five weeks ago, I'd come back to attend the funeral of Cassie Beaumont, the younger sister of my high-school boyfriend, Colby. The service was unspeakably sad. Mrs. Beaumont was so crushed by the grief of losing another child that it hurt to look at her. Vanessa, her only surviving offspring, had delivered the eulogy with tears streaming down her cheeks. When she spoke of Colby and Cassie now being together on the other side, it took all my self-restraint not to bolt from the church and keep running.

It hadn't been easy, coming face to face with the Beaumont family again. Back in December, I'd unearthed the truth about

Colby's murder ten years previously, when we'd both been high school seniors and desperately in love with each other. But my investigation had set in motion a chain of events which brought more grief, and legal woes aplenty, to the Beaumont family. Mrs. Beaumont had once been closer to me than my own mother, so it cut deep when, at the funeral, she was merely polite. Vanessa had glared at me coldly, then pulled me into a fierce hug and sobbed on my shoulder for long minutes before glaring at me again and storming off without a word.

A realtor sign stuck out front proclaimed the house for sale. No doubt Mrs. Beaumont had no desire to rattle around alone inside its vast interior. According to my father, she was now living at the family's old vacation home on Martha's Vineyard and in the process of getting a divorce. She was probably learning, as I had, that when you leave town, the past doesn't stay behind. It goes right along with you.

"Come on, let's go get those keys," I said to the dogs.

The guard on duty at the gatehouse was a muscle-bound guy with no neck and a loose-lipped smile.

When I enquired about the keys, he said, "Sure, here you go," and handed me a full bunch.

"Why didn't you give them to me when I signed in?"

His face crinkled as he thought about that for a long minute. Then he said, "You didn't ask."

"Slower than molasses on a cold day," I muttered.

"What's that?"

"Nothing. Thanks for these. C'mon, Darcy, Lizzie, let's go." I tugged on their leads, but both dogs were wantonly begging the guard for attention. Darcy licked the guy's fingers, and Lizzie lay on her back, exposing her belly for a rub.

"You staying here long? Can I come over and visit sometime?" the guard said, crouching down to tickle the dogs on the silky white fur of their chests. "The Andersens have ESPN, don't they? We could hang out and watch a few hockey games."

"I already have a boyfriend."

Kind of. If I counted the presence that I sometimes thought I sensed by my side.

"Hey, I don't mind sharing," the guard said.

I yanked Lizzie and Darcy away and we walked back to the house where I unpacked my car and lugged my suitcase upstairs, tripping over the dogs on every other step. The guest bedroom's décor had me sighing so hard that Lizzie tilted her head at me in concerned curiosity. The double bed was trimmed with a scalloped night frill, covered with a pink check comforter, and topped with white lace cushions. A vase of dried lavender flowers stood on the doily-topped bedside table, and three porcelain butterflies took flight across wallpaper patterned with tiny pink rosebuds.

It was enough to induce a seizure in people with healthier brains than my own.

There was nothing to be done about the floral drapes, but I grabbed the cushions, coverlet, doily and flowers, and stashed them in the main bedroom, which was decorated in the same fussy style, but in shades of baby blue.

Downstairs, I checked the contents of the refrigerator and immediately forgave the Andersens their stylistic excesses because, judging by the bottle of pinot grigio sitting on the top shelf beside a covered plate of spaghetti and meat sauce, they clearly had good hearts. Filling a glass with ice cubes, I topped it up with wine and then sat down to read the list of instructions I'd found lying on the dining room table, weighted down by an ugly porcelain clown.

The directions told me what — and when — to feed the dogs; listed emergency numbers; explained where I'd find the breaker box and extra blankets; gave detailed instructions about trash collection and thermostat operation; urged me to eat anything from the refrigerator or cupboards and, I was relieved to see, supplied the password for the wi-fi. Attached to the list was a copy of their itinerary with their contact information, plus a twelve-page-long list of rules and regulations for the Estate. I shoved it all into the mail tray on the hall dresser and stuck the clown into a neat row of figurines on a shelf in the living room.

The dogs vacuumed up the kibble I poured into their bowls in less time than it took me to reheat my meal in the microwave, then they sat at my feet, staring up at me while I ate. Their pleading eyes followed every movement of my fork, and their pitiful whines finally induced me to feed each a few saucy strands of spaghetti, in clear violation of item seventeen on Mrs. Andersen's list.

After supper, I set my laptop on the desk in the study and tried to dredge up a smidgeon of motivation to put in some work on my thesis, but was saved from doing more than looking up the precise definition of "proximity maintenance" by an incoming call on my cell phone.

"Hi, Mom," I said and, before she could ask, added, "Yes, I arrived safely."

"Well, thank St. Christopher for travel mercies!" my mother said, then yelled into the background, "She's safe, Bob!" To me, she said, "Your father was beginning to worry."

"I was just about to call you," I lied.

"We were hoping to see you tonight."

"Oh. Tomorrow, maybe? I'm beat."

That was true. I was kidding myself about getting any work done that night. Besides, I had weeks and weeks to finish it — it could wait until the morning. At that moment, the lightbulb in the desktop lamp flickered and then went out. It seemed like a sign, so I switched off my computer.

"Are you all settled in? What's the place like?" my mother asked.

I strolled to the living room, glancing around. "It's very neat and very ... *nice.*" From the shelf beside the TV screen, the porcelain clown leered at me, its red grin reminding me unpleasantly of the guard at the gatehouse. "Too nice actually." I pushed the figurine further back on the shelf and turned it around to face the wall. "So nice, it's kind of creepy."

"Gracious, Garnet, what nonsense you talk."

"That's rich, coming from you!" I protested.

My mother was the mistress of malapropisms and mangled language, and the undisputed queen of far-fetched beliefs and silly superstitions.

"How can anything be *too* nice?" Without waiting for an answer, she began rattling on about all the things we were going to do now that I was in town. "Jessica Armstrong's gallery has a new show, and wouldn't it be wonderful to take your two fur-babies to the Dog Chapel in St. Johnsbury and have them blessed? St. Francis, you know! We could do the tour and tasting at Sweet 'n Smoky Maple Syrups, and did you ever do the Windsor cheese trail?"

I tested the couch and found it amazingly comfortable.

"Mom, I'm here to work on my thesis. We're not going to be spending that much time together."

Whenever my mother and I were in each other's company for more than half an hour, she rubbed my nerves raw with her linguistic and metaphysical meanderings.

"Yes, dear, but you will need to take a break *sometimes.*"

"I'll swing by tomorrow," I promised.

"Come for dinner. I'll make Mexican."

"The real kind? With meat?" According to my father's weekly calls, my mother was going through a phase of cooking with tofu and chickpeas. And "Quorn," whatever the heck that was.

"If you insist," she said. "Sweet dreams, and may the goddess grant you restful sleep."

I wouldn't need any divine assistance to sleep — my eyes were already drooping. Lizzie was curled up fast asleep at the other end of the couch, in violation of another of Mrs. Andersen's rules, and Darcy snored on the carpeted floor beside my feet.

The dogs were behaving normally around me. That was a huge relief because after the weird reactions I'd received from cats and dogs during December, I'd worried that this dog-sitting gig might not be a cakewalk. But the beagles hadn't whimpered or growled at me, or stared off to my left side as if seeing something that wasn't there.

My brain seemed to be behaving normally, too. In December, I'd been haunted by strange symptoms — being overwhelmed by intense feelings that weren't my own, hearing words inside my head, and having visions and seeing memories of things I'd never witnessed in person — but I'd experienced nothing weird since then.

Almost nothing.

There'd been a few odd things, but I'd chalked them up to coincidence, post-traumatic stress disorder, and a fertile imagination. True, at Cassie's funeral I'd felt swamped by soul-crushing sadness, but surely that was just grief, and a reaction to being in the very church where, ten years before, I'd sat through the funeral of her brother, Colby, who'd been the love of my life. Yes, my mind had teemed with unfamiliar images of Cassie as a little girl, but maybe I'd just recollected long-forgotten memories.

The one thing that did still baffle me was that wherever I sat — at the counter of my favorite bar in Beacon Hill, on a crowded subway car, in the waiting room at the dentist — the seat to the left of me invariably remained unoccupied. I had yet to find an explanation or rationalization that accounted for that particular peculiarity.

"Time for bed," I told the dogs.

I let them out into the yard for a last pee before tucking them into their baskets in the laundry room. They peered out from beneath their blankets, but the moment I turned to leave, they jumped out and followed me to the kitchen door. Hardening my heart against the guilt-inducing entreaty in their liquid brown eyes, I shut the door firmly behind me. Mrs.

Andersen's instruction on this had been underlined for emphasis — _no dogs on the beds!_

I took a long shower, letting the hot water soothe my elbow and shoulder, which ached from where I'd banged them on the toilet and bathroom floor. Before getting into bed, I stood at my bedroom window, nibbling a nail and staring out into the darkness for long minutes. Somebody was taking their own dog for a late walk up the road. The park across the way was deserted, lit by the yellow glow of streetlights. Wind whipped at the flag on the pole in my neighbor's front yard. Ned was out on his porch, swinging the tube of a large telescope up toward the sky. It was a clear night and the viewing would be good, but he must be a dedicated stargazer to be out in this cold.

Downstairs, the dogs whined and scratched at the door, pleading to be let out of their kitchen prison. I closed my drapes, burrowed under my duvet and, yawning, stared at the rosebud wallpaper on the wall beside the bed. Up close, by the faint light filtering through the drapes into the room, I could make out forms and faces in the patterns.

I remembered doing this as a child, finding images in the pattern of the paint or wallpaper and making up stories about them. _Pareidolia_ — my sleepy mind dredged up the term for the psychological phenomenon of finding meaningful patterns, especially human figures and faces, in random data. If I remembered correctly, it had something to do with the activation of the fusiform brain region.

My own fusiform neurons must have been firing energetically just then because I could see smiling baby faces in some of the petals, and extended hands in the shapes of the leaves. My gaze kept being pulled back to the gap between the buds where the shape and shading exactly resembled the creepy face of a stern old man. In my imagination, he looked like a devil — the serrated edges of the surrounding rose leaves formed sharp horns, the thorns made slanted eyes, and the wedge of white between adjacent stalks and stems was his pointed beard.

The shape was repeated about every five inches in the pattern. I tried to estimate how many of them — hundreds? thousands? — must be on the walls of this room, watching me. At some point in my calculations, under the gaze of countless fiends, I fell asleep.

− 3 −

The next morning, I forced myself to put in a few hours on my thesis, using the theory of phenomenology to explain unique individual narratives of the grieving process. Riveting stuff.

Just like the dogs pacing the room and whining at the front door, I longed to get outside and stretch my legs. At eleven o'clock, I gave in to the temptation to take a break. Promising myself that I'd return to the mystery of mourning later, I shrugged on my parka, dumped my phone, a bottle of water and an apple into a small backpack, grabbed my knitted gloves and beanie, and asked the dogs, "Want to go for a walk?"

Those words, they understood. They leapt up and ran to the door, yelping with excitement. I fastened their leashes, grabbed a couple of poop bags and stepped outside, locking the door behind me — it would take more than the three-hour drive from Boston to Pitchford to shed my big-city paranoia.

It was freezing outside. There was no wind, but the feeble March sun was blotted out by dense gray clouds which threatened to add more snow to the piles that lingered in shady spots. Pushing the leads over my wrists, I shoved my hands deep in my pockets, fiddling with the two crystals that still nestled there. One, a light mauve lepidolite stone, was a gift from my mother, who swore it would assist me in decision-making. The other, a purple amethyst I'd found at Plover Pond, was supposed to be good for sharpening my "third eye."

Darcy and Lizzie were eager to resume hostilities with the ducks, but I steered clear of the park and strode up the hill to the copse of trees at the very top of the estate. I had planned to walk the perimeter of the whole property, but when we reached the fence, I discovered a gate secured with just a bolt. So much for the estate's advertised "hi-tech impenetrable security." Beyond the gate, a path disappeared invitingly into the woods beyond.

"What do you say we go for a *real* walk?" I asked the dogs, eager to burn off both their and my restless energy.

Darcy yelped once and Lizzie did a little dance on the spot, which I took to mean they were in favor of an adventure, so we headed out. The trail was overgrown in places and littered with sticks and the odd fallen tree. The ground underfoot was spongy with the mulch of pine needles, leaves, moss and lichen. Snow lay lightly on branches and against the north sides of boulders and tree trunks, but here and there, yellow coltsfoot flowers were testing whether spring had routed winter yet. The trill of waxwings high above me added a high-pitched harmony to the gurgled *conk-a-reee* of an early blackbird and the rapid drumming of grouse in the underbrush below. Spring wasn't here yet, but it was on its way.

Lizzie seemed determined to sniff as many trees as possible, but Darcy was more interested in those that sheltered birds and other creatures in their branches. He refused to budge from the base of an enormous beech until a bushy-tailed squirrel sprang onto the branch of a neighboring tree and disappeared from view.

The path headed downhill for a way, then leveled out and curved around to the left, belting the base of the hill. We walked almost all the way around to the north side, and I was contemplating turning back when our path merged with another trail coming up from below. White tails wagging furiously, the dogs sniffed the intersection in excitement, perhaps picking up on smells that had been absent from our route.

I used the moment to catch my breath and was gulping water from my bottle when Darcy gave a sudden loud yelp and took off at top speed, yanking his leash out of my hand. A second later, he was out of sight, apparently hot on the trail of some irresistible scent.

Oh, crap. Day two of my job and I'd already lost a dog. Weren't you supposed to be better at adulting by the age of twenty-eight?

When I'd told Professor Perry I'd be baby-sitting beagles, he'd laughed uproariously for several minutes and wished me luck. Then he'd said, "Be warned, beagles are hounds, originally bred for the hunt. That means they bay and howl like the devil himself day and night, and you should never let them off the leash in an open area because once they catch a scent, they'll chase it all the way to its source. Which usually means losing their owner."

I'd thought he was exaggerating. I'd been wrong.

Lizzie strained at her own leash, yowling and barking, eager to follow her mate. At least I still had her — that would help me track him down, wouldn't it? We set off at a jog along the path, following the route I thought Darcy had taken. While I could see neither hide nor hair of him, I could still hear distant baying.

Alternately cursing and calling for Darcy, I half-ran, half-stumbled along the climbing trail, until we reached the tumbledown remains of an old chain-link fence. Rusted signs declared the area beyond to be the private property of Rare Rock Stone Works and warned that trespassers entered at their own risk.

I knew this place. I recognized the signs and the fence — more dilapidated now than it had been when I was a teenager — and knew what lay in the center of the clearing beyond it. My heart kicked into a faster rhythm because although I could tell by the volume of Darcy's agitated barking that he was close by, I also now knew that he was in danger.

This part of Vermont was riddled with quarries. Most of them were for granite, slate and marble, some with vast tunnels that burrowed into the sides of hills and mountains. On the other side of this fence lay a quarry, abandoned in the seventies when carving out slabs of the dark-green serpentine rock used for floors, countertops and fireplace facings became too expensive in a market flooded with cheaper imports from India and Eastern Europe. The deep hole left behind had filled with water from a nearby spring and soon became a favorite summer swimming hole for Pitchford's teens.

The path that had merged with the one the dogs and I had

been walking was a short one which led down to a parking lot just off the highway. Because it was hidden from view by a thick border of hedges, that lot had been a favorite make-out spot for many a couple, including Colby and me.

In the summer before I left Pitchford, I'd spent many golden days up at the quarry, swimming and drinking beer with Colby and my best friend, Jessica, and other seniors from Pitchford High. Although the pit had steep sides, it was possible to hike down to the bottom, where a couple of smooth rock terraces made an ideal spot to laze and tan when the sun was overhead.

The quarry itself wasn't enormous — maybe about three hundred feet deep and about one hundred and fifty by two hundred yards across — with ledges jutting out at varying levels along its vertical rock faces. Everyone agreed that the murky pool at the bottom was seriously deep. Some said it went down sixty feet, some said ninety, but no one knew for sure. That didn't deter the cliff-jumping thrill-seekers who regularly hurled themselves off the ledges. I'd thought myself brave leaping off a ten-foot-high ledge, but others — mostly guys, there was a reason women tended to live longer than men — had spent hours carelessly diving and somersaulting off ledges way higher up, plummeting into the cold, dark water below, their shouts and splashes echoing off the high quarry walls. Between the underage drinking and adolescent delusions of invincibility, it was a wonder none of us got killed or paralyzed.

That serpentine quarry was the spot above us where Darcy's barks now came from.

My yells and whistles for him were met with a renewed

frenzy of yaps and yelps. There was no help for it, I'd have to follow him and physically haul him back.

"Wait," I told Lizzie. She ignored me. "Stop. Whoa." No, that was for horses. "Stay?" She tilted her head at me. "Stay!" I repeated firmly. "Sit."

She sat but looked ready to bolt at any moment, so I tied her to a section of fence, knotting the leash twice. Ignoring the signs which threatened to prosecute my trespassing ass, I stepped over the sagging fence and made my way between scrubby bushes and thinning trees toward the center of the clearing at the top of the hill, where tufts of dried grass, jutting through the snow like dark stubble on a white face, crunched beneath my feet.

When I caught sight of Darcy, my gut went cold, and my knees felt suddenly unsteady. He stood perilously close to the edge of the hole, barking and staring at something down below.

"Darcy, Darcy, come here, boy," I cajoled through a tight throat.

He turned to face me, whined, and then resumed his scrutiny of the pit whose sheer sides fell away mere inches from where he bounced on his paws.

I edged over to him, but when I reached down to grab the trailing end of his leash, he leapt sideways, slipping on the loose gravel at the sloping lip of the quarry. Swallowing hard, I edged closer to Darcy, talking to him in a singsong hypnotic voice, trying to soothe him into standing still.

"Darcy, hey boy, please stay cool. Just sit and stay and don't move any closer to that edge, okay? Good boy, Darcy, good boy."

His leash now lay on the ground, parallel with the side of the hole. The handle dangled over the edge. I inched closer, keeping up the soothing murmurs.

"I'm just going to step on the leash, Darcy. Stay cool." I trod down on the closest section of it, pinning it in place. "And now I'm going to grab it, please don't freak out and pull me over the edge into oblivion, okay? I've already died once and have zero desire to do it again."

Moving as slowly as I could, I bent over and grasped the leash. Wrapping it securely around my hand, I kept my muscles braced against another possible lunge. Although Darcy was safe — or at least *safer* — now, I felt no relief. On the contrary, my heart was racing, a cold sweat beaded my top lip, and my heavy limbs rooted me to the spot. Despite the evidence of rapid puffs of frosty air from my mouth, I felt like I couldn't breathe, like the air was being sucked from my lungs. Was I having a panic attack?

No. No!

The words were loud in my mind, and in a voice that wasn't my own. As though magnetized, my head turned, and I peered over into the looming abyss below. As I stared, the high, perpendicular sides buckled and undulated in my vision. Dizziness surged.

And I saw the cause of Darcy's upset.

− 4 −

Approximately one hundred feet directly below me, a wide snow-covered ledge jutted out from the quarry wall. On it, spread-eagled on the snow, lay a body.

Long black hair fanned out in a grisly halo, melding with a pool of blood, dark against the frozen white. Black-clad arms and legs lay at impossible angles. The absence of life lay heavy and solid as a shroud over the still form.

I dragged Darcy several yards back from the edge of the quarry before removing my gloves and fumbling in my backpack for my phone. A single bar of signal came and went. Fetching Lizzie, I pulled both dogs down the path, hoping to find a spot with a stronger signal.

I forged through the scrub and trees to where a huge boulder erupted from the ground some twenty yards off the path and tied the dogs to a couple of sturdy bushes. Darcy flopped down — clearly exhausted by all that running and barking — and Lizzie immediately began digging in the dirt under a bush. I clambered up the rock, slipping and scraping the palm of one hand on my way to the top, then checked my phone's screen. Two bars. Hands still shaking, I called the cops and returned to the path to wait for their arrival, leaving the dogs at the boulder, where they'd be out of the way.

Less than an hour later, the quarry was abuzz with local cops, a State Police Search and Rescue team wearing vivid orange jackets, and a couple of paramedics whose services would be of no use to the poor woman in the quarry.

Ryan Jackson, Chief of Pitchford's tiny police department, was in charge of the scene. Once he'd directed everyone to their tasks, he came over to where I stood a little way off the path, hands in my pockets, clicking the crystals together like worry-beads. For an awkward moment I wondered if I should give him a hug. I *wanted* a hug, wanted for just a moment to lean against someone solid and strong, especially if that someone was Ryan Jackson.

But as I took a step toward him, he said, "Hey, Garnet. Here you are at the scene of a death again."

"Yeah."

"I didn't even know you were back in town."

From his tone, I could tell he wasn't overjoyed that I hadn't let him know.

"I only arrived yesterday afternoon," I explained.

His slate-gray eyes scrutinized me for a moment. "You're shivering. Can I get an extra jacket for you? Or a blanket?"

I shook my head. It wasn't the cold that had me shaking.

"Up to giving me a statement?"

"Sure."

Speaking into his phone's recorder, I told him what I'd found and how, leaving out the part about my panicky reaction at the side of the pit. We were just finishing up when a heavyset police officer with a grimly excited expression came up to Ryan.

"Garnet, this is Officer Veronica — Ronnie — Capshaw. Ronnie, this is the witness who found the body."

She gave me a nod and handed Ryan a plastic evidence bag. "We got into that Jeep Renegade in the lot down below, and I think we've got a probable identity on the dead woman."

Trying to be unobtrusive about it, I edged close enough to see that the bag contained a driver's license.

In a low voice, Capshaw said, "And there was a note on the passenger seat."

Blue paper.
A trembling hand holding a piece of pale-blue paper scrawled with big, loopy handwriting.

The flash lasted only a moment, and then my vision cleared, and I saw the cop pass another evidence bag to Ryan. Inside was a sheet of pale-blue paper, creased along two folds.
What the hell?

Curious, I sidled up behind Ryan and peered over his shoulder to read the note.

Dear Bethany,
  I'm so sorry to do this to you. I know I'm leaving you with a mess to handle. I think you've known, or guessed, for a while now that this was coming — you've always known me better than I've known myself. I know you'll

26

be angry with me for making this choice, but honestly, I
can't continue living this kind of life.
   All my love,
   Laini xoxo

"Suicide, sir?" Capshaw asked, catching me snooping and shooting me a disapproving look.

I stepped back and pretended to be checking my phone.

"Looks like it," Ryan replied.

There was a commotion at the edge of the quarry as the recovery team winched the rescue stretcher up over the lip of the pit. When they carried it down over the fence to the yellow-taped perimeter of the scene, Ryan held up a hand for them to stop. He unzipped the top of the black body bag strapped to the stretcher and compared the face inside to the photograph on the driver's license.

Sighing, he turned to his officer. "I think it's her, Ronnie, but we'll need a formal identification. Find a family member or good friend."

"I'm on it."

She disappeared back down the trail while Ryan tried to close the body bag. But the woman's hair had gotten caught in the zipper, and it wouldn't go all the way. Giving up, Ryan signaled to the two men holding the stretcher that they could go on. As they stepped over the police tape, one of the men turned his ankle on a rock and stumbled. The stretcher tipped sideways toward me, and I glimpsed a section of white forehead bordered with a streak of dark blood and a clot of gore matting the black hair above. I thrust out a hand to stop it tipping onto me. My palm landed on the body bag, and my fingers touched that cold skin, that sticky mess.

Images and sensations fluttered into being inside my mind.

Laughing, I flick my long hair back from my face.
"What?" I say. "You can't be serious."
My laughter turns to nervousness. To fear. I can feel the fierce sting of it flooding my body. It's so cold up here, but I'm sweating.
"Stop. What are you doing?"
Pressure on my chest. Hands pushing.
"No. No!"
A sudden shove. And I'm over the edge.
Falling, falling.
Tumbling through space.
An endless instant of rushing air.
The wind steals my breath.
I want to fly, to float free, to—
Impact.

The wave of shock sent me toppling to the ground. I could hear the stretcher guy apologizing profusely — he thought he'd knocked me over — and Ryan was at my side, helping me to my feet.

"I'm okay. I'm fine," I said, then turned away and deposited the remains of my breakfast behind a nearby bush.

"Here." Ryan handed me a handkerchief and a bottle of water.

A little hysterically, I wondered who still carried handkerchiefs.

Cops, that's who. For wiping tears, vomit, blood and brains. I muttered my thanks, rinsed my mouth and spat, wiped my face and brushed splatters of sick off the toes of my boots. Pushed away that terrifying infinity of when I fell.

No, when *she* fell.

"Can you…?" I passed him the bottle and held my hands underneath as he poured, rubbing the fingertips that had touched that face. I wanted soap and a scrubbing brush.

"I'll get Ronnie to type up your statement," Ryan said. "You'll need to come in to check and sign it, but tomorrow will be fine for that. You can go home to your parents' now."

I wiped my hands against my jeans, trying to rub off the sensation that lingered there. "I'm staying at Bill and Nancy Andersen's house in the Beaumont estate — house-sitting and looking after the dogs while they're away this month."

"So you'll be here for a while this time?" Ryan said, a smile teasing at the corner of his mouth.

Back in December, when I was investigating Colby's death, I'd spent a fair amount of time with Ryan. True, for a while I'd suspected he might be a cold-blooded killer, but really, I'd been happy to be proved wrong. Because Ryan was a good guy — smart and funny, and attractive too, with his black hair, vivid gray eyes and tall, lean build. I'd kissed him once, and when I'd popped back into town in February for Cassie's funeral, we'd met up for drinks. It had been fun, but we'd both known I was going straight back to Boston, so we'd kept it light.

Now, with me in Pitchford for the whole of March, we could, if we wanted, pick up where we'd left off. *Was* that what I wanted? I wasn't sure. The thought of opening myself up to a relationship scared me. Because back when my heart had stopped beating in Plover Pond's frozen depths, it hadn't been the first time I'd died. Not really.

The first time I died was when Colby was killed. That's when I'd shut down, pulled back from human connection, retreated into a decade-long winter of emotional numbness, and vowed never to love again. There had been some slight thawing of my frozen heart in the last few months, but I wasn't yet sure that I was capable of falling in love again, let alone eager to try.

But I was getting way ahead of the game. Ryan hadn't offered a relationship. Hell, he hadn't even asked me out for a cup of coffee, and already I was sniffing out reasons to avoid seeing him again.

"Ronnie will give you and the dogs a ride back," Ryan said, summoning his junior officer.

"Thanks," I said, grateful for the offer because suddenly, I felt utterly exhausted. Walking all the way back to the estate was more than I could face. All I wanted was a hot bath, a giant mug of bitter coffee and a couple of Tylenols for the headache behind my eyes.

I'd already taken a few steps down the path when I turned back. "Hey, Ryan, that woman's death — could it have been murder?"

His brow creased. "Why would you think that?"

"Just ... just a feeling."

Yeah, a feeling of being pushed.

– 5 –

I walked down the path to the parking lot in a daze, towing the dogs along behind me; they seemed eager to return to the excitement of the quarry.

Just exactly what had I experienced up there? Seeing and hearing and feeling things that weren't my own — this could *not* be starting all over again. I was done with it. Had been done with it ever since I solved the mystery of Colby's murder. I'd only been inundated with his experiences because he'd been Colby, because I'd known him so intimately and had never fully let him go, never truly accepted that he was dead and gone. But once I'd identified his killer, and justice was done, the weirdness had subsided.

I'd made peace with the fact that he was dead. I'd given myself permission to heal and to start living again. And I'd known — *known* — that all this bizarre shit was over and done with.

So, what the hell had I just experienced? I didn't know the dead woman, didn't think I'd ever even met her. So why was I seeing her last moments, hearing her last words, and feeling her terror? I tried to tell myself that I was imagining things. That I'd dreamed up a version of her death in my heightened state of distress, that what I'd experienced while standing next to Darcy at the edge of the quarry had indeed merely been just a panic attack. I told myself that must be it.

But I didn't believe it.

Officer Capshaw opened the back of Ryan's police SUV so the dogs — both with muddy paws, and Lizzie with a stick between her teeth — could jump inside. Either my driver just wasn't a chatty Cathy, or she was annoyed at having to leave the action up at the quarry in order to chauffeur me home, but the ride back to the Beaumont Estate was done in silence, which suited me fine.

Inside the Andersen house, I went directly to the downstairs bathroom to wash my hands, shuddering as I remembered the sight and feel of that body. I kept seeing flashbacks of the white face, the hair as black as coal, the halo of red around her broken head as she lay like some macabre version of Snow White on her frozen bed in the quarry. I pushed the images out of my mind and changed my clothes. As I threw my jeans, shirt and underwear into the washing machine, I used a psychological grounding technique to anchor myself in the present.

Four things I could see — stains on my jeans, laundry detergent, the extra-hot setting on the machine, the red tin of dog treats on top of the refrigerator.

Three things I could hear — panting dogs, the washer starting its cycle, a dripping faucet.

Two things I could feel by touch — the wool of my sweater, the scarred surface of a wooden chopping board.

One thing I could smell or taste — mint.

The kitchen smelled faintly of mint. Nice. I should get some of whatever product was the source of that scent for my own tiny kitchen back in Boston.

I filled the dogs' water bowls and swallowed an entire glass myself, noticing that my hands still weren't completely steady. I needed something stronger. Opening the refrigerator, I was shocked to see that less than a glass of wine remained in the bottle on the top shelf — I'd clearly drunk too much last night.

Someone famous once said that the true test of character is what one does when nobody's watching, which made me an unrepentant lushy pants because I downed the last of the wine directly from the bottle. I *did* throw the empty bottle into the glass recycling bin, so at least I was an eco-friendly lushy pants.

In the living room, I parked myself on the couch in front of the TV and began channel-surfing. Images of people in orange jackets swarming around a familiar scene arrested my attention. A local news channel was already at the quarry, showing a carousel of repeating footage — lingering shots of the bloodstained snow on the ledge at the quarry; forensic experts in white protective suits and booties packing up their gear; rescue workers and state police leaning up against their vehicles in the lot below while they smoked and checked phones, enjoying the respite before the next alert of danger or death.

When the images were replaced by live footage of a reporter, I turned up the volume then tossed the remote aside.

"The identity of the woman found in the quarry is known to police but is being withheld until her next of kin are informed," he said solemnly.

I recognized this guy — he was one of the reporters who'd covered the story when Colby's murder had finally been solved. He had perfectly coiffed hair and an impressive set of brilliantly white teeth which he loved to flash in a smile so wide it was unsettling. Right now, he wore a grave expression perfectly suited to the occasion, but his eyes glittered with excitement. No doubt he was enjoying the opportunity to report on something more newsworthy than warnings of heavy snowfalls and icy roads.

While I watched, I dug the nail of a forefinger into the rough edge of skin beside my thumb, picking and tugging until I worked a filament of skin loose.

According to police, The Hair solemnly announced, "No foul play was suspected."

He tilted his head a fraction and sighed, wordlessly conveying that suicide *was* suspected, and then briskly urged me to stay tuned for developments in the story. If what I'd experienced at the quarry was real, and much as I didn't want it to be, it sure as sugar had felt like it was, then I might be ahead of the news on this story.

A warning growl drew my attention to where Lizzie lay on the carpet, jealously defending her stick from Darcy. No, not a stick — it looked more like a bone. Even as my conscious mind tried to recall whether Mrs. Andersen had outlawed bone-chewing in the living room, my subconscious was taking in the color, size and shape of Lizzie's treat, automatically comparing it to my memory bank of dog bones and concluding that something was very wrong.

I noted the strange curved arch, like an elongated comma,

the creamy bone showing through the brown dirt and discoloration, the ends — one smooth, one knobbly. It looked horribly like a rib. A human rib.

Wanting to examine it more closely, I reached for it. Lizzie bared her teeth and seemed set to do battle with me if I tried to wrest it away from her.

"Hey!" I yelled at her. "Drop that."

Probably more in surprise at my harsh tone than in obedience to my command, she opened her mouth and let the bone fall to the carpet. I snatched it up.

The impact slammed into me like a blow. I heard no words and saw no images. A black nothingness saturated my field of vision. Paralyzing terror swamped me. At the point of contact with the thing in my hand, I was plugged into a source of something ancient and primal which contracted my stomach into a tight knot, slowly squeezed the air from my lungs, and dried my mouth. A deep, creeping darkness, like distilled eons of fear and dread and despair, filled me with crushing heaviness, tugged me down.

With a sharp cry, I dropped the bone and fell back onto the couch. Wiping a clammy, trembling hand across my mouth, I sucked in ragged breaths of air, blinking as my vision restored itself and I returned from the void, back to the warm, bright room where the TV promised I'd be "in good hands" if I bought their insurance. Darcy yawned from his spot at my feet, and Lizzie was back to gnawing on the bone.

I cursed — long, loud and savagely. This was a whole new level of disturbing.

After a few minutes of deep, slow breathing, I was able to

stand. I searched the kitchen, then returned to the living room wearing a pair of rubber gloves and carrying an old grocery bag and a couple of dog biscuits. Luring Lizzie away with the treats, I tentatively touched the arched bone with one gloved finger. Nothing. I snatched it up and stuffed it into the bag, then hung it on the hook with the dog leashes, well out of the dogs' reach.

Then I called Ryan.

"So," I said, "my dog found a bone."

– 6 –

"Dog finds bone? Alert *The Bugle*," Ryan said on the other end of the phone. His tone was good-natured, but I could hear the strain of the day's events in his voice.

"Thing is, she found it up at the quarry," I said. "And I think it might be human."

"Damn."

"It looks really old."

I was hyperaware of the fingers and palm of my right hand. They didn't tingle, precisely, but I couldn't shake the sense that they'd been contaminated by touching that bone.

"Do you know whereabouts she found it?"

"I think so."

I described the huge boulder in the thicket of bushes way off the path. While I spoke, I went upstairs to my bathroom. Washing my hands would at least remove any microbes from my skin, though I doubted it would cleanse the dark taint lingering in my mind. When I got to the basin, cold water was dripping from the faucet. I shoved the lever to the left. What I needed was hot water, and lots of it.

A thought occurred to me.

"I could be completely wrong, though," I said to Ryan. "About it being human, I mean. It's probably from a moose or a deer."

That would be the most logical explanation. Why hadn't I thought of it immediately?

"We'll check. Ronnie and the forensic team will search that spot in case there's more to find, but I'll come over and get the bone from you now."

"Okay, see you soon."

With Ryan on his way, I probably didn't have time for a shower, but I scrubbed my hands thoroughly with a nailbrush, wincing as the soap and hot water stung my scraped hand. Then I washed my face and, still feeling unclean, brushed my teeth, too.

I turned off the faucet, checked it wasn't dripping, and then texted my mother, telling her something unexpected had come up and we'd need to reschedule supper to the next night. Ryan arrived a few minutes later. The dogs, predictably, launched into a cacophony of barking. My heart lifted a little to see his face, though I wished he was visiting under different circumstances.

When he bent over to pat the dogs for a moment — Lizzie was leaping up against him, whining for his attention, while Darcy was snuffling around his boots — I snuck a look at his rear. Nice and lean. I pulled my gaze away before he caught me checking out his booty, and led him inside the house.

Not wanting to go near the bag with the bone, I merely pointed him in the direction of it. He peered inside the bag and grimaced. "Oh yeah, I'm pretty sure that's a human rib. The

Medical Examiner's office will confirm it."

"I touched it, and Lizzie chewed on it," I confessed, watching as he donned latex gloves to drop the bone into a large evidence bag. "And this is going to sound funny —"

"Funny-haha, or funny-strange?"

"Strange." Definitely strange. I began chewing on a nail, then remembered what my fingers had touched and dropped my hand.

"Let's hear it."

"When I touched it, I felt —" How to say this? "I got a bad feeling, like a sense that there's something ... wrong with it."

"It's a human rib, Garnet, found in the wilds. I'm guessing our John or Jane Doe didn't have a peaceful death at home with family gathered around singing *Swing Low, Sweet Chariot*. You wouldn't need much imagination to think that this" — he waved the bagged rib at me — "has some unpleasant history."

That made sense. Of course a human bone found where this one had been would likely have some bad story attached to it. I would unconsciously have known this, and my imagination might have rushed in to create the accompanying visceral "soundtrack" of doom and gloom. But while my rational mind seized on this perfectly logical explanation, the rest of me remained unconvinced.

Because I hadn't imagined it.

What I'd experienced had been deeply disturbing, terrifying even. It hadn't been the normal thrill of horror — that almost pleasant mixture of excitement, relief and morbid fascination — that a person sometimes feels when they brush up against remote tragedy. There was nothing normal about what I'd felt.

"Yeah, that's true, but …" My voice trailed off as I weighed the wisdom of saying more.

For one thing, I liked Ryan. I thought he might be interested in me, too. I didn't want to ruin any good opinion he might have of me.

Back in December, he'd witnessed some of my strange behavior, but I'd never explicitly told him what I'd seen and heard, and I'd ducked his questions on how I'd known facts I shouldn't have been able to, merely telling him my conclusions must have been lucky guesses. But back then, I'd been convinced I was going crazy, or that what I was experiencing was temporary. Now I was starting to think differently.

So, I teetered on the edge of a cliff of my own. Should I take the leap and tell Ryan Jackson the truth? Trusting didn't come naturally to me; it came harder than when my seventeen-year-old self leapt off the high ledge at the quarry and fell into the water hole below. Back then, I'd been buoyed up by beer and Colby's encouragement. Now I was stone cold sober, and on my own.

I thought again of that woman lying broken on the frozen ledge at the quarry, saw a flashback — black, white and red — of her crumpled body. According to my gut, and what I'd "seen" and felt, her plummet off that cliff had not been voluntary. The cops, however, seemed set to write her death off as suicide. How much did that matter to me?

With Colby, I'd felt I owed him, that I needed to ensure justice was done for his sake. But this victim was a stranger to me. Did I owe her anything? I thought maybe I did, that maybe we humans were all bound together by an invisible web of humanity, and that we owed each other a duty of care. Bottom line: if that had been me lying dead on the snowy ice, and someone else suspected I'd been murdered, I'd want them to speak up.

The irony of an atheist speculating about what she'd want when she no longer existed to have any preferences or volition wasn't lost on me.

"But?" Ryan prompted.

"We're going to need coffee for this."

The dogs followed us into the kitchen, but as soon as they realized that no food was in the offing, they flopped into their baskets. I put on the coffeemaker, and keeping my gaze on the machine so that I didn't have to see Ryan's expression, I tried to explain this strange stuff in a way that wouldn't sound embarrassingly insane.

"I never told you this, but in the weeks after I drowned, I had a couple of strange experiences — episodes, I guess you could call them — when I felt and saw and kind of heard things."

The first drops of coffee trickling into the pot were loud in the silence that followed.

"What, like flashbacks or memories?" Ryan asked.

"Yes, both of those. But they were of things *I'd* never experienced. They were other people's memories," I said, risking a glance at Ryan to check his reaction.

He didn't laugh. But he didn't say anything else, either. No doubt he was waging an inner war between amused incredulity and innate good manners.

"The memories — they were mostly Colby's."

Ryan's lips tightened a fraction.

"Look, I know it sounds insane," I said, before he could. "For a long time, I thought that it *was* insane, that I was having a mental breakdown, or that my symptoms were due to post-traumatic stress or concussion. I even checked in with my psych professor, and for the record, he didn't think I'd gone off the deep end."

Ryan nodded, perhaps relieved to see I could appreciate the absurdity of what I was saying and had taken appropriate measures to have my mental state assessed. That while I may have boarded the express train to Woowooville, I hadn't yet reached the end of the line.

The coffeemaker sputtered and I poured us each a cup. Ryan took his with cream but no sugar; I took mine black and bitter, like I had ever since I'd drowned. Like Colby had taken his. I sipped it, welcoming the searing heat.

"And then all the weird stuff stopped." More or less. "I thought it was gone for good."

"But it's back?" Ryan asked.

"When I touched that bone, and before, at the quarry, I experienced more ... funny stuff."

"Was that when you turned as white as a sheet and fell over?"

I nodded, waiting for him to dismiss the incidents, or at least make light of them.

Instead, he said, "Your eyelids were fluttering. Same as they did that time I found you going fetal at the Pond."

I shrugged. I would've thought that when I saw the flashes, my eyes would behave as they did in dream sleep — moving rapidly from side to side as they scanned the inner scenes playing out in my mind's eye.

"So, what did you experience?" he asked, sounding genuinely curious.

I explained what I'd felt at the top of the cliff and when I'd accidentally touched the body. The fear and panic, the feeling of having been pushed. How I'd had a flash of the blue note paper a microsecond before I'd actually seen it, and that it hadn't felt like *déjà vu.*

Ryan watched me closely while I spoke and nodded noncommittally when I finished.

"You said something about the bone. Did you get a feeling then, too?"

"Yes, as soon as I touched it. But that was different."

I worried at a rough edge of a fingernail with my teeth, then stopped when his gaze flicked to my mouth. My decade-long struggle with anxiety expressed itself in two horrible conditions officially called onychophagia and excoriation — nail-biting and skin-picking. I knew the habits were gross, but they were also automatic, and when I was especially anxious — like now — the urge was almost irresistible.

Ryan leaned up against a counter and sipped his coffee, as if settling in to hear all the details. "Different how?"

I couldn't find words to explain it and feared it would sound ridiculous even if I could, so I merely said, "I didn't hear or see anything specific. It just felt —" *Evil*, that was the most accurate word for it. "Bad," I finished lamely. "It shook me to my core."

I stared at Ryan, trying to assess his reaction to what I'd told him, but his expression was unreadable. If he felt the extreme skepticism which I suspected he must, he hid it well; there was no snort of laughter and no eye-rolling. As a cop, he had to be used to hearing some wild stuff.

Eventually, he said, "I can see this has shaken you, and you think it means something —"

Before he could utter the big fat "but" on the tip of his tongue, I interrupted. "It did with Colby."

Ryan's brows drew together. "What do you mean?"

"The stuff I saw and heard in here" — I tapped my temple — "and the feelings I got, that's how I figured out who'd killed him."

He scrubbed a hand across his mouth. "I wondered how you knew some of that stuff. Are you saying Colby sent you clues?"

"I know it sounds bizarre. And I'm not claiming to be a psychic or anything," I babbled, already regretting my decision to spill the beans.

He gave me a long, assessing look. "And are you still … in contact with Colby?"

"I don't think so."

He opened his mouth as though to speak, closed it again, frowned harder and then said, "To be honest, Garnet, I'm not sure what to do with this."

Me either, buddy.

He finished his coffee and began jingling his car keys, clearly eager to be gone.

"Could you just check it out — that woman's death? Don't automatically assume it's suicide, okay?" I said as I saw him out.

"Sure."

And I couldn't tell if that was a "Sure, I'll investigate thoroughly" or a "Sure, whatever lady, just let me get the hell away from your crazy ass."

Either way, I figured no romantic dinner invitation would be coming my way anytime soon.

– 7 –

On Monday morning, while I was deep in an article on the role of pre-loss dependency in chronic grief, the doorbell sounded. At once, the dogs began barking furiously, but they stopped at once when they saw who it was — my neighbor, Ned Lipton. Today he wore a yellow bowtie and held a snow shovel.

"Can I clear your path for you?"

"Sure, thanks," I said, although only a scant inch of snow had fallen in the night.

"You're most welcome," he said and set to work, humming tunelessly, while Lizzie and Darcy romped around his feet, messing where he'd cleared and generally getting in the way.

I stood awkwardly on the top step, unsure of the etiquette for this. It felt wrong to stand and watch him work, and even ruder to return inside and leave him working, but the bitter wind made light work of my thin sweater. I was just about to go back into the warmth of the house, good manners be damned, when Ned said, "I saw the police were at your house yesterday. Twice."

His carefully casual tone didn't fool me — this was the real reason why he'd come over: to snoop.

"Yeah," I said.

"Nothing wrong, I hope?" he asked, his keen gaze fixed on my face.

"They're investigating a possible crime."

He peered over my shoulder as though he thought the crime had happened in the house. "What happened?"

"A body was found in the old serpentine quarry."

"I saw that on the news! So, you're involved in that?"

"Tangentially," I said, offering no details. I had a sneaking suspicion that Ned was the local gossip, and I wanted to keep his nose well out of my business. "Look, I'm freezing," I said, hugging my arms. "I'm going inside, but thanks for clearing the path."

He gave a friendly wave, and leaving him humming as he swept the path, I returned to my work. By lunchtime, my brain was fried, so after wolfing down a bacon, peanut butter and pickle sandwich, and drinking a bottle of beer, I crashed on the couch and napped until woken by plaintive whines and warm tongues licking my face. Me being better at decoding dog-speak than Lizzie and Darcy were at understanding my commands, I took this to mean that they were hungry.

"Give me a minute to wake up, okay?" I said, rubbing sleep from my eyes, wiping dog spit off my cheeks, and wondering how I'd slept so deeply with the television volume so loud. The Hair was back on the news, not even trying to hide his excitement as he described the latest developments at the quarry.

"Police have confirmed the discovery yesterday of the

skeletonized remains of an unknown person, found in the immediate vicinity of the decommissioned Rare Rocks Serpentine Quarry just outside Pitchford, Vermont. The identity of the deceased person is not yet known, and although the remains are clearly old, police will need to wait on the Medical Examiner's report before they can estimate a date of death. The remains are believed to be unrelated to the body found in the quarry yesterday by a passing hiker."

It occurred to me that, as the passing hiker who'd found the body, it was strange that I hadn't been contacted by the media for comment. Had Ryan withheld my identity to protect me from being harassed?

"That person has been positively identified as thirty-nine-year-old Laini Carter," the reporter continued. "She headed up the marketing division of the Sweet and Smoky Maple Syrup Company and is survived by her brother."

Laini Carter. That's who she'd been. And only thirty-nine years old. Again, I felt what she had as she fell, tumbling through the air, breathless, almost flying. I pressed my fingers hard against my eyes and pushed my feet against the floor, forcing myself back into the present.

My phone rang, startling my eyes open.

"Hey, kiddo, we were expecting you at six o'clock. Where are you?"

Crap. I'd forgotten that I was supposed to be having supper with my parents.

"I'm on my way, Dad."

I fed the dogs, locked them in the kitchen and set off for the house on Abenaki Street where I'd grown up. My mother flung the front door open before the bell finished its chime.

"Come in, come in, it's cold enough out there to make milk cows give icicles!" She tugged me inside and enfolded me in a tight embrace before stepping back to inspect my face. "Your eyes are still different colors," she said, sounding pleased about it.

My mother's eyes were bright, her cheeks rosy, her gray hair neatly curled, and she looked like she'd lost a couple of pounds. Being back behind the counter of her esoteric store, Crystals, Candles and Curiosities, dispensing wacky wisdom and joss sticks to the county's metaphysically minded citizens, was obviously doing her good. Dad looked the same as ever, maybe more relaxed than the last time I'd seen him. Mom being back at work and out of his hair was no doubt suiting him fine, too.

Mom ushered us both into the dining room, which looked much the same as it had back when I'd lived there. The old spinning wheel still sat in the corner, a basket of dried flowers rested on the sideboard and the table was set for three with Mom's blue-patterned china.

"Are you hungry?" she asked, taking her usual seat and lifting the lid off a serving dish. "I've made turkey enchiladas."

Immediately, I diverted to the kitchen and rummaged through the condiment bottles inside the refrigerator, looking for something with a kick. Squinting at the label on an old bottle of sliced and pickled jalapenos, I saw they'd expired over a year ago. They still looked okay to me. A little pale, maybe.

Back at the table, I handed the jar to my father to inspect. "Think these will kill me?"

"I wish you wouldn't eat dodgy foods, kiddo. It's going to catch up with you one day."

"Oh hush, Bob, Garnet's got the gullet of a goat; she can stomach anything," my mother said.

That was probably true. I piled a heap of the chilis — unappetizingly limp and mushy — onto my plate and took a bite. Not bad.

"Did you see the news?" Dad asked, using his knife and fork to divide his enchiladas into bite-sized pieces. "They found a body at the old quarry."

"Correction," I said. "*I* found a body at the old quarry."

Dad paused with his fork halfway to his mouth, and Mom's eyes bugged with astonishment. I took a big bite of jalapeno-topped enchilada, savoring the burn that was already raising a faint sweat on my brow.

Under a barrage of questions, I filled my parents in on how I'd stumbled across the corpse of Laini Carter. My father, who had a gruesome fascination with murder and serial killers, insisted on hearing every detail of what I'd seen, but like the cops, he seemed to think the death was probably a suicide and not worth getting too fired up about. So I threw him a bone, telling him what Lizzie had dug up.

He perked up immediately. "Well! That could be a murder, couldn't it? And you had the bone with you at the Andersens'? What did it look like? I wish you'd called me — I'd have liked to have seen it."

"Dad, has anyone ever told you that you're pretty strange?"

He chuckled loudly, but *someone,* I noticed, was being uncharacteristically quiet. I glanced over at my mother. She was studying me intently, her face bright with excitement. *Uh-oh.*

"What?" I demanded.

"You encountered *Death*."

She said it like that, as if death had a capital letter and was a presence that I'd hung out with up at the quarry, the two of us getting better acquainted as we traded amusing anecdotes about mortality.

"And?" I asked, though I had a pretty good idea what was coming.

"Did you *see* anything?"

"Trees, snow, rocks. A body."

"You know what I mean, Garnet! Did you have any *visions*? Get any messages from the beyond?"

I hesitated, nibbling on a fingernail, knowing that if I told her what I'd experienced, she'd grill me with a hundred other questions and pepper me with far-fetched theories of what was happening to me. Better to deny anything had happened.

But I'd paused too long.

"You did!" she said, thumping a fist on the table so hard that her knife rattled on her plate. "I *knew* it."

Dad sighed and forked another portion of turkey into his mouth.

"I had a funny feeling at the top of the quarry, but I think it was just vertigo," I fudged.

"You aren't heightaphobic," she said, like a lawyer pouncing on a witness's lie.

"Acrophobic."

"Don't try to distract me, young lady. What else happened at the quarry? You tell me every single thing right now!"

– 8 –

"Sorry to disappoint you," I told my mother, "but nothing much happened."

Dad said, "You may as well come out with it, because your mother won't stop until she knows everything."

He wasn't wrong, so I told them what I thought I'd felt and heard at the top of the quarry, and what I'd experienced when I'd touched the body on the stretcher.

"Psychometry!" my mother declared.

"Huh?"

"You're a psychometrist, dear."

"No, I'm not."

"It's a form of ESP that occurs when you touch an object with residual memory and pick up *emanations* from its energy field, because the past is always *entombed* in the present via atom exchange."

"Setting aside the fact that I have no idea what you just said and fully believe it made no sense, can we just back up a minute? A psychometrist is a psychological professional who administers and scores psychometric instruments like IQ and aptitude tests."

"Are you sure, dear?" she said, with that politely incredulous look she always gave me whenever I said anything inconveniently logical or scientifically true.

My mother would find it easier to believe that a posse of leprechauns had carried me off to the end of the rainbow than to trust any of Newton's laws.

"Yes, I'm sure," I snapped. "I've got— I've almost got a master's degree in psychology; I know what psychometrics are."

"Don't bite my head off, Garnet. That might be what psychometrics are. But *psychometry* is the skill of object-reading. It definitely is." She gave a firm nod, as if the question were settled.

"You people can't just co-opt established terms for your woo-woo nonsense," I said, outraged.

Blithely ignoring this, she continued, "The old term for it was psychoscopy, but nobody calls it that anymore. Goddess, this is so exciting! Objects get infused with energetic signatures, you know, especially of past traumatic events. And now you have the psychic ability to read the residual energies inside them through touch, to possibly even connect to their previous owners! I wonder ..."

Her gaze wandered around the room, and I knew exactly what was going through her mind. She was searching for an item on which I could test my "object-reading" abilities.

"Did you feel anything when you touched the bone?" Dad asked.

Mom's head snapped back around, and her gaze locked onto my face.

"That was different," I told my father. "It wasn't the same

as when I touched the woman's body. It felt — I don't know — horrible. Bad."

My father stared at me, his face creased in concern, although I couldn't tell if he was worried about my sanity or just alarmed at the prospect of being outnumbered two-to-one by the crackpots in his family.

"What did you *see*?" Mom said.

"Darkness."

She sucked in a breath and then, with a thrill of horror in her voice, said, "The presence of evil!"

Despite this being exactly what I'd felt, and even what I'd thought, I was instantly irritated.

"No, it wasn't. It was me knowing that there could be no good reason for a human rib to be lying out in the wild," I retorted, flinging Ryan's explanation at her.

"Your second sight is growing in power, Garnet. You can deny it all you like, but you have the *Gift*."

I faked a yawn. "I'm really tired, guys. Would you mind if we called it a night?"

"No problem, kiddo," Dad said, no doubt sensing the argument that was looming.

"Hold the telephone," Mom said. "We haven't decided what mother-and-daughter activities we're going to do."

"I need to work," I reminded her.

"You get some work done tomorrow, and we can have an outing on Wednesday afternoon when I have an assistant in the store. We could have lunch in town, or I could do a tarot reading for you, if you like?"

"How about that maple syrup tasting you suggested before?

You said it was at the Sweet and Smoky factory?"

I felt a strong compulsion to go and see the place where Laini Carter had worked, and to check whether I could pick up anything more.

"I doubt they'll be running tours now, dear. That poor woman isn't even cold in her grave yet. I wonder when the funeral will be?"

So did I. Maybe I could sneak in and see if I got anything more.

"There won't be a funeral," Dad said. "No memorial service of any kind. Just a cremation."

"Fancy that!" my mother said, clearly shocked at this flouting of the conventional formalities.

"According to the grapevine, she was an atheist. Her brother, who hails from the South, is coming up tomorrow and meeting with the Medical Examiner in Burlington to formally identify the body, or some such thing. And then he'll be in Pitchford on Wednesday to meet with the police."

Mom and I stared at Dad, amazed by this flow of information.

He smiled back. "I got the whole lowdown from Hugo."

Hugo was the owner of the town's old hardware store, and he knew almost everything about everyone. In fact, he knew things about people which even they didn't — because they weren't true.

"I'll call tomorrow and find out if the factory tours are running," Mom said, collecting the empty plates.

I helped her with the dishes and on my way out went to say goodnight to my father, who was sitting in the living room with a thick forensic textbook open on his lap.

"I've been reading up about skeletonized remains," he said, cheerfully. "Did you know old bones can be black, white, brown or red, depending on the chemical and mineral make-up of the soil in which they've lain?"

"I do now," I said.

"They've even found jaw bones from medieval Greece which are stained green from the copper coins placed in the mouths when they were buried — fare for the mythical ferryman who would take them across the river Styx and into the world of the dead."

I pressed a kiss on his forehead. "Well, whatever their color, *my* bones are weary. Goodnight, Dad."

Catching me at the front door, my mother said, "It worries me that you had that bone in your house. You might be contaminated."

I'd thought the same thing, but I'd been worried about germs.

She pressed a bundle of rolled, dried leaves into my hands. It looked like a massive joint.

"*Mom?*"

"It's white sage for smudging, dear." At my blank look she explained, "You light this end and then walk around every room of the house, waving it in the air."

"Why?"

"It's an ancient ritual for purifying your space from harmful spirits. And these" — she handed me a small paper bag — "are bath salts. Epsom salts to reduce stress, relax the muscles and detoxify the body."

"You can't extract toxins from the skin, Mom."

"Plus, sea salt for a spiritual cleanse, and baking soda to pull out blockages from your aura. And I put some vanilla essence in, too."

"What's the vanilla supposed to do?"

"It just smells nice, dear." She slid me a look that implied it was wacky to think vanilla essence might have metaphysical properties and gave me a white gauze bag with five small gemstones inside. "This is a seer kit."

From the living room came the sound of Dad snorting.

I said, "A what, now?"

"To increase your psychic abilities," she explained. "Azurite for the third eye, and bloodstone to keep you open but grounded. Bloodstone will help your sex life, too, and goodness knows you could use some energizing in that area!"

I scowled at her.

"Turquoise, of course, and labradorite for clairvoyance, and moonstone because you're so reluctant to embrace your abilities. And moldavite" — she indicated a green stone — "to give your spirit guide something to latch onto."

"What spirit guide?" I snapped.

"Colby."

Stunned, I took a step back. My mother thought Colby might still be hanging around, guiding me? Back in December, Cassie had told me about a psychic medium who'd insisted that Colby hadn't fully "moved on" to the other side, that he was trapped in "a limbo of unknowing." If that was true, then surely solving his murder would have freed him? I didn't want him still hanging around.

Or did I?

My mother studied me through narrowed eyes. "Hmmm. Or would your spirit guide be Johnny?"

"Johnny? Johnny who?"

"Your childhood spirit companion."

"My childhood *imaginary friend*," I corrected.

"Well, whoever's guiding you, the moldavite will help. Now, quartz is essential for seeing, of course," my mother continued, "but I'm assuming you still have the piece you picked up at the pond?"

I would rather have swallowed it than admit to my mother that I'd kept the unusual stone — purple at one end and clear at the other. With a jolt, I realized it had been in a pocket of the parka I'd worn on my hike to the quarry. That I'd been fiddling with it shortly before I'd gotten that vision of Laini Carter.

"Always keep these on you," she said, closing my fingers around the crystals.

"So, just to be clear, I must use the stones to attract psychic phenomena, and the bath salts and sage to repel them?" I said, but my sarcasm was wasted on her.

She beamed at me, clearly delighted that I was such a fast learner.

"That's exactly right, dear!"

– 9 –

After a day's hard work on Tuesday, I made a late-afternoon run to the grocery store in town; I was running low on food and had used the last of the coffee trying to caffeinate myself into productive alertness. Plus, I was going to need more alcohol. And chilis — definitely chilis. Bizarrely, the Andersens had nothing spicier than ground white pepper in their kitchen cupboards.

What had once been my father's mom-and-pop grocery store on Main Street was now a Best West supermarket. I wandered the aisles, snagging a bottle of Sriracha and a jar of pickled Mucho Nacho Jalapenos (fatter, longer and hotter than their common cousins) along with basic groceries and a bunch of snacks — chips, salsa, several packets of sour Skittles and a giant bag of Barnum's animal crackers. As a nod to good nutrition, I grabbed some ripe tomatoes and grapes from the fresh produce section, before I steered my cart to the wine aisle for a bottle of pinot grigio and a six-pack of beers. That was when I saw her.

Jessica Mantovani, who'd been my best friend back in high

school when she was still Jessica Armstrong, was standing staring at a shelf of expensive-looking chardonnays. With her sleek bob of auburn hair, her subtle makeup and cashmere coat, she looked just as elegant as the last time I'd seen her — at Cassie's funeral. On that day, Jess had given me a silent nod and a look as cold as a penguin's ass, clearly still angry that due to my investigative efforts, her lover had been arrested on a bunch of charges.

While I pondered whether to march up and greet her or make a cowardly retreat — the latter option appealed way more — Jessica glanced up and saw me, forcing the issue.

"Hi, Jess!" I walked over to her with arms open and a smile glued to my lips.

She didn't hit me or push me away, but she didn't return my hug either.

"Didn't know you were back," she said, with no hint of enthusiasm.

"Yup." I explained about the house-sitting and then, to break the awkward silence that followed, added, "Hey, let's get together and have a chat. You know, catch up and … clear the air?"

After a moment's hesitation, she said, "Okay."

"You could come around for dinner."

She arched an eyebrow at that. "You cook now?"

"Good point," I said. "Drinks at the Tuppenny Tavern?"

"Lunch, at the Frost Inn," she said. "Friday at twelve-thirty would work for me."

"It's a date!" I said, my tone overly cheery.

"Well," she said, turning her back on the chardonnays and

cabernets, "I need to get going."

"Your boss at the gallery nitpicky about working hours?" I joked, because Jessica *was* the boss, and owner, of the *Art on Main* gallery.

The slightest flicker of a smile flitted across her expression. "I promised Nico that I'd get him a nice steak for dinner."

"Oh, right."

In the decade since high school, Jessica had become a modern Stepford wife — slim, perfectly groomed, and effortlessly juggling the tasks of raising children, running a business, and getting meat and potatoes on the table for her spoiled husband. It was impressive, but also disconcerting, because she was now so different from the girl I'd once known.

Back in the Andersens' minty kitchen, I let the dogs out for a toilet break and fed them another serving of the kibble, topping each bowl off with a juicy chunk of the rotisserie chicken I'd brought home from the store for my supper. I ate on the couch in front of the television, checking to see whether there was anything new on either of the quarry stories. I had to search through the channels to find the local news channel again, because the TV was on a different station when I switched it on. An electrical appliance behaving oddly? I could just hear my mother telling me it was a sign of a ghostly presence.

Eventually, I found the right channel, but there were no updates on the story and no live crossings to The Hair. Perhaps he'd taken the evening off to deep condition his tresses. The repeat footage of the quarry gave me flashbacks of the woman's corpse in the pit and on the stretcher, killing my appetite.

I fed the remains of my meal to the dogs, then poured myself a large glass of wine and took a deep, candlelit bath, sprinkling in my mother's salts, which smelled like freshly baked cupcakes. I should have felt relaxed as I soaked in the steaming water, but instead, I grew increasingly edgy. Being in this bathroom, with its pink tub, tiles and towels, was like being stuck inside the rosy depths of a giant conch shell. Bathrooms should come in any color as long as it was white.

I picked at the scabs on my scraped hand by the light of the flickering candle while I reviewed the day, trying to identify the source of my unease. I'd put in a good day's work, so no guilt or anxiety there, and I'd taken care of the dogs. Maybe I was dreading the upcoming lunch with Jess — it was bound to be uncomfortable — or perhaps I was still experiencing the increased autonomic system arousal of post-traumatic stress. Given the events of the day before, that made sense, but it didn't make me feel any more relaxed.

I cut short my bath, wrapped myself in one of the fluffy pink towels and brushed my teeth. A sensation like a faint itch prickled behind my shoulder blades. I froze, feeling the fine hairs on my arms lift and goosebumps pucker my skin. Someone was watching me; I could feel it. I spun around.

No one was there.

Of course no one was there. The only eyes in the bathroom apart from my own mismatched pair were the beady black ones of a sappy mermaid statuette on the shelf below the mirror. *Damn these freaky figurines!* I shoved the vile thing inside the cabinet beneath the basin and slammed the door shut, but I still felt the flesh-creeping sensation of not being alone.

The rib bone. Maybe my mother was right — she was bound to be *sometimes*, if only according to the law of probabilities — that it hadn't been a good idea to bring human remains into the house. What if I'd brought some spiritual presence in along with the bone? *Oh joy,* I thought sourly. Either I was imagining things, or I'd just discovered another unpleasant aspect to this whole psychic tangle.

As soon as I'd gotten back from the previous night's dinner at my parents' house, I'd tossed the sage blunt in the trash. Now I half-wished that I *had* moseyed through the house, smoking away the bad vibes.

The dogs, however, didn't seem at all agitated by any possible ghostly visitation. They were stretched out, sleeping, on the top of my bed.

"Oh, no you don't, you charm-monsters. You get down right now!" I ordered them, pointing at the floor.

Reluctantly, they jumped down and nestled together on the floor beside my bed, Darcy resting his head on Lizzie's paws. I slipped into the ratty old T-shirt I always wore to bed and half-cajoled, half-carried the dogs downstairs to settle them in their baskets. Back upstairs I snuggled into bed with a crime novel. Despite the eerie moaning of the wind outside and the sounds of the unfamiliar house settling around me — creaks and rustles in the ceiling and cracks of the floorboards — I was feeling better. The sensation of being watched had faded and I could breathe more easily. Maybe I'd just imagined it, after all.

But, as I drifted off to sleep, I thought I caught a faint whiff of cola-flavored lip balm. The type Colby had always worn.

When my phone on the bedside table rang the next

morning, Sting's *Every Breath You Take* was playing so loudly and clearly inside my head that it took a few moments to realize there wasn't a radio playing the song in my bedroom. I'd been dreaming about Colby. I strained to recall the dream images, but it was like trying to hold mist between my fingers.

"This is Officer Ronnie Capshaw from the Pitchford Police Department."

"Oh, right. Hi," I croaked groggily.

"Have I called too early?"

I thought I detected judgment in her tone.

Blinking sleep away, I squinted at the time display on my phone. Seven-thirty. Way too early.

"Not at all," I replied.

"We'd like you to come into the station this morning to check and sign your statements about what you found at the quarry. Is eleven-thirty convenient?"

"Sure." I could drop in before I met my mother for lunch at twelve-thirty.

She ended the call without further niceties. I slumped back into the pillows, but drifting back off to sleep was impossible. I could hear the hounds whining and scratching at the door downstairs. Was this what having kids was like — being on-call all the time? It was probably worse. Dogs didn't need to have diapers changed or be driven to ballet lessons.

Running on still-sleepy autopilot, I let the dogs out into the yard, put on the coffeemaker, and poured some muesli into a bowl. When I opened the refrigerator to get milk, I was taken aback to see that there was only a scant inch of wine left in the bottle from last night. Damn, I hadn't realized I'd drunk that much. Again. *Better watch the sauce*, I warned myself. It was enough that I was turning into an oddball. I didn't need to become a drunk, too.

I kept my nose fixed to the thesis grindstone for two uninterrupted hours, nibbling on sour Skittles while I worked — a trick which helped keep my fingers out of my mouth. Afterwards, I took the dogs for a long walk around the estate, goggling at the mansions with their snow-iced topiary and three-car garages.

When I passed the gatehouse, the muscly guard trotted over to walk beside me for a way.

"How *you* doin'?" he said, Joey-Tribbiani style. "My name is Doug. That's *God* spelled backward with a little bit of *u* wrapped up in it."

My eyes rolled so hard they nearly came loose entirely. The dogs, who clearly liked this clown, leapt up against him, begging for attention.

"And your name is Garnet," Doug said.

"I know, right?"

"Sooo … I'd like to hook up sometime." He extracted a folded piece of paper from his pocket and tried to hand it to me. "Here's my number."

"Oh, no thank you, I already have one."

He frowned for a moment, then returned it to his pocket. Did he keep a whole collection there, for ease of distribution?

"What's with your eyes?"

"What do you mean?"

"They're different colors."

"No way! *Really*? I'll need to get that seen to."

He nodded. "There was a reporter sniffing around here this morning. Soft-looking guy with hair like a girl. Thought he was gonna cry when I denied him entry."

"Uh-huh." I tugged at the dogs, keen to get away.

"He asked a lot of questions about you, but I told him nothing. Sooo ... maybe I could come around to your place later to receive your *demonstration of appreciation?*" he sang the last words, walking beside me. "I don't mind your crazy eyes."

"Wow." I stopped and faced him. "I have no words. I mean, I do, but it's a string of four-letter ones."

"What's that supposed to mean?"

"It means *no.*"

He folded his arms, and the seams on his jacket strained. "You're not very nice, are you?"

"It's been said." I marched off.

"Hasn't anyone ever told you that you catch more flies with honey than vinegar?" he called after me.

I turned around and, walking backward, yelled, "But you catch the *most* flies with corpses."

Back at the Andersen house, I took Ned up on his offer to babysit Darcy and Lizzie, because I didn't know what time I'd be home.

"Any further news on Laini Carter?" he asked as I handed over the dogs on his doorstep.

"Not that I know of."

"I knew her."

"You did?"

"She used to live here on the estate. In that double-story over there." He pointed to a house on the far side of the park.

"Then she moved out, and I couldn't see her anymore." He looked put out by the fact.

"Oh, were the two of you dating?"

"What? No! I wasn't in her league."

"What was she like?" I asked.

"She was beautiful," he said simply. "Why don't you come in and have a cup of coffee, and we can chat about her?"

I glanced at my wristwatch. "I can't, I have an appointment in town in fifteen minutes."

"Of course, of course," he said. "Some other time." And, humming, he let the dogs inside his house.

– 10 –

Officer Veronica Capshaw stood planted behind the front desk at the Pitchford police station like a solid oak, set to withstand any storms within its red brick walls. When I'd first met her up at the quarry, I'd been too upset and confused to notice much about her, but now I saw that she was in her late twenties, with black eyes, square hands, and a no-nonsense manner. On this March morning, she was dealing with a lady with tightly permed gray hair and the lemon-sucking expression of the perpetual complainer.

"Why, I almost ran over one on Route 100 near the Brookford turnoff the other day after church! Wearing dark clothes and a blue helmet — well, that's not very good for visibility, is it? Not a speck of reflective gear!" she said querulously. "My son's a cyclist, but he always wears the correct apparel *and* he has flashing lights on his pedals. People need to be more careful and more aware." She held up a fistful of flyers with the proselytizing fervor of a zealot.

Noting my arrival, Officer Capshaw raised a hand to stem the woman's babble. "I'll be with you in a minute," she told me and then turned to the complainer. "I understand, Mrs. Posillico, but you will have to get permission from the town clerk's office to stick those on lamp posts or in any other public place."

The woman's face fell. Perhaps she already knew that Town Clerk Michelle Armstrong would never allow her town's cutesy *ye olde village* vibe to be despoiled by homemade safety posters.

"Can I stick one on your notice board, at least?" she asked.

"You're most welcome to, ma'am."

While the old lady rearranged the notices on the cluttered corkboard to make a space for her flyer, Capshaw beckoned me over.

"Is Ryan in?" I asked. "Can I see him?"

I was anxious to touch base with him — to find out how the investigation was going. *If* the investigation was going.

"Chief Jackson is busy with other matters," she replied.

While I tried to figure out what this meant — whether Ryan wanted to avoid me after my crazy confidences, or whether I was overanalyzing a simple statement as psych students tend to do — she extracted two sheets from a manila folder on the countertop.

"This is your statement about finding the body at the quarry, and this is the one about the bone," she said. "Read them carefully. If they are correct in all respects, sign over here."

"Do you have a—?" I began, but she was already answering the phone.

"Yes, sir, I'm listening. Uh-huh, uh huh ... Outside the school?" She scribbled an address on a piece of paper. "Burning *donuts*? In a pile, or what?"

JO MACGREGOR

She caught me tracking this fascinating conversation and tapped a finger on my statement. I moved a foot to the side and obediently began reading.

"Well, what did he say when you confronted him?" Officer Capshaw asked the caller. "I see ... Of course. Your name? ... Contact number?" More scribbling. "I'll get out there as soon as I can, sir."

She slid me a look which clearly conveyed that I was the person delaying her swift reaction to this emergency, and I returned my focus to the documents. They were concise, accurate and neatly typed; she'd even spelled my name correctly. Unsurprisingly, it made zero reference to any of the strange things I'd experienced. Had Ryan shared any of that with her?

She left the front desk, went down the short passageway that led to Ryan's office, and I heard her telling him, "I need to head out to the school, Chief. I got a report that Zakary Weber is setting donuts alight in his food truck and tossing them into the street, as a protest against the elections." There was an unintelligible reply, and then she replied, "Damned if I know."

I worried at a filament of skin beside my pinkie nail while I waited, wondering if I dared just march over to Ryan's office.

"I'll let you know, boss," I heard her say, and then she was back at the desk, attention on me. "Well? Is it all there?"

"Yes, if you just want the facts."

"What else would we want?"

Instantly I regretted saying anything, but she was looking at me like she wouldn't budge until she had her answer.

"Nothing, really. I just thought ... maybe my thoughts or feelings? Hunches?"

70

She gave a short, mirthless laugh. "You're a shrink, right?"

The term rankled a bit. *I* used it all the time, but it was like making Jewish jokes — you had to be one to tell them.

"No, I'm not a *psychologist,* yet," I said, emphasizing the correction.

"Well, shrinks — oh, excuse me, *psychologists* — may be interested in feelings and hunches." She said the two words like they were dirty. "But we cops deal in facts."

"Then these are one hundred percent factually correct," I said, taking her pen and signing both statements. "Have there been any developments in the Laini Carter case?"

She tilted her head and eyed me impassively, before saying, "We don't generally make a habit of keeping witnesses updated on our investigations, Miss McGee."

"Right."

"If that's all" — she placed a service bell and a sign reading *ring for attention* on the counter "— then I'll escort you out."

Outside, she waited until I was driving away from the station before climbing into her police cruiser. Not very trusting, was Ronnie Capshaw. On the other hand, she *was* a good judge of human nature, because I merely circled the block, pulled back into the parking bay I'd just vacated and, glancing left and right to check Ronnie wasn't hiding somewhere ready to pounce on me, snuck back into the station. I didn't ring the bell before marching through the low swing-door beside the front desk, but I did knock on the door of the chief's office before entering and plonking myself in the chair across the desk from Ryan.

"Hey," I greeted him. "How's the Carter case going? Any leads?"

"Hello, Garnet. Do take a seat. And how are you today?"

That brought a wry grin to my face. "You're determined to teach me some manners, aren't you? Okay then, I'm very well, thank you. And how are you today?"

"Peachy."

"So, any developments?"

"Not really."

"I thought maybe the autopsy results would be through by now."

He made a sound like a shrug.

"Are they?"

He nodded grudgingly.

"*Well?*" I demanded. "You know it'll be in *The Bugle* anyway. Are you going to make me wait to read it?"

He sighed. "The ME says the cause of death was massive trauma to the brain, presumably occurring at impact. And if that didn't kill her, then the multiple devastating injuries throughout the rest of her body would have."

"And the manner of death?"

"Undetermined. He says the injuries are consistent with either a fall or a jump. Which means it could be either an accident or suicide."

"Or homicide."

He shrugged an acknowledgement. "Are you hungry?"

Was this a lunch invitation? "Why do you ask?"

"Because you're eating yourself."

He pointed to my mouth, where I'd been gnawing on a nail. Abashed, I put both my hands in my lap, interlinking the fingers and clenching them tightly to keep them from straying.

"How do *you* think she died?" I asked.

"Odds are, it'll turn out to be suicide. Her boss says Laini Carter had some serious problems in her life."

"What does her brother say? Did you interview him yet? He's in town, isn't he?"

"And how do you know *that*?"

Discerning a hint of discomfort in his voice and expression, I said, "Don't worry, it didn't come to me in a vision."

Ryan's face colored, and I knew I'd been correct in my assumption. He was not copacetic with what I'd told him on Sunday. That bothered me. And it bothered me *that* it bothered me, that I cared what this man thought of me.

"Does Laini's brother think it was suicide?" I pressed.

"He'd better hope it was. Because if it's murder, he's the chief suspect," Ryan said, and by his rueful expression, I figured that, in his embarrassment, he'd blurted out more than he intended to reveal.

"Oooh!" I leaned forward in my chair, all ears. "Why's that?"

"Garnet, you're a witness in this case, not an investigator."

"Yeah, your bouncer out there" — I jerked my chin toward the front desk — "told me that cops aren't in the business of keeping witnesses updated on cases."

"Ronnie said that? She's a tough cookie. Takes no shit from anyone."

Swinging from side to side in his swivel chair, he watched me plot my next move with an expectant expression just lifting one edge of his lips. His very nice lips.

I pulled my gaze away from them and asked, "What about

Laini's phone — did you get anything off that?"

"Even if I had any information on that — which I don't, because it's still with the techs who're trying to extract the data — I wouldn't tell you, because again, that's police business."

I blew out a frustrated breath. "Ryan, you're being very …" — I searched for the right word — "tiresome."

He gave a bark of laughter and ran a hand through his black hair but still said nothing. I wasn't ready to give up on trying to prise something out of him, though.

"Got *anything* back from forensics yet?"

He didn't reply, but I got my answer from the flit of his gaze to a couple of labeled evidence bags resting on his desk.

"Are those hers?" I asked.

He nodded, and before he could stop me, I grabbed the closest one.

"Hey!" he protested.

The clear plastic bag contained Laini Carter's driver's license, and although the card was smudged with sooty powder, I could still make out the details.

"Can I try touching it?" I asked hesitantly.

"I'm amazed you're asking permission," Ryan said sarcastically.

"Please?"

Looking ill-at-ease, he began, "Garnet —"

"It can't hurt, right? I mean, it's already been fingerprinted and stuff, hasn't it?"

He didn't exactly give me the go-ahead, but he didn't demand the bag back either. I opened the zip lock an inch, glanced at him, then opened it all the way. Still he said nothing.

I tipped the card out of the bag and into my left hand and then held it between both my palms.

Ryan sat very still, eyes fixed on me. "Anything?"

"Not really." A slight tightening in my head, perhaps. A faint frisson of something — Excitement? Turmoil? — that was over almost before it began. Disappointed, I peeked at the other bags, trying to make out what was inside them. "Maybe it needs to be something more personal?"

Ryan scrubbed his hand across his mouth and held it there a moment, as if holding back words. Then, seeming to come to a decision, he passed another of the bags to me. Inside was a necklace in rose gold with a pendant in the shape of a wagon wheel, or perhaps it was a daisy with its petals cut out, inside an outer circle studded with bright diamonds.

"Was this hers? Was she wearing it when she died?" I asked.

"You tell me."

I opened the bag and spilled the necklace into my hand. Again, I felt that rippling of alertness, like an awakening to the object in my hand, a sudden electric awareness of it, and the top of my head grew tight. But I got nothing more.

I met Ryan's curious gaze and shrugged. "Maybe I need to concentrate?"

He held up his hands in a *don't-ask-me* gesture.

I shut my eyes, closed my hand around the necklace, and tried to send my attention to the cool metal, focusing hard as though listening with an inner ear for the slightest silent sound. It took a moment, and then it began.

– 11 –

Inside my closed hand, the chain and pendant pulsed faintly, like the heartbeat of a living thing. My whole body responded — tensing, pulling into itself. Behind my closed lids, my vision went bright, then images began to flicker.

Two people — a tall woman in cycling gear, her long black hair swept up into a tight ponytail, and a broad-shouldered man with brown hair graying at the temples. He holds out a blue velvet jewelry box to her, opens the lid so she can see inside.

She gasps in delight. "It's lovely! Thank you, thank you," she says, planting quick kisses all over the man's face.

"Put it on," he urges. "I want to see you wearing my gift."

"I may never take it off. The charm brings good luck, you know." She hands it to him and spins around, offering him the back of her neck.

He loops it across the front of her throat and fiddles with the clasp. Leaning in close to the nape of her neck, as if to see better, he inhales deeply. His expression is one of hunger and longing and grim satisfaction.

She dances over to a full-length mirror on the wall and studies herself from several angles. "It's gorgeous, Carl! You really shouldn't have."

"I knew you wanted one."

"Just a little silver one would have been fine. This must have cost a fortune. Did you get it specially made for me?"

"I wanted it to be unique, as exceptional as you are." He smiles as he sighs. "I just wish you'd let me put a ring on your finger instead of a chain around your neck."

Her face falls. "Oh, don't start that again."

"I want you to be my wife," he says, meeting her gaze in the mirror.

She turns to face him. "You want me to belong *to you," she corrects him, lifting a pale hand to gently stroke the stubble on his jaw. "But I can't. I can't belong to anyone, you know that."*

He leans his face into her hand, but his expression is unhappy, angry even. "You've never tried!"

"I've never tried flying to the moon, either, but I still know it can't happen." She kisses him on the lips. "I'm going for a ride now. And if I get mugged for this beautiful bling, it will be entirely your fault for being so generous!"

With a giggle, she twirls out of the room and is gone.

The man, alone now, snaps the velvet box closed and hurls it at the mirror.

The scene faded. I realized I was panting and made myself take a deep breath as I doubled down, trying to see more. But all I got was a shimmering vista of trees — rows upon rows of them, with short, twisted trunks and thin, silvery leaves — bathed in golden sunshine. The image wavered and then disappeared.

I opened my eyes, suddenly aware that they were watering. My fingers were prickling with an electric tingle.

"Are you– are you crying?" Ryan asked.

I wiped my eyes. "No, just leaking."

"Did you get anything?"

"Yes. A man, Carl — Laini's boyfriend, I think? — gave her this. He wanted to marry her; she wasn't interested. And she was a cyclist."

Ryan drew back his head in surprise.

"And then that part ended, and I saw lots of trees." I considered for a moment. "I think they were olive trees."

"You saw *olive trees*?"

Registering his mystified expression, I said, "I'm not an expert, okay? I can't direct this. I just get what comes to me."

"Sure. Anything else?"

I slid the necklace back into its bag and returned it to the desk, shaking my head slowly. "Not really."

But there had been. Along with the images I'd seen, I'd experienced sensations that weren't easy to identify. A constricting heaviness in the first scene and a more open, light feeling when I'd seen the olive groves. I rubbed my hands together. The pins and needles had faded, but a faint awareness, a sensation like I had eyes in my fingertips, lingered.

Ryan and I sat in uneasy silence for a while. I didn't know what to make of my visions, and he clearly didn't know what to make of me.

Eventually, I cleared my throat. "So, what about the bone Lizzie found? Anything more on that?"

"It's human."

"I already knew that much from the news."

"It's old."

I gave him the look that deserved. "Do you have an identity on the victim yet?"

"I guess I can tell you that much, because it'll be released to the press. We found a medic-alert bracelet at the scene. It belonged to one Jacob Wertheimer, who went missing in 2009. So it's likely that's who our vic is, although we'll only be sure when the ME's office confirms the dental records."

"There's something you're not telling me." I didn't need to be psychic to know that he was holding back; his face was a study in suspiciously careful blankness. "Oh, c'mon, Ryan, this is like pulling teeth. Tell me! *Please.* Pretty please? Pretty please with a — what was it, a Heineken? — on top," I begged.

He looked pleasantly surprised that I'd remembered his favorite brand, but instead of answering me, he stood up, stepped over to the glass partition which looked out onto the hallway, and stood for a long minute with his back to me. Weighing his options? I kept quiet.

Turning to face me, Ryan asked, "When you touched that bone, did you see anything specific?"

"No. I just had an oppressive, dark feeling. Why?"

"Remember that old serial killer case I told you about?"

I did. Back in December, Ryan had told me about a serial killer who'd been operating in New England around the time of Colby's death in 2007. Although they'd been murdered in a variety of different ways and dumped in different spots, all the victims had been young gay men.

"You're not saying this is one of his victims?" I asked, amazed.

"Looks like it."

"How do they know?" When he looked reluctant to answer, I said, "I won't tell anyone, Ryan, I promise. I *pinky-promise!*"

I reached out and linked a baby finger with one of his as I spoke. Did he feel the same little zing of contact that I did?

"You literally have me wrapped around your little finger." He gave my pinkie a squeeze and then released it. "According to the FBI, the killer left an item behind with every victim."

"Don't serial killers usually *take* something from their victims?"

Trophies, that's what they were called. Many serial killers liked to keep reminders of each of their kills in macabre collections — a lock of the victim's hair, something from their wallet, a piece cut from their body — to help them remember the victim and recapture the pleasure of the kill.

Ryan nodded. "This guy is different. He thinks he's special. He *wants* us to know it's him. Signing his work like it's a piece of art or something," he said, his voice thick with disgust. "Of course, he might have *taken* trophies, too, no way to know that. Anyway, the fact that he left something of his own behind at each body dump scene was kept from the media back then to prevent copycats, and so the FBI would know something that only the killer knew. That would help them definitively identify him if they ever caught him."

"That's how they knew Colby wasn't one of his victims? They didn't find the thing with his body?"

An image of Colby's body — white and waxen, lying behind the yellow barrier of police tape at Plover Pond — flashed through my mind, a momentary memory of horror.

"Yeah," Ryan said, dropping back into his chair.

"And this corpse up at the quarry — they found one of the things with it?"

"So they tell me."

"What was it? Can I touch it?"

I felt a strong pull to find out more about that murder, even as my body recoiled at the thought of going anywhere near that oppressive sense of fear and evil again.

Ryan blew out an amused breath. "*I* don't have it. I don't even know what it is, yet. The FBI has jurisdiction on this."

I tried to recall what I knew of the serial killer case. Something didn't add up.

"You told me those murders stopped the year after Colby died, so in 2008. But if this guy, Jacob Whatshisname, only went missing in 2009, that means —"

"— that he went on killing after we thought he'd stopped, yeah. It means maybe he just got better at disposing of the corpses. It means we may still find more victims hidden out there," Ryan said grimly.

"So, you think the killer picked up this young man somewhere nearby, then took, or forced, him to the quarry and killed him? Or maybe killed him somewhere else and just dumped his body there?"

"Could be. But the last time he was actually seen was on campus at UVM in Burlington, so for all we know that's where he was taken. Maybe he was even killed there. Nine years on, there's obviously no evidence of whether he walked up to that quarry or was dragged or carried."

"Do you think the killer planned to drop the body in the pit but got tired and hid it in the brush?" I asked.

"Could be," he said again.

"But you don't think so."

"I think it was a pretty specific place to dump a body, right beside that big boulder."

"It would have made finding and accessing the body again easy?"

"That's my theory. He wanted to visit it again. And maybe he did."

Killers frequently *did* visit the corpses of their victims again. I knew this from a guest lecture on homicide in our recent psychopathology unit. The visiting expert had explained that killers enjoy a special intimacy with their victims. They often prefer the non-threatening, non-judging compliance of the dead — posing and sometimes mutilating the bodies, or playing with them like a child would with a rag doll. A small percentage of such perpetrators return to have sex with the corpse — necrophilia being the ultimate in control and degradation of the victim — or to masturbate to fantasies of what they did while reliving the high of the kill.

The expert had told us that Ted Bundy, who often returned to his victims to dress their bodies and sometimes even paint their nails before photographing and having sex with them, had once explained to an interviewer, "When you work hard to do something right, you don't want to forget it."

"Then again," Ryan continued, "the perp may just have dumped it there in a shallow grave because it was a good spot well off the path, so it wouldn't be discovered immediately. That would give him time to be well away from the Pitchford area by the time it was found, if it ever was. And in the meantime, the elements, insects and animals preying on the corpse would destroy most of the forensic evidence. If he'd dumped it in the quarry, it would have been found sooner by kids going there to the swimming hole."

Fall leaves, their vivid scarlet and amber hues fading to brown, drift down. A breeze blows them up against the base of the boulder.

"He did it in fall. Around the end of fall," I said, speaking slowly. "Am I right?"

Ryan looked startled. "He went missing in November. Did you– did you just get a vision?"

Had I? I couldn't be sure.

I shrugged. It was difficult trying to distinguish glimpses of something that had once happened and that I was tuning into in some psychic way, from intuitive hunches, or from even just picturing the scene and having my imagination fill in details. I'd always done that.

Didn't everybody?

– 12 –

After the visions I'd had at the cop shop, I was feeling tired and sluggish, and not at all in the mood for lunch with my mother, especially since she'd insisted we meet at Dillon's Country Store and Café.

"I'm pretty sure I'll be *persona* totally *non grata* there, Mom," I'd complained.

I didn't look forward to coming face-to-face with Judy Dillon, since I'd been partly responsible for bringing legal troubles to her family a few months back.

My mother pooh-poohed my concern with an airy hand. "Judy should be *grateful* for what you did. Besides, you can't avoid her forever, so you may as well get it over with. As your father would say, 'Eat the toad!'"

"Frog," I'd muttered, knowing that although she was wrong on the wording of one of Dad's favorite expressions, she wasn't wrong about getting the inevitable over with.

Parking in Main Street, I noticed that the Sweet and Smoky Syrup Emporium was closed, with an explanatory notice stuck on the front door and a black ribbon tied around the door handle. Again, I felt the compulsion to learn more about Laini Carter, to speak to the people she'd worked with, to find out more about her life and her death. Especially her death.

A big man clutching a marmalade cat to his chest sat on the bench outside Dillon's, asking the patrons on their way in to buy him lunch.

"Hey, Lyle," I said.

He studied me for a few moments while his cat stared off to the left side of me.

"You're back," he said in his low rumble of a voice. His cat narrowed its eyes and hissed at me.

"Can I buy you a sandwich?"

"I like hot beef on rye. Toasted. No pickles."

"I remember," I said, pulling the door open.

"No pickles!" he called after me.

Inside, Dillon's was warm to the point of being stifling. I hung my coat on the hook at the door and joined my mother at a table in the center of the restaurant. While she chattered away about inanities, I rubbed at my temples, where a dull headache throbbed. I needed coffee — where was the waitress already? Glancing over my mother's shoulder, I saw a pretty woman with long strawberry-blond hair striding toward us, a look of fury on her face.

Uh-oh.

Judy Dillon marched up to our table and stood, hands on hips, glaring down at me. Her mouth opened and closed a few times as she seemingly struggled to find words. I suspected if we weren't in her place of business, she'd have given me a serious piece of her mind — and maybe even the back of her hand — but she needed to be polite in front of her other customers. Was that why Mom had chosen this restaurant? Sometimes, my mother was cannier than I tended to give her credit for.

Judy's gaze traveled from my new boots up to my old sweater, while a succession of emotions chased across her face — outrage, dislike and finally, resignation.

"So," she finally said, "you're back, are you?"

"I am."

She gave a *hmmph* of displeasure. "Are your eyes stuck like that, then?"

"I guess."

"You could get contact lenses, you know? Wear a brown one over your blue eye, and then they'd match."

"I could." I kept my answers brief and neutral, minimizing the risk of saying something that would give Judy an excuse to lay into me, because she still looked like she was itching to.

"May we order?" Mom asked.

"I'm not a waitress here anymore," Judy said. "I'm the *manager.*"

"Congratulations," I said.

Judy sniffed. "But I guess I can give your order to the kitchen."

"I'll have the scrambled egg and smoked salmon popover," Mom said.

"I'll have …" I scanned the menu, then tossed it back onto the enameled top of the table. "Could you just bring me an Irish coffee? Extra, extra hot."

"Daytime drinking?" Judy said, smirking at this evidence of my moral slackness.

"Make it a double," I said, defiantly.

"It's your liver, I guess." Taking the menus, she sashayed back to the kitchen.

"*Extra* hot! And no sugar," I called out after her. My mismatched eyes weren't the only consequence of my death that remained. I still had Colby's dislike of anything too sweet.

"Why aren't you eating?" my mother asked me.

"I'm not hungry."

My stomach felt like I'd swallowed a tragedy-sized lump of serpentine.

"I hope you're not coming down with the flu."

Sore head, fatigue, no appetite — it *felt* a lot like the flu. But the beings that affected me weren't microbial.

As though *she* could read *my* mind, Mom said, "Any more messages from the beyond?"

"Not a one."

"Nothing funny happening when you're alone at home? No more signs or visions?" She looked as eager as a kid on Christmas morning.

I didn't like lying to her, but right then I had neither the inclination nor the energy to get into what I'd experienced at the police station, so I threw in a distraction.

"My television changes channels by itself."

She clapped her hands together and clasped them against her chest. "That's a sign, Garnet, a definite sign! The electrics always go wackadoodle when there's heightened paranormal activity in the vicinity. The spirits love to play static and to change stations on the radio."

"It was the TV."

"Same difference. It's their way of trying to communicate. Oh!" she gasped. "You know what you need?"

A genetic test to confirm that I was in fact her biological daughter despite us having so little in common?

"I'm sure you'll tell me," I said.

"An EVP recorder!"

"A what, now?"

"An electronic voice phenomenon recorder. It's a special kind of tape recorder that captures sounds the human ear doesn't — like spirit voices. Ghost hunters use them all the time."

I snorted. "You mean those gadgets the Winchester brothers run around with on *Supernatural*?"

"No, that's an EMF meter — it measures the electromagnetic frequency given off by paranormal beings."

I rolled my eyes.

"EVP recorders are channels of communication between us and the discarnate," she said solemnly.

"*Discarnate*? Is that even a word?"

"The best kind are Panasonic DR60 recorders. They came out in the 1980s and were supposed to be the latest, greatest and up-to-datest dictation recorders because they used a chip not a cassette tape. But then customers started returning them in droves because when they played back their recordings, there were these very peculiar sounds on the sections when no one was speaking!" She looked at me as if expecting an amazed reaction to this tidbit of history. When I gave her a bewildered look, she continued, "They thought the recorders were *faulty*, you see. But really the machines were extra good, so they were picking up paranormal communications! If you listen very carefully to the recordings, you can hear what the spirits are saying."

That sounded like auditory pareidolia — the tendency to incorrectly perceive meaningful sounds where there's just random noise. But I could also think of a bunch of other reasons for the "peculiar sounds." Static, background or white noise would be the most likely explanations, but the recorders might surely also be picking up faint radio signals, interference from other nearby electrical equipment, or even the internal operating noise of the device itself. And, of course, the "spirit voices" could simply be deliberate hoaxes by fraudsters.

"They go for a fortune these days," Mom continued. "My friend Bettina says people sell them for a fortune on eBay and Greg's List."

"Craig's."

"What's that, dear?"

"Craigslist."

"That's the one! Bettina says they go for $1500 and more —"

"Are you *serious*?"

"Which just goes to show how valuable they are."

"Just goes to show how gullible people are, more like."

Judy arrived with our drinks. "One cappuccino and one Irish coffee, extra hot, no sugar, with a *double shot of whiskey*." She said the last few words loudly enough for everyone in the vicinity to hear.

A thin man at a nearby table turned around to look at us, then returned to reading his newspaper.

"That's Kennick Carter, Laini's brother," Judy whispered to my mother. "Poor thing, he looks devastated."

"Oh, my!" Mom craned around Judy's midriff to get a good look, but the man had his back to us again. "And is he from the South?"

"Could be. His accent sounds like a little bit of everywhere."

"He looks nice — what I can see of him," Mom said.

"All you can see of him is his back," I pointed out.

Talking to my mother, Judy said, "He's attractive from the front, too, in a rakish kind of way."

"*Rakish?* What is he, a pirate?"

A calculating look came over my mother's face. "Do you know if he's married?"

"*Mom*," I said in a warning tone.

It wouldn't be the first time she'd tried to find a beau for me. She still believed a new romance could fill the hole left by the loss of my first love.

She was wrong.

"How long is he in town for, Judy?" she asked, sending the man another evaluating glance.

"Dunno. Would you like me to ask him for you, Garnet?" Judy said with an evil smile.

"No, I would not," I snapped, irritation rising along with a dull flush.

"Your loss," she told me.

"Please make me a hot beef on toasted rye and a tuna salad, both to go. On the sandwich, hold the pickle, and on the salad, hold the salad and the dressing."

"So, basically, you want a tub of plain tuna?"

"Yeah."

"Your money," she said, giving me a look that clearly

conveyed she thought I was cracked before heading back to the kitchen.

"Well, now, where were we?" my mother asked.

"Quite far down the rabbit hole," I said and took a sip of the coffee. It was almost too hot and almost too bitter — just perfect.

"No, I think we were talking about EVPs."

"Mom, let me tell you a story. There's this huge astronomical observatory in Australia that has an enormous radio telescope which picked up strange signals for seventeen years. No one could figure out what they were. The scientists — and these were genius-level astrophysicists, mind you — were baffled. The best explanations they could come up with for the mystery signals were that they were due to distant lightning, or" — I paused dramatically — "to radio signals coming from a distant galaxy."

My mother's eyes widened in anticipation. I took another slug of coffee.

"Of course, those explanations didn't account for why the signals were only detected during the daytime," I said. "Anyway, they were convinced it came from the earth's atmosphere or way beyond."

"Signals from outer space!"

"Not so fast," I said. "A couple of years back, a doctoral student figured out that the radio signals were interference coming from the microwave in the staff kitchen." My mother's face crumpled in disappointment. "When the staff, who only worked there in the daytime, used it to heat their lunch or coffee, and opened it while it was still cooking, it caused the strange signal which the telescope detected if it happened to be facing the kitchen at that moment. *Voila*! Mystery solved."

"Well, that's very interesting, dear, but what's that got to do with the price of cheese in China?"

"The signal wasn't what they thought it was, it was *interference*. Just like on your E-recorders."

"EVPs."

"The human brain has evolved to recognize patterns even when none exist."

"They do exist!"

"Plus, there's a psychological phenomenon called priming. People who believe in — what did you call them? *Discarnate* entities — well, those people hope and even expect to hear speech, and so they do. But it's not really there." My mother took an indignant breath, but before she could speak, I added, "And I'll bet they always hear the words in their own language. They do, don't they? That's because they're imagining it!"

"It's not imagination, it's proof! It's *science*. Thomas Edison came up with the idea, and he was one of the brightest minds ever."

I downed the last of my coffee. "Yeah, well, I'm not spending $1500 on a defective voice recorder, no matter what old Edison thought."

"Maybe you could try using the recorder on your cell phone?" Mom said, sounding doubtful.

Judy came to our table just then, made a fuss of setting my mother's food down for her, and dropped the wrapped sandwich and a can of tuna in front of me. "Can I bring you another Irish coffee, with a double shot of whiskey? If you like, I could hold the coffee."

She was gone before I could reply, even though I was feeling better — which just proved the whiskey had been purely medicinal — and would've liked to order something to eat.

After a few minutes of alternating her attention between her popover ("This is delicious — you're missing out, dear!") and Laini's brother ("Poor fellow, he's not eating either, and he looks like he could use a square meal and a good woman to take care of him,") my mother announced, "I've just had a brilliant idea."

"An even better one than the EVP?"

"You could offer to help him."

"Help who?"

"Your father's worried about you, you know?" Mom pointed an accusing fork at me. "He says you need to start earning a living. I mean, you're almost thirty!"

"I've just turned twenty-eight."

"And when you finish your thesis, they'll want the assistant's job at the psychology department back, won't they? To give to a student who's still registered. And then how are you going to provide for yourself?"

It was something I'd been worrying about, too.

"He might even be willing to pay you a fee."

"Who, Dad?"

"No, Laini's brother." She shot another glance at the man, who was tucking a couple of bills into the check folder.

"Pay me for what?"

"For helping him!"

Was she suggesting I get a job as a companion to console and feed the bereaved? "Mom, I'm lost."

She waved the fork at me again, dropping a piece of egg

onto the table. "You're being deliberately obtuse! Lawdy, if there ever was a donkey as obstinate as you, I never met him. I mean, of course, that you could help him solve the mystery of his sister's death."

"*Ohhh*," I said, finally getting what she was on about. She wasn't matchmaking after all, at least, not in any romantic kind of way. "Oh, no way!"

"With great talent comes great responsibility, Garnet, and you have the second sight in spades."

"No. Way," I repeated.

"You could turn it into a business, like a private eye."

"Are you drunk?"

"I can see it now" — she wrote big letters in the air — "*McGee Paranormal Investigations*. No, wait, I've got it! *Garnet McGee — Psychic Detective!*"

Laini's brother stood up to leave, and to my horror, my mother waylaid him as he passed our table.

"Mr. Carter? I'm Crystal McGee, and this is my daughter, Garnet."

He looked a bit bewildered but shook her hand.

"I wanted to give you my condolences on the sad loss of your sister. She was a wonderful woman."

As far as I knew, my mother had never even met Laini Carter.

"Thank you," he murmured.

"It must be so difficult not knowing exactly what happened."

"*Mom*," I warned.

"But my daughter here could help you with that — she's a psychic detective."

"*Mom!*"

"She solved a murder here in Pitchford last Christmas."

Kennick Carter blinked in confusion. "I'm sorry, what?"

"Please ignore her," I told him. "She's not right in the head."

"She has the second sight, you know," my mother continued, unperturbed. "She gets messages from beyond the veil, and sometimes when she touches objects, she gets readings. And she's had visions about *your sister.*"

"Mom, stop talking now," I told her fiercely, my face hot with anger and embarrassment. To Carter, I said, "I'm so sorry to have bothered you."

"Here, let me." My mother slid the folded newspaper right out from under his arm and scribbled something on a margin. "This is her name and number, in case you want to make use of her services."

I hid my face in my hands and shook my head. When I looked up again, Carter had gone.

"I have never been so embarrassed in my entire life," I said. "That poor guy must think we're nuts."

But my mother had a very satisfied expression on her face. "I think you'll be getting a call from him," she said.

"Oh, yeah? You think he's the sort to contact random weirdos, do you?"

"I think he's the sort who likes to take a chance. Didn't you see what he was reading?"

"Uh, the newspaper?"

"The horse-racing results."

– 13 –

I had checked the laundry basket, my drawers and under the bed, and was feeling around the drum of the dryer for a missing pair of panties — my favorite white lace ones — when my phone rang.

I grabbed it off the counter and answered, "Garnet speaking."

"Hi, this is Kennick Carter. We met yesterday at Dillon's Café in Main Street?" His voice was deep, with a slight Southern lilt.

"Oh! Hi. Look, can I just apologize for my mother ambushing you like that. It was rude. I'm so sorry."

"I've been thinking about what she said, though. Can we meet and discuss whether you could possibly help me?"

"Really?" I said, taken aback. "I mean, okay, sure. When? Where?"

"Would now work for you? I don't know this town very well, but how about that Tavern place at the bottom of the hill, near the pond?"

"Give me a few minutes to finish what I'm doing." Translation: give me a few minutes to change out of my scruffy sweatpants and stick some makeup on my face. "I'll meet you there at two-fifteen."

I gave up the underwear search — clearly my panties had joined that black hole of lost socks and hair ties that lurked in the ether — and got dressed. I was in two minds about taking this gig. On the one hand, I was curious to learn more about Laini Carter's life and death, and to check out the man Ryan said would be the chief suspect if her death had been a murder. On the other, I was terrified of falling into my mother's loopy world of foolishness and never being able to climb back out. For now, curiosity was leading by a nose.

When I arrived at the Tuppenny Tavern, Kennick Carter was already waiting, leaning up against a black BMW. I studied him as I walked over. He was tall, with a thin face and the same black hair and pale skin as his sister. He wore a long, beautifully tailored camelhair coat that I immediately coveted, and expensive-looking leather shoes, but I could see why Judy had called him rakish. The too-long hair, the dark shadows under his eyes — and the world-weary expression in them — and the way he held his cigarette between thumb and forefinger, gave him a slightly dissipated look. He looked like a modern-day Byron, only with a mole high on his left cheek where the poet might have worn a beauty patch.

His gaze flicked between my eyes, but he made no comment on their mismatched colors, and he didn't offer to shake hands. Interesting. He wasn't wearing gloves, so was he a germaphobe or just lacking in manners? Or was he wary of making skin-to-skin contact with me given what my mother had told him about my getting psychic impressions from touch?

"I'm so sorry for your loss," I said.

"Yeah." He pinched his cigarette out between his fingers and tossed the butt in a trashcan. A muscle worked in his cheek.

"Should we go inside to talk?" I asked.

"It's too crowded and noisy in there. I'd like a little more privacy for this," Kennick said, giving me a strange sideways smile, his face turned away but his eyes still on mine. "How about down there?" He indicated the elevated pier that stretched over the beach and jutted a good thirty or forty yards into the pond.

I shivered. The afternoon was white with cold. Icicles dripped from the roof eaves, and a thick mist ghosted in off Plover Pond. I would have welcomed the cozy interior of the tavern and something hot to drink, but the customer is king and all that, so I merely fell into step beside him.

"Your mother says you have second sight?" He spoke without any hesitation or doubtful inflection, like he thought her claim was entirely credible.

"Look, I should warn you, she exaggerates horribly. I'm not a licensed private investigator. I'm not even sure I'm a psychic. I sometimes see and hear things, but I really have no idea what I'm doing."

"She said you'd had a vision about my sister."

"Yeah, a couple, I think. At the quarry, I got a strong feeling that she'd been there with somebody, and that they were arguing. I don't know who it was, or what they were talking about, but I felt … I think she was pushed." I glanced across to gauge his reaction, but he said nothing. "And then yesterday I had another vision."

"What was that one about?"

"Your sister had a necklace. I think it was given to her by her boyfriend."

Kennick shrugged. "If you say so."

"Oh, I was hoping you could tell me more about it. It had a very unusual design."

I described the wagon-wheel shape of the diamond pendant.

"That sounds like a chakra," he said.

"Aren't those supposedly energy zones in the body?"

For all my mother's ramblings about chakras, I still had no very clear idea what they actually were.

"The wagon wheel — usually with sixteen spokes, sometimes with eight — is the emblem of the Roma. It symbolizes constant movement and progress. It resembles the Hindu chakra wheel as a nod back to the Roma people's Indian origins."

"The Roma people?"

"The Romany. The people who disrespectfully get called 'gypsies.'"

"Laini liked Romany things?"

"Sure. She was Romany after all."

"What, like literally?"

"Yes. Well, she was born Romany, but hasn't — hadn't — lived that life for many years. I guess hardline Romany would have considered her a *gorger*, or *gadji*." At my blank stare, he added, "Non-Romany."

"Wow."

We'd reached the end of the pier, and we both looked out over the pond. The surface was a lattice of thin, fractured ice floating on water as dark as death. Gripping the handrail, I pulled my gaze away from the water and stared instead in the direction of the far bank, now lost in the drifting mist.

"Tell me about your sister. Who was she?"

"We come from a long line of circus folk. My father ran a circus, Carter and Cooper, which mostly worked the southern circuit — Georgia, Louisiana, the Carolinas, though once we went all the way through Tennessee and Kentucky to Illinois. Never again — too cold." He shivered at the memory. "Laini rode the ponies until she grew too tall. Then she did the poodle act and juggling. It didn't really matter what she did, though. She was so beautiful that people came just to watch her, rather than the act."

"What did you do?" I couldn't resist asking.

"I was no good in the ring, but I had a good gig with a shell game in a side tent." He gave me that odd sideways smile. "As a little boy I had such a cute, innocent face that it was hard for the rubes to realize I was cheating. When I grew older, I manned the ticket office. By then, my father was grooming Laini to become ringmaster. I think he wanted her to take over the business eventually."

"Not you?" I asked. He was, after all, the older brother. "Or your mother?"

"She died when we were young." He tapped a cigarette out of a crumpled packet and lit up. "But being a circus boss wasn't in Laini's nature. Or maybe it was too *much* in her nature, because she never wanted to be tied down to one thing. She was a good kid, but as she got older, she got ... restless. Even packing up the tent and moving to the next town wasn't enough change for her, because the circus and its people stayed the same, you know?"

I nodded. I might not know about an itinerant lifestyle, but I knew about having to pack up, leave the past behind and start afresh someplace new.

"She left when she was nineteen, did a couple of years at college," Kennick said.

"Studying what?"

"Marketing, but she didn't finish her degree. Every now and then she'd come back to the life for a year, maybe two, and then she'd skip off again. When my dad died and we finally wound down the circus, she moved to New Orleans with me. Got a job running promotions for the big aquarium there. She did very well for herself, too — she had a good head for business, and she could sell ice to an Eskimo. But after a few years she got restless and ran off with a cattle baron from Colorado to play at being a rancher's woman for a while."

I brushed a strand of hair out of my face. "How'd she wind up in Vermont?"

Both the land and the culture of New England seemed about a million miles away from balancing on a pony in a Louisiana circus.

"She knew Bethany Ford — the owner of the syrup business where she worked? — from when they were kids. They got in contact again a couple of years ago, and Bethany offered her the marketing position at Sweet and Smoky. So Laini shed her chaps and leathers, put on a business suit, and came up to this godforsaken frozen neck of the woods you call Pitchford."

"Is this where she met her boyfriend — Carl, I think his name is?"

"Carl Mendez, yeah, I think so."

"They weren't married?"

"No, she wasn't the marrying type." Kennick took a long drag on his cigarette, blew it out sideways from the corner of his mouth. "Laini was ... like a butterfly, flitting from bloom to bloom, drinking life's nectar. She didn't want to be caught and pinned down in anybody's collection."

"Like a butterfly," I repeated softly, feeling like I was finally getting a sense of who the dead woman had been.

"Perhaps *butterfly* isn't the right word. It makes her sound superficial, which she wasn't, not really. She always jumped in with both feet — into every job, every relationship, every gig. She *immersed* herself, learned what there was to learn, threw her whole heart into the place and the people. But always, sooner or later, she moved on. Started over in a brand-new life."

"She sounds impulsive."

"I guess."

"Impulsive people make rash decisions."

"She didn't kill herself, if that's what you're getting at," he said flatly.

"Are you sure of that? If she had problems at work, or in her relationship ...?"

"She'd just have packed her bags and moved on." He turned his back to the pond, leaning against the rail. "She didn't even want to be in one place after she *died*. Last year, she came down to New Orleans to visit me for a few days, right? We drank too much bourbon and got maudlin. Started talking about death, what we wanted to happen with our bodies after we died. I told her I wanted a full-on New Awlins jazz funeral with a horse-drawn hearse and a brass band bringing up the second line of the parade."

"And what did she want?"

"No funeral and no burial. 'Cremate me, and then fling my ashes into the air and let them be carried wherever the four winds take them!' That's what she said."

I picked at a splinter of wood sticking up from the railing. "Do you know any problems she might have had, anyone who might have wished her ill?"

"No. We'd get together once or twice a year, but we didn't have regular contact."

"I see. And — look, I'm sorry to have to ask you this — but do you know who benefits from her death?"

Looking uncomfortable for the first time, he finished his cigarette and flicked it into the pond. I frowned down at where it sizzled on the water — I didn't approve of littering.

"Well?" I asked.

"Isn't it usually the woman's partner who kills her?"

"Who inherits her money?"

"I do." Again with that sideways smile. It was starting to unsettle me.

"All of it?"

"Nobody can find a will. It doesn't look like she ever made one. Typical Laini."

"So, she died intestate, and you're her next of kin?"

"That's why I want to hire you. If it was murder, they'll look at me first. I want you to prove my innocence."

Or to make it *look* like you want to prove your innocence, I thought, trying to peel the jagged sliver of wood off from the railing and succeeding only in driving a splinter under my thumbnail. I pinched it out using my front teeth and pushed my thumb down hard on the rail until the nail went white, a thin streak of red bisecting the nailbed.

"Speaking of hiring, what do you charge?" Kennick asked.

I had no idea. I racked my brain, trying to remember what private eyes on TV shows quoted as their rates, and came up with nothing but a sense that I was a complete fraud.

"Why don't we see what I find out first, before I take any of your money?" I said.

"Okay, but let me give you something for expenses in the meantime."

Taking out his wallet, a black leather one with a tiny horseshoe discreetly stamped on one corner, he counted out five twenties and handed them to me.

"You're a gambler. You like to bet on the horses?" I said.

His head snapped around to me in surprise, and his fingers fumbled as he made to return the wallet to his pocket. It fell to the ground, and I quickly bent to retrieve it.

"You saw that? You just got a vision?"

"I saw this" — I tapped the horseshoe motif — "and yesterday you were reading the racing results."

His shoulders relaxed a little. "Oh."

Had he been worried about what I might have intuited?

My fingers, still clutching his wallet, tingled. My scalp tightened, and my eyes began to water.

A torn betting slip crushed underfoot.
Bitter cursing.
Resentment.

"But you've been down on your luck recently." The words were out of my mouth before I could stop them.

He took the wallet from my hands, the wariness back in his face. "You're the real deal. You're a reader."

He pushed off from the rail and began walking back up the pier. I strode to catch up with him. Our footsteps sounded strangely muffled on the wooden boards as, ahead of us, the red glow of the Tavern's neon sign emerged from its veil of mist.

"What do you do for a living?" I asked Kennick.

"I'm a financial advisor," he said with a bitter laugh and another sideways smile.

I said nothing, but it seemed to me that a financial advisor with a gambling problem was like a shop teacher with missing fingers.

"So," he said as we reached the parking lot, "what's your plan of attack?"

"Sorry?"

"How will you investigate this?"

Good question.

"Um, I need to speak to Laini's boyfriend, I guess, and the people who worked with her."

"I'm on my way there now — to the syrup factory. You can come with, and I'll introduce you to Bethany Ford if you like?"

"That would be great, just please don't call me a psychic detective."

I walked with him to his BMW, which even I — no car expert — could tell was an expensive model. Kennick Carter clearly liked to project the appearance of someone who was financially successful, even though the reality might be very different. I wondered if there were more discrepancies between his appearance and reality.

He unlocked his car with a remote and opened the passenger door for me.

"Get in," he said.

– 14 –

I took one step toward the open passenger door of Kennick Carter's car, then stopped abruptly. I'd just convinced a man with a lucrative motive for murder that I did in fact get real psychic visions and might be able to identify Laini's killer.

"Um … I'll meet you there," I said.

I followed the black Beemer out of town. About two miles down Route 100, a sign marked the turnoff to the Sweet and Smoky Syrup factory. The dirt road snaked through the dense woods, rising up a steep hill and then sinking down through the mist and dark shadow. If Laini had looked like a tragic sleeping beauty, then this felt like we were headed through an enchanted forest to the castle of the weak king and wicked queen. I half-expected to see seven little people with pickaxes heigh-hoing their way to work between the trees, or a handsome huntsman clutching a heart dripping blood.

It was sugaring season in Vermont — the time of year when daytime temperatures started rising while the nights were still below freezing, driving the sap up through tree trunks. Across the state, farmers would be tapping the sweet sap of maples and boiling it down into the famous syrup. Smalltime operations tended to use the traditional method of drilling a spile into the tree trunk and collecting the flow of sap in steel pails hung below. This old-fashioned way of doing things was supposedly kinder to the trees, but the Sweet and Smoky outfit, I saw as I drove deeper through the forest of red, black and sugar maples, used the newer, more efficient technology of vacuum extraction.

Plastic tubing plugged into the trunks high up on the trees, drew out the sap and fed it into thicker tubes which pulled it downhill to the pumping station and processing plant. The long sap lines crisscrossed the woods in a lattice of blue, red and green plastic, held up by trees and iron stakes. It was a bizarre sight — like the maples were hooked up to intravenous lines, only these tubes were drawing the lifeblood *from* the trees.

Neat rows of fast-growing firs bordered the winding dirt road. They were still saplings, but in a few years, they'd mask the unsightly sap-collection in the woods behind. As we drew near the factory, the avenue of saplings ended, revealing huge maples plugged with spiles and cute pails dangling beneath — a picturesque display presumably set up to charm visiting tourists.

There were no tourists that day, however. The large notice board at the entrance to the parking lot announced that tours of the sugar works, along with the children's program and sugar-on-snow events, would resume the following week. I pulled into a parking bay beside Kennick's car and looked around. To the right was the sugar shack — an enormous shed with red clapboard siding, white-trimmed door- and window-frames, and a gabled metal roof from which a chimney billowed snowy plumes of smoke and steam into the air. A sign above the door declared, "May your sap run strong and sweet!"

The building directly in front of me matched the style of the sugar shack but had glass fronting. Gold lettering on the windows pronounced this to be the factory outlet of the Sweet and Smoky Syrup Company, purveyor of Vermont's finest hand-crafted maple syrup, candy and cream. It, too, was closed, although the lights were on and I could make out someone moving around inside. A sign to the side of the shop directed "staff only" to the offices behind.

The smell of woodsmoke and boiling syrup hit me as I climbed out of the car. Kennick Carter was still in his BMW, talking on his phone. When he motioned for me to give him a minute, I nodded and walked over to the store, cupping a hand against the glass to peer inside. The clerk inside was counting bottles and making entries into a tablet — stock-taking? So, the business hadn't entirely shut down out of respect to Laini Carter. I ambled across the lot to the sugar shack, but before I could peer inside the open sliding doors, a short man in blue overalls stepped out. Wiping his hands on a grease-stained rag, he peered out at me from a face as wizened as a walnut shell.

"There's no tours today, lady." His voice was low, gruff and in no way friendly.

"I'm not here for a tour. I came to talk to Bethany Ford. Mind if I look around while I wait?"

I tried to take a step around him, but he blocked me.

"I'm Jim Lundy, the custodian of the sugar shack," he said, like he was announcing himself to be Prince Regent of the empire. "And you can't come in. There's no tours and no one to do the tours. Laini always does the tours." A spasm of intense emotion crossed his face. "And Laini is dead."

Flashbacks of her dead body — in the quarry, on the stretcher — threatened. I curled my hands into fists and dug my fingers into my palms, trying to stay grounded in the present while Jim glowered at me, seemingly ready to tackle me to the ground if I attempted to penetrate his sanctum.

"Garnet!" Kennick had finished his call and was beckoning me over to where he now stood with two people.

I recognized the man immediately. Medium height with graying hair and as square as a refrigerator — this was the man I'd seen giving Laini the necklace. The woman was a few inches taller than my five foot five, with a lovely, fine-boned face framed in soft blond curls. She reminded me of an old-time Hollywood movie star — Grace Kelly, or perhaps Ingrid Bergman.

"Bethany, Carl, this is Garnet McGee. She's a special consultant who's assisting the police with their investigation into Laini's death," Kennick said. "Garnet, this is Bethany Ford, Laini's boss, and Carl Mendez, her partner."

They looked less than enthusiastic at meeting me. I shook both their hands, and though I'd been half-braced for the contact, I picked up no readings. Carl's hands were bare, but Bethany was wearing a pair of dove-gray leather gloves. I needed to get a pair of those for myself; they looked both elegant and warm and might help with keeping my fingers out of my mouth.

"What kind of a special consultant?" Carl Mendez asked, his gaze doing the usual flick between my differently colored eyes.

"Uh …" I began.

"Victim analysis," Kennick said smoothly.

"Victim?" Bethany Ford said. There was concern in her voice, but not a hint of a frown marred the smooth space between her brows. Botox?

"I don't believe my sister committed suicide," Kennick said.

Mendez shot him an assessing glance, suddenly alert. Bethany Ford's expression, however, was one of compassion shot through with pity.

"Oh, Kennick, this must be so very, very hard for you." She shifted her gaze from brother to lover. "For both of you."

Honestly, it looked like it was hardest for her. Her eyes were swollen, her makeup smudged, her nose red, and she looked exhausted.

"I need to go," Mendez said.

"I'd like to chat to you about Laini," I said to him. "Can we set up a time?"

"No."

He turned on his heel and stalked off across the lot. Bethany Ford hurried after him, and at his car, they embraced. Did I imagine it, or did the clinch last just a second too long for a condolence hug?

Bethany returned to us, apologizing for Mendez' abrupt departure. "He's devastated, just devastated. Well, we all are, I guess."

His car disappeared, but she remained staring into space, lost in thoughts, or perhaps memories, that had her dabbing her eyes with a tissue.

"Ms. Ford —"

"Bethany. Everyone calls me Bethany."

"Bethany," I began again, "I realize this is a difficult time, but could you spare me a few minutes? I'd like to find out more about —"

"I'd do anything to help Laini and her family with this tragedy, but right now is not the time. I've just lost my best friend," she said, smoothing her hair with a trembling hand.

"Right. I'm very —"

"And it's taking everything I've got to keep the business on the rails and to sort out Laini's affairs. Which reminds me," she said, turning to Kennick, "the paperwork for you is in my office. Should we try to get that settled now?"

She and Kennick set off around the side of the store toward the offices, while I trailed behind like an uninvited child. Feeling a prickle on the back of my neck, I glanced over my shoulder and saw Jim the custodian standing on the side porch of the store, watching me.

− 15 −

I caught up with Kennick and Bethany as they entered the office building. They paused in the hall, where a blue mountain bike with thick tires hung on a rack on the wall, with a matching helmet on a hook beside it.

"This was Laini's," Bethany said, resting a hand on the bike.

Immediately, I knew I needed to touch it. But Bethany and Kennick were blocking my way.

"I think you should have it," Bethany told Kennick. "Take it with you when you go."

She sounded eager to give it to him. Perhaps it pained her to have to keep walking past that symbol of Laini's vitality. I wished she would walk past it right then, so I could grab a hold of it.

Kennick didn't seem to want it either. "No, you keep it. Or give it away."

"I thought maybe your kids ...?"

"They're still on tricycles and training wheels."

Bethany nodded, and then led the way upstairs.

I lingered behind, laying first one, then both hands on the

bike's handlebars. I got no images and no words, and nothing from the helmet either. Hurrying upstairs, I caught up with the other two outside Bethany's office, where a round-shouldered, mousy-haired woman with bright-blue fingernails was updating her with messages.

"The printing guy's on the phone and refuses to go away until he speaks to you," she said.

"Oh dear," Bethany sighed. She consulted a square high-tech watch on her wrist, and then said, "Denise, take Mr. Carter to Laini's office." To Kennick, she said, "There might be some of her things you'd like to have."

Bethany disappeared into her office while Kennick and I followed Denise to an office at the end of the hall. It was small and decorated in neutrals with pops of vivid color — an emerald-colored pen holder, a scarlet orthopedic cushion on the typist's chair, a yellow mousepad on the desk. The room was dominated by an enormous picture window with a magnificent view of the woods and mountain ridges beyond. Unusually, the desk was pushed up against the window so that Laini, when she sat in her chair, would've had her back to the door. It wasn't the sort of setup I'd be comfortable with, especially with odd men like Jim on the premises.

"She chose this office because of the view?" I asked Denise.

"Yeah. She was supposed to get one of the bigger offices, but she wanted this one."

She handed Kennick a cardboard box for any keepsakes he wanted to take and left us to it.

My gaze gravitated to a two-picture photo-frame on the desk. In one of the photographs, younger versions of Laini and her brother laughed as they high-fived clouds of purple cotton candy. In the other, Laini rode a painted horse on an old-fashioned fairground carousel. She sat sideways on her horse, holding the pole with one careless hand, while the other arm was flung out behind her, where her dress rippled in the breeze. Her face was filled with joy, and there was a wildness there, too. She truly had been exquisite.

"I gave her this," Kennick said, handing it to me. After a few moments, he asked, "Anything? From touching the picture, I mean?"

"No. Sorry."

I walked around the office, trailing fingers across surfaces, picking up items that might have carried her imprint — a stapler, pens from the holder, the computer keypad and mouse — but my hunch that she hadn't been much attached to objects was growing stronger. If only I could grasp the view through the window in my hands.

An object on the top shelf in one corner of the room caught my eye — a soccer-ball-sized globe of the world resting on a brass stand and axis. Standing on Laini's chair, I grabbed it and gave the earth a spin as I climbed back down. Tiny pearl-headed push pins had been pushed into different spots around the world — Egypt, India, Spain, Iceland. I placed my hand on the globe, blotting out Africa and Europe, then closed my eyes and concentrated. Bright light and colors coalesced into an image of Laini twirling the globe, randomly touching a place and sticking a pin in where her finger landed. A moment later, the image dissolved.

Kennick, rifling through papers on Laini's desk, hadn't

noticed my absorption, and I decided against telling him what I'd seen, because I hadn't really seen much. As I lowered the globe into the box, Denise reappeared, telling Kennick that Bethany could see him.

"You," she said to me, "need to make an appointment."

In her office, I sat down in a chair and waited while Denise scanned Bethany's schedule on her computer. My thumb throbbed — could a splinter shard be stuck in there? To stop myself sucking it, I rammed my hands deep into my pockets. The amethyst and lepidolite were still in my right pocket. In my left, the gauze bag of crystals from my mother had spilled its contents so that I now had a bunch of new stones to play with. It was soothing to turn the crystals over and over, feeling their cool smoothness beneath my fingertips.

"I could squeeze you in for fifteen minutes next Friday at seven o'clock," Denise said eventually.

"In the *morning*? Anything later? And preferably sooner?"

"It's next Friday, or April."

"I'll take Friday," I said, but I must have looked disappointed, because she gave me a small smile.

"What was it in connection with? I know most of what there is to know about the business. Perhaps I could assist you?"

"I'm helping with the investigation into Laini Carter's death."

"Oh? How?" She sounded doubtful.

"I'm trying to find out more about Laini. Can you tell me what she was like?"

Denise pulled a face that might have meant anything. "Beautiful."

"Everyone says that."

"I mean, not just pretty, but like a different species kind of beautiful. People would stare at her, like she'd put a magic spell on them. It was funny to watch."

Denise didn't sound amused, though. I got the sense that she hadn't been one of those who'd been entranced. What must it have been like for her, working with two very attractive women, both of whom were probably about as old as she was, but who wore their age so much better?

"That's why Bethany still had her do the tours even though there was more important stuff to do up here," she said. "Because the visitors would lap up her every word and then go on to spend a fortune in the store."

"I need petty cash," a voice behind me growled.

Startled, I spun around. Jim was standing in the doorway, tugging on the jug-ears set low on the sides of his head. Though he spoke to her, his gaze was fixed on me.

When I was a little kid, maybe five or six years old, we'd played a game called Kingy, which scared me stupid whenever I was tagged as "king." You had to turn your back on a line of kids standing about twenty yards away and yell out, "K-I-N-G spells king!" before spinning back around. While your back was turned, the other kids could sneak toward you — the first kid who got near enough to touch you, won — but as soon as you spun around to face them, they had to freeze on the spot. If you saw them move, they were out.

Then you had to do it again. Turn your back. "K-I-N-G spells king!" Spin around. And they'd be closer. And closer. I'd been terrified by the shuffling and sniggering behind me, the sense of threat creeping up on me. Dread grew, anticipating the moment I'd be grabbed, possibly engulfed by the whole gang. Even knowing what was surely going to happen didn't prevent me screaming when a paw clamped down on my shoulder. It had always freaked me out.

I felt like that, now, with Jim. Every time I turned around, he was behind me, standing a little closer.

"For the milk. Three dollars and fifty cents," Jim said, stepping up to the desk and handing Denise a crumpled receipt.

She grabbed a bunch of keys from her desk, unlocked a drawer and refunded Jim, tossing the crumpled receipt he handed her into her in-tray. Still he lingered, standing right next to where I sat. He smelled of smoke and sweat.

"Was there something else, Jim?" Denise asked.

I jumped as a bell trilled beside me. Jim fished an old kitchen timer out of his chest pocket, carefully reset it, and then melted away out of the office.

"When we're doing a boil, he has to tend the fires under the evaporators constantly," Denise explained. "They need a wheelbarrow of wood about every nine minutes so as to keep the temperature even, or the syrup could get grainy."

"So, Jim, he's a little …?" I let the question dangle.

"I thought you wanted to know about Laini."

"Right, yeah, I do. She was the head of marketing here?"

"Uh-huh, and she's also the VP." Denise shook her head. "She *was*, I mean."

"When did she join the company?"

"Two years ago, it must be. She and Bethany were friends from way back when, but they hadn't been in contact for years. Then

Bethany found her on Facebook. Well, everyone's on Facebook, aren't they?" As she spoke, Denise fiddled with her keys, rubbing each one before letting it slide down the ring to join the rest and moving onto the next. The movement of her fingers, with their long, turquoise nails, was hypnotic. "And Bethany just handed her the job on a silver platter — no interview required — even though Laini knew nothing at all about the business. She didn't even like maple syrup, can you believe it? She told me that once. I mean, who doesn't like maple syrup?"

"I *love* it. So … was she good at her job?"

"Yeah," Denise said grudgingly.

"What will happen now, then?"

She shrugged. "No one's indispensable." A slight smile lifted the corners of her mouth. "And who knows? The next person appointed to that position might be even better."

The phone on the desk buzzed then.

"Uh-huh, sure. I've got it," she told whoever was on the other end of the line. Dropping the keys on her desk, she rifled through a stack of papers, extracted one and stood up. "Bethany needs me."

"She sounds like she'd be lost without you," I said, ingratiatingly.

She nodded. "Sit tight, I'll be back in a couple of minutes."

As soon as she was out of the door, I snatched the bunch of keys and held them between both hands, pushing my mind into their curves and crenellated edges. My body tightened, as though all my nerve ends were waking up and gathering into a single focal point of attention. Light flickered behind my eyes.

Here we go.

– 16 –

Behind my closed eyes, images shimmered into existence.

Two women — one with a glossy fall of black hair, the other with short, mousy-brown curls — sit opposite each other at a long table. In a boardroom.

Laini's face is drawn tight with concern. Denise's is flushed a dull red.

"How long has this being going on?" Laini asks. Her voice is low, controlled.

"It's nothing. I told you I just borrowed it until the end of the month."

"Denise, I suspect this" — Laini taps a spreadsheet lying on the table between them — "is the least of it."

"Prove it!"

"I don't need to prove it. I'll leave that to the experts. I just need to tell Bethany."

"She won't believe you. You think you're so special because you're pretty, because of your past? Lipstick and

sequins!" she sneers. "Well, you're not special. I've been here since this business started. She trusts me. She needs me!" she hisses, sending a drop of spittle onto the polished surface of the table.

"I really think it'll be best if you tell her yourself. Come clean. She'll let you go quietly — she won't want any negative publicity."

Denise's hands bunch into fists. For a moment it looks like she'll hit Laini. But then her face crumples, and her head sags onto her hands.

"I can't lose my job. I can't. Please, Laini, please. My son ..."

"You tell her, or I will."

"What are you *doing*?" a loud voice intruded.

The keys were snatched out of my hands, and I blinked my eyes open to see Denise staring down at me in deep suspicion.

"Sorry, I– I ..." I couldn't think of a plausible excuse. I just looked at her, open-mouthed.

"What are you staring at?" she demanded.

A thief, I think.

Eager to get away, I stood up. "Mind if I have a stroll around the yard downstairs while I wait for Kennick?"

"Knock yourself out," she said, stashing the bunch of keys in her desk drawer. "But don't annoy Jim."

As I left, my gaze was drawn to a collage frame of family snaps. One photograph caught my attention.

"Is this your son?" I asked Denise.

Her face softened. "Yeah, that's Christopher, my baby boy."

The kid in the picture — seventeen if he was a day — was

laughing. He sat strapped in a wheelchair, elbows pulled tight against his body, wrists bent downwards, spasmed hands contracted all the way back against his forearms.

I glanced back at Denise, but she said nothing, and I left.

Downstairs, outside the office building, I headed straight for the sugar shack and slipped inside, keeping a sharp lookout for Jim. Enveloped in billowing clouds of fragrant steam, I looked around. Maybe, judging by the vintage exterior, I'd been expecting peachy-cheeked lasses in gingham dresses stirring copper pots over open log fires, because the sleek array of hi-tech equipment came as a surprise. There were huge stainless steel tanks filled with clear sap, tall machines labeled "Reverse Osmosis" and "Filter," a huge open pan bubbling over an iron boiler with closed doors — that must be where Jim shoveled in the wood — and multiple closed vats with pipes running to a room on the right-hand side of the building. Through the glass partition, I could see bottles on a production line being filled with amber liquid, sealed with lids, and wrapped with labels before being stacked in boxes by two workers.

A voice behind me asked, "Can I help you?"

A woman wearing a white coat and a protective net over her hair was smiling at me expectantly.

"No, thanks. I'm just waiting for Bethany and Denise," I said, trying to sound like I was inside the shack on official business. "They said they'd only be a minute or two."

"Okay, then. Please don't touch anything."

I forced a laugh. "I wouldn't dare! I know how Jim hates that."

She nodded, checked a reading on the boiler, made a notation on her clipboard and walked to the bottling room. Knowing that Jim would be back at any minute to feed the fires, I crept past the boilers, heading deeper into the factory. There wasn't much more to see, though, and the sweet smell of boiling syrup was beginning to make me feel sick. I was about to turn back when I spied a room in the far corner of the building. "Custodian's Office", read the sign on the closed door. When I got no answer to my knock, I checked that no one was watching and went inside.

If a person's working space is any reflection of the inside of their head, then Jim was one crazy, mixed-up fellow. The room — more workshop than office — was a mess. Tools, pipes and the assorted innards of machines lay scattered on workbenches and the floor. A pinup calendar hung lopsidedly on one wall. Above the dates circled in thick red marker and the indecipherable notes scribbled in its margins, Miss March — a lissome redhead with breasts as large as cantaloupes — gazed out at the mess. Against the far wall, a filing cabinet with papers spilling out of its open drawers stood alongside a tall steel locker which had coils of blue tubing stacked on top.

With no clear idea of what I was looking for, I snooped around — touching a wrench and the calendar, riffling through the paperwork, poking through drawers. One of these was stocked with breath mints, gum, a comb, a nail grooming kit, a tube of industrial-strength hand cleaner and two cans of spray deodorant. Did Jim spruce himself up for a special lady before he left work at the end of the day?

I had just opened the tall locker and was staring at the coats and overalls hung on the rail inside when I heard the trilling of Jim's alarm from nearby. A quick glance around the office confirmed that the only possible hiding place was inside the locker, so I climbed in, pulling the door closed behind me. It was hard to keep from falling back out because the uneven contents of the base of the locker, which I figured to be boots, made my balance precarious. The door wouldn't shut all the way, but that was probably a good thing because it was suffocating inside, with a funky odor that made me switch to mouth-breathing.

As quietly as I could, I slid some of the hangers aside to make room for my face between the coats. Then I froze. Someone had come into the office. Low mutters and metallic clanging followed. My fingers, gripping the sharp inside rim of the door, started to cramp. Something soft and silky brushed against my cheek, but I didn't dare brush it away for fear of making a sound. Every time I moved my face, even a fraction, it tickled my cheek or lips. I could only hope it was a spider's web, and not the critter itself.

One final loud clank and then silence. Had he left? I forced myself to count to thirty before opening the locker door another inch and peering out. The room was empty, the door ajar. *Time to get the heck out of here.*

I stepped out and, wanting to arrange the hanging coats back in their original positions, turned back around. Then I gasped and shuddered as though a bucket of icy water had been hurled in my face. The back of this closet was strange and unusual, but it sure as maple sugar was not a magical doorway to Narnia.

And what had been tickling my face was no spider's web.

– 17 –

When I drove into town late Friday morning, I was still feeling disturbed about what I'd seen in Jim's locker the previous day. I needed to tell Ryan Jackson all about the creepy contents, but I reckoned it could wait until that afternoon. Ryan had called first thing in the morning to ask if he could come around at three o'clock "in an official capacity." Would he be interested in hearing about my vision of Denise and Laini, I wondered, or like Officer Capshaw, would he just want the facts?

Before meeting Jessica for lunch, I swung by Hugo's Hardware. I'd heard more noises coming from the Andersens' ceiling, and I wanted to buy a couple of mousetraps to stick up in the attic. Hugo welcomed me into his cluttered store like an old friend and chuckled when I admired his sweatshirt. It was black and emblazoned with a white skeleton riding a Harley Davidson above a motto that read *Sons of Arthritis — Ibuprofen Chapter*.

"Christmas present from my grandchildren," he said.

I noticed that his breath had lost none of its pungency since the last time I visited; Hugo was a fan of raw garlic sandwiches.

He snapped his suspenders and asked, "What can I do for ya today?"

"I need to buy some mousetraps."

"Hmmm." He tugged on his long white beard and crinkled his brow at me. "Now I stock dog food, birdseed, things in cardboard boxes, all the sorts of things rats like to eat. Though they also eat drywall and plastic cables, did ya know that?"

I considered. "Maybe?"

"But do you see me setting any mousetraps around my store?"

"I'm guessing that's a no."

"Right ya are," he said, pointing a gnarled finger at me. "Know why that is?"

"Because you don't have mice?"

"You betcha. Want to know the reason I don't have mice?"

"Mousetraps?"

"Poison!"

Blue eyes twinkling with excitement, he limped over to a high shelf lethally stocked with packets of rat poison, boxes of slug bait, bottles of weed killer and an old rusted can that, ominously, didn't specify its contents.

"Now, these blue blocks will do the trick very nicely. Turns their blood to water, and makes them thirsty to boot, so they go outside and die there, and you won't have any rotting rat corpses stinking up your attic," Hugo said with grim satisfaction.

"Yeah, but it poisons owls and any other wildlife who eat them out there," I said.

"Mother Nature is tough that way."

Ignoring the illogic of this, I said, "I think I'd prefer traps."

He squinted at me. "Are ya sure it's mice up there? Did ya see them scampering about?"

"No, but I've heard them."

"Could be you've got yourself a squirrel infestation, or some bats in your belfry." He guffawed.

"You could be right about that, Hugo." More right than he knew. "How would I know whether it's mice or rats?"

"Ah, now, that can be tricky, telling the difference. You'll want to go up there and check for droppings."

"*Urgh.*"

"Mice droppings are tiny and will be scattered all over the area. Squirrel droppings are bigger and smell the worst. Rat droppings, now, they have pointed ends and are darker. Your average rat will leave 25,000 droppings in a year, did ya know that?"

"I do now, and kinda wish I didn't."

"You'll be wanting one of these for when you do a site inspection," Hugo said, handing me a protective face mask. "You don't want to be catching the plague from inhaling dust from their droppings."

"Don't you sell mousetraps?"

"Of course I sell 'em," he said, looking at me like I was crazy to ask. "Right this way."

He led me past shelves stacked with power tools, pool chemicals and fishing tackle, asking over his shoulder, "So, you're back in town, then?"

"For a while."

"Taking care of the Andersens' place while they're gone, I hear?" Hugo heard everything. He was the heart of the town's

127

grapevine. "Over at that big golf estate outside of town. Golf! Men with sticks chasing a little ball around." Hugo tutted and shook his head at this folly. "Well, that's not all that happens there. I could tell you a thing or two about those people. I know things."

"You sure do know a lot, Hugo. Do you maybe know what happens in Fight Club?"

"Eh?"

"Never mind. Where should we look next — for the mousetraps?"

"Hold your horses," he chided me. Lifting a storage box off a shelf, he blew dust off its lid and peered inside. Then he shook his head. "Nope, not in here."

I suspected the old devil knew exactly where they were but wanted to prolong our chat.

"Tell me what you know about the people in the estate," I said, not averse to hearing his gossip.

"That guard at the gate now, big fella" — he held his hand away from his sides like a gorilla — "with a thick neck."

"I know the one you mean."

"Name of ..." Hugo peered at me from under beetling white eyebrows.

"Doug."

"That's the one. Dirty Doug. He's got an eye for the ladies."

"I noticed."

"And he's been at playing nug-a-nug with Mrs. Murphy."

"Nug-a-nug?"

"Shaking the sheets, doing the dirty, getting the old hanky-panky!" He cackled. "Catch my meaning?"

"Loud and clear."

"Works his way through the ladies, he does." He eyed me keenly.

"Not with me, no way!" I said.

Looking disappointed, he bent over to examine another shelf, which I could see at a glance contained no mousetraps.

"Got any gossip on my neighbor, Ned Lipton?" I asked.

Hugo straightened, stroking his beard. "Lipton, Lipton … Fussy sort of fellow? Wears bowties?"

"That's the one."

"He's an architect, designs houses. And he's on the lookout for flying saucers, did ya know that?"

"Aliens?"

"You betcha. He had me order a telescope a while back. Said his binoculars weren't strong enough. What's he looking for if not UFOs?"

"Maybe stars or asteroids or meteor showers?"

"Ha!" Hugo barked, clearly skeptical.

"Any news on Mrs. Beaumont?"

Hugo shook his head sadly. "She's been at Martha's Vineyard for the last coupla months. Since that poor lass of hers passed."

He sighed and, limping back to the front of the store, retrieved two mousetraps from under the counter.

"There you go. But they won't work, you mark my words. Rats and mice are clever critters. They ain't going to fall for these traps."

"Then why do you sell them?"

"Because people buy them!" He wheezed another delighted

cackle. "The greeny beanies in this town don't want poison."

He showed me how to set the trap, pulling back the spring-loaded lever and hooking it onto the trigger plate. I jumped when he released the retaining bar and the lever snapped down.

"Will it kill them instantly?" I asked.

"Depends on how big they are. This trap will break a little mouse's neck immediately, but if it's a big, tough old *rat* you've got up there" — he held his hand apart to indicate the length of a large cat — "then this might only keep him in place, wriggling and squeaking, until you finish the job yourself." He demonstrated wringing the rodent's neck, complete with a squelchy sound effect. "And don't let him bite ya! You can get rabies or rat-bite fever from rodents."

The poison was looking more attractive by the minute.

"Okay, then, do you have a bigger trap — one that would work on a rat?"

He beamed at me. "What you want is the Verminator!" Retrieving a trap that looked big and strong enough to snap the paw off a grizzly, he said, "Course, a little mouse won't be heavy enough to trip *this* one."

Hugo glanced from one device to the other, then looked expectantly at me.

"Fine, I'll take one of each."

"Now, don't you be baiting them with cheese. The only rodents that like cheese are the ones in the Loony Tunes. What you want is a pea-sized blob of peanut butter, or a soft candy like a gumdrop. These'll do you nicely." He grabbed a packet of gummy bears from a stand on the counter and added it to my growing pile. "Line the traps up along the bottoms of the walls, but at right angles, and be careful when you set these things. That big contraption will take your finger off as quick as a guillotine."

"Right."

"And don't touch the bait with your fingers, leaving your scent all over it to warn the rats — use rubber gloves. You'll be a size medium." He plonked a pair on the counter and slowly began ringing up the pile of items on an ancient cash register.

"So, what can you tell me about Laini Carter?" I asked, trying to sound casual.

"I heard tell you're investigating her death."

"Where'd you hear that?"

Hugo tapped a finger to the side of his nose.

"What do you know about her?" I asked.

"What do *you* know?" he replied.

"Quid pro quo, huh? Alright, Laini Carter came from circus folk. Did you know *that*?"

His thick white eyebrows rose. "Is that so?" I could almost see him filing the juicy tidbit away in his store of gossip.

"Your turn," I said, handing over my credit card.

"Pretty as a princess, she was."

"I knew that already."

"And full of life. Always ready with a smile." He processed the payment. "Her boss, now, surname of Ford."

"Bethany."

"That's the one. Pretty, too, but sharp and hard. *Efficient.*" He said the last word like it was an insult.

"Really?" This didn't gel with my impression of her the day before. She'd seemed lost and confused. Then again, grief did that to a person, as I well knew.

"She's never been in here but one time. Always buys from the superstore near Randolph, instead of supporting locals," he grumbled bitterly. "Wouldn't put it past her to kill Laini because she was prettier." He packed the Verminator and the mousetrap into a sturdy brown bag. "Laini, now, she had a good heart. She used to buy birdseed from me for the wild birds and salt licks for the deer. I worried about her."

"You did? Why?"

Hugo hooked his thumbs under his suspenders. "It's a funny thing about beauty, but people always want to catch it and keep it. And sometimes … sometimes they like to break it. Like those vandals always smashing statues and throwing paint on monuments. I saw a fella on the TV, an artist, put his own painting through a shredder! Can ya believe that?"

"Did someone want to break Laini?"

He dropped the rest of my purchases into the paper sack and rolled the top closed.

"One time, she was in here buying this and that, and when she left, she took a flyer off my counter. A fella had left a pile of them here, see? Advertisements."

"For what?" I asked.

Hugo sighed and handed me the bag. "For self-defense classes."

– 18 –

Lunch with Jessica Armstrong was a brisk one-hour affair in the dining room at the Frost Inn, where the walls were decorated with a variety of portraits of Robert Frost and the poetically-themed menu offered items such as the Road Less Traveled Salad (Parmesan, pomegranate and brussels sprouts) and Fire and Ice Dessert (deep-fried ice cream).

I ordered a Lovely, Dark and Deep Steak (aged rib eye with red wine sauce) and a beer. Jessica ordered a Nature's First Green Caesar salad and sparkling water.

"Wait," she said as the waiter was about to leave with our orders, "is there raw egg in the Caesar dressing?"

"Yes, ma'am, it's made the traditional way," he replied.

"Then I'll have the chicken salad instead. No mayo."

Once we had our drinks, I asked, "How are you doing, Jess?"

"Okay. Good, I guess."

I wondered how she was handling the still-recent loss of her father but didn't know how to ask, so instead I said, "How's your mother?"

"Fighting fit." Jessica gave me a wry smile. "She positively *loathes* you. Says you've brought scandal and heartbreak to this town, and irreparably damaged the local economy."

Jessica's mother, Michelle Armstrong, was the town clerk and treasurer, which pretty much made her the closest thing to a mayor Pitchford had. She was on a mission to turn the town into the heart of New England tourism, and anything that got in the way of that — even justice for a decade-old murder — was taboo.

"And here I was expecting the key to Pitchford for my efforts."

"Yeah, don't hold your breath."

The waiter brought our drinks, and I took a long swallow of beer. "And Blunt? How's he doing?"

Jessica's brother was a long-time drug addict, one of the victims of Vermont's plague of heroin addiction, and quite possibly even more of a thorn in Mrs. Armstrong's side than I was.

Her face hardened, and instead of answering my question, she said, "How are *your* parents?"

"Fine, a little older and frailer. My father's still a gem, and my mother's still a kook."

I felt a bit bad saying this, because I figured I was more-or-less a kook now, too. Also, to my chagrin, I was discovering that my mother wasn't always wrong, as I'd assumed for most of my life. In fact, one of the most upsetting aspects of this whole psychic thing was how often my mother was being proved right. Not in everything, of course — I still believed most of her far-out theories and bizarre practices were ludicrous and without any basis in reality — but enough to trouble me and make me question my once-certain view of the universe.

The waiter arrived with our food, and I dug in. Jessica pushed pieces of lettuce and shavings of Parmesan around on her plate as I told her about my studies, and she caught me up on news about her family and life. Her twin sons were wonderful, Jessica said, they'd just turned four, and judging by their finger-painting creations, they were all set to become artistic prodigies just like their father. Jessica's husband was a temperamental artist who, on the only occasion I'd ever met him, I'd found to be arrogant and demanding. She seemed to still be in love with him — or at least, I thought, as she raved about how he was currently taking the art world by storm with his recent mixed-media series on *Disconnected Identity in the Connected World,* she was still smitten by his talent.

"He's been booked for an exhibition in New York, at the end of May," Jessica said.

"Wow, that's great." I swallowed the last of my beer and looked around for the waiter to order another. "And he must be so pleased about the baby."

"What baby?" she asked, startled.

I gestured at her midriff. "You're expecting, aren't you? A little girl?"

She glanced down at her still-flat stomach. "How did you know that?"

Good question. I tried to think. "Didn't you mention it earlier? Or maybe in the store the other day?"

"No. I haven't told anyone yet, not even Nico. I just confirmed it at the doctor this morning. And I don't know the sex yet."

"Oh."

"So how did *you* know?" she demanded.

My mother would no doubt have some theories, but I merely said, "Lucky guess? Or maybe because you're not drinking, and you were worried about eating raw egg?"

She seemed mollified by my explanation. "Look, please don't tell anyone yet. I haven't decided– Just keep it under your hat, okay?"

I kept my expression neutral as I mimed zipping my lips and tossing away the key, but inside my mind was racing. Had Jessica been about to say, "I haven't decided whether to keep it," or only something like, "I haven't decided when I'll break the news"?

She wasn't showing yet, but I had an idea that pregnant bellies didn't become obvious until around the fourth or fifth month. It was early March now, and I'd interrupted her and her lover getting it on in the back room of her gallery just before Christmas, so it was entirely possible that the baby wasn't even her husband's.

While we ate, we chatted about safer topics — my life in Boston, the closing down of the local high school due to lack of students, a local project to encourage the nesting of peregrine falcons — before she dropped her fork and called for the check.

"Sorry, I need to get back to the gallery."

"No problem, I need to get moving, too. I'm meeting Ryan Jackson this afternoon."

Jessica gave me a knowing look. "Oh, yes?"

"Not like that," I said hurriedly. "It's about the Laini Carter investigation. You know I found the body?"

"I read that in *The Bugle*."

"Did you know Laini Carter?"

"A little. Enough to know she was brilliant at her job. That syrup business had been chugging along for ages, but it was only when she joined in the last couple of years that it started to fly. She dragged it into the twenty-first century in terms of marketing — set up a fantastic presence on social media and apparently grew a huge email database. She raised the bottom line significantly. I don't know how they're going to cope without her."

I waved aside her attempt to pay for the bill and handed the waiter my credit card.

"I tried to poach her, more than once."

"You tried to do what?" I asked.

"I tried to get her to do marketing for the gallery, but she wasn't interested, not even in doing a few hours on the side. And my mother tried to persuade her into doing some publicity and promotion work for the town, but she declined that, too," Jessica said.

"Did she say why?"

"Initially I thought it must be because she wanted to give her all to Sweet and Smoky, or maybe that her employment contract didn't permit her to do work for other organizations. But when I asked her about it, she said she didn't need more stakes in the ground, or something like that. I didn't understand what she meant but didn't want to pry."

"Do you know her boyfriend, Carl Mendez?"

"Not really. He and Laini occasionally visited the gallery, and once he bought one of Nico's paintings, an oil, I think. But

I do recall this one time when they came in together and he wanted to commission Nico to do a portrait of Laini. Well, that was a no from the get-go. Nico creates art when inspiration strikes; he captures what the muse sends him. He's not in the business of painting pretty ladies." Jessica gave a little laugh and bit her lip. "I mean, I don't want to sound patronizing. Laini wasn't *pretty* — she was … extraordinary. So beautiful, you couldn't even be jealous, you know? It's like *she* was the work of art."

I signed the credit card slip, nodding.

"Anyway, before I could turn them down, Laini herself told Carl no. And then she insisted on buying him a painting for his bedroom wall. I remember that she said it like that, 'A painting for your bedroom wall,' and not '*our* bedroom wall.' It struck me as odd, because they were a couple, and everyone knew they were living together at his place." Jessica picked up her handbag. "Maybe she didn't feel completely at home there."

Or maybe Laini hadn't been quite as committed to the relationship as Carl had.

– 19 –

Back at the Andersens' house, I was greeted with a fury of hysterical delight by Lizzie and Darcy. Really, everyone ought to have a dog just to be on the receiving end of that kind of welcome. As I tickled their tummies and smoothed their silky ears, I detected the hint of mint on the air again. My mother would say it was a ghostly presence. If so, it smelled like the house was being haunted by the ghost of Pepsodent past.

I put on the rubber gloves Hugo had sold me, grabbed the mousetraps, gummy bear bait, a flashlight and a broom — in case I needed to defend myself against any rodent attacks — and headed upstairs. The dogs sniffed excitedly at the ladder when I pulled down the trap door to the attic and watched with interest as I climbed up. Once my head and shoulders were in the dark space above, I paused and whacked the broom head on the wooden boards a couple of times to scare away any rats that might have plans to bite my face or bats who wanted to take up occupation in my hair.

"I'm coming in!" I yelled, feeling both stupid and nervous.

I shone the flashlight around the interior, lighting up storage boxes stacked against walls, a pile of magazines, a crate of empty beer and soda bottles, an old mattress and an antique wooden rocking horse which cast crazy shadows as the beam of light hit it. I climbed up another step and turned around to cast the beam on the back of the attic, then yelped and slipped down two rungs as the light caught the unmistakable reflection of an eye. Heart hammering and hands suddenly slippery with sweat, I forced myself to climb back up, pick the flashlight up from where I'd dropped it, and shine it back to where I'd caught the gleam.

A doll. It was just a vintage porcelain doll sitting on a dressing table. But my sigh of relief hitched in my throat as I climbed up another step and took in the full scene. The doll was large — big enough to ride the rocking horse, for crying out loud — and missing both legs. One round glass eye peered directly at me, while the other was closed in a grotesque wink. Teeth — too many and too pointed for an infant — showed in the baby's smile, which was smudged from some long-ago application of lipstick. The doll's naked torso was propped up against the mirror of a child-sized dressing table with a cracked, spotted mirror that reflected my horrified face back at me. On top of the dressing table lay a pink brush and comb set, still tangled with a fuzz of long blond hair.

"What the hell?" I whispered, my eyes watering as they always did when I was scared.

The doll leered back at me, silent and still as the grave. Cursing the creepy contents of the house, I retrieved the rodent traps and baited them as quickly and carefully as I could. Using the broom to shove the traps deeper into the attic space, I tried to align them with the walls as Hugo had advised, irrationally aware of the single glass eye watching me from the darkness behind my head. Then I scrambled down the ladder and shoved the trapdoor closed, returning the spooky doll to the full darkness of its tomb and returning myself to the creepy house where such things were kept in the attic.

I was beginning to have some serious doubts about the Andersens.

I knew the doll and dressing table in the attic were most likely just the old toys of a kid who'd once lived here, but still, I had a bad case of the heebie-jeebies. It was getting increasingly difficult to distinguish between what was real, what was crazy-but-maybe-real, and what was just plain crazy.

What had happened at lunch with Jess was a case in point. I'd told her I'd just guessed she was pregnant, and my justifying explanations made sense. The only problem was, they weren't true. Because I hadn't guessed, I'd *known*. Just like I knew her fetus was female. And how could I know something without knowing how I knew it?

Back in the kitchen, I stowed the broom and gloves, poured myself a strong cup of coffee and, craving noise and a sense of company, turned on the radio — an old-fashioned model with manual dials and an extendable aerial.

"The National Operational Hydrologic Remote Sensing Center estimates northwestern Vermont has accumulated 7-10 feet of snow in total this season, and —"

The announcer's voice cut out, and loud static sounded through the kitchen. Lizzie whined.

"I know, right?" I said to her. "One of the most annoying sounds in the universe."

I grabbed the radio and, leaning against a counter, turned the dial slowly, searching for a station with some upbeat music or a nice frenzied political debate. Anything to distract me from my unsettled state of mind. But the entire FM range gave only static, sometimes soft and sometimes loud enough to make Lizzie protest. I switched to AM. More hissing, until — finally, a song. It was one I recognized: *Somebody's Watching Me* by Rockwell.

I danced across the kitchen to nuke my lukewarm coffee in the microwave, singing along loudly, "People say I'm crazy, just a little touched." I could totally relate to those lines. Maybe a little too much? "I always feel like somebody's watching me," I sang, then stopped. The song pretty much captured exactly how I was feeling. Paranoid and unbalanced and a freaking mess. Had I somehow affected the radio or intuitively found this song? Was that even possible?

Accepting these abilities was hard for me. *Ego-dystonic*, that was the correct psychological term for it. It didn't sit comfortably with my sense of self, with who I knew myself to be. Correction — with whom I'd once *believed* myself to be. I'd been trained as a scientist, schooled to test hypotheses, experiment under controlled conditions, to focus on what was observable, measurable and provable, and deduce objective conclusions from the data. The psychic phenomena I'd experienced, on the other hand, were varied, unpredictable and subjective, a complete inversion of scientific method and understanding.

I wasn't eager to believe in any of it, so it was unsettling and embarrassing to discover how I'd shifted to being more or less willing to do so.

The microwave beeped, the song ended, and an advertisement for Burger King began playing. Lizzie settled in her basket, head on paws, back to normal.

Another aspect that bothered me was exactly how this whole psychic thing worked. How come I sometimes got flashes or visions spontaneously, like I had at the top of the quarry, while at other times I had to concentrate, like with the keys and the necklace? Why did I sometimes have to touch an object and other times not? I needed to know the rules.

I fired up my laptop, opened a blank Excel spreadsheet, and made a vertical list of all the visions and flashes I'd had. I named columns for each of the factors that I thought might be variables, such as whether the vision had occurred spontaneously or after concentrating, if I'd touched an object or person, or known the individual in the vision, whether there were strong emotions in the vision, and if the event portrayed had happened recently. Then I worked down the list, checking the boxes of the conditions that applied to each vision.

The panicky feelings I'd experienced at the top of the quarry, and which I was now sure had been Laini's rather than my own, had come to me spontaneously, I hadn't had to touch anything, and it was a memory of a high-emotion event that had happened very recently.

With Laini's body in the bag, though, I'd had a fuller vision — was that because I'd touched her? Realizing I'd touched both her body and the body bag, I checked both relevant columns, then paused, running fingertips over the ends of my nails, automatically searching for rough edges while I pondered. Laini had been dead when I touched her, so did that make her an object, or should she still be classified as a person? I compromised by dividing the *touched person column* into *alive* and *dead* and checking the latter, along with *strong emotion* and *recent*.

I'd had to concentrate to get readings on Laini's necklace and the globe — perhaps that was because they weren't in themselves connected to something with high emotions. The bone was not recent but surely was very high in emotion, or — the thought popped into my head before I could stop it — attached to a restless spirit. My scientist brain, the one analyzing my experiences for a common and predictable pattern, refused to create a column for that particular variable.

Back in December, all of Colby's visions had come spontaneously, and I'd been inside them, inside *him* looking out, rather than on the outside watching the scene play out like a video. Was that because we'd been so close, or because he'd been "sending" them to me?

I created two more columns — *inside* and *outside* — and checked the relevant boxes for each vision. I'd been inside Laini, too, when I experienced what she had at the top of the quarry and when she fell. But I hadn't really seen anything, I'd just felt her emotions and body sensations. I added columns for these.

I stared down at my spreadsheet, searching the data for patterns. I saw none. I'd keep updating the file with my experiences, though, in the hope that eventually I'd figure out the rules of engagement in this strangest of games. As I hit *save*, the doorbell chimed. Ryan had arrived for our official meeting.

Pushing the barking dogs aside and futilely ordering them to be quiet, I opened the front door.

"Oh!" I said, surprised.

Because Ryan wasn't alone.

– 20 –

F BI agent Ronil Singh, of the Rutland field office, was the poster boy for tall, dark and handsome, and so pointedly polite that I immediately suspected he was visiting me under sufferance.

I offered my visitors coffee, and when I went to the kitchen, Ryan, Darcy and Lizzie followed.

"You told the FBI about me?" I said.

"Is that a problem?" Ryan asked.

I set a tray with cups, cream, sugar and some of the animal crackers I'd bought in town. Ryan grinned when he saw these, grabbed a gorilla and bit its head off.

"I always figured cops were supposed to be skeptical unbelievers," I said.

"I always figured cops were supposed to believe the evidence."

"What evidence?"

"I checked on the necklace."

"And?"

"Carl Mendez did give it to Laini, and he did have it

specially made. And she was a cyclist."

So, the vision had been accurate. That pleased me. Scared me a little, too.

Ryan helped himself to an elephant and a cougar. "Go on, you can say it ..."

"*What?*" I said, all innocence.

"You told me so."

"I did, indeedy. And I've got more, but it'll have to wait."

I put the coffee pot on the tray and handed the lot to Ryan to carry into the living room, where Agent Singh was standing, staring at the figurines on the shelf. *If you think those are creepy, you should see the doll in the attic, bud.*

Singh sat down only after I did and accepted a cup of coffee, but he left it untouched for the rest of the interview. Darcy snuffled at his feet, and Lizzie put her front paws on the couch beside him, begging for affection.

"Sit," Singh said, and to my surprise, they did.

"Agent Singh is one of the investigators on the Jacob Wertheimer case," Ryan said.

"You're not here about Laini Carter?" I asked.

"That's not under our jurisdiction, ma'am," Singh replied.

"Right." I sipped my coffee. "So, how can I help you?"

"Officer Jackson here contacted us because he believes you may have some" — Singh hesitated, clearly searching for the right words — "extraordinary knowledge of the crime?"

"Knowledge? No, I don't *know* anything. I just sometimes get ... *impressions* when I touch objects or visit places where something traumatic has happened."

"I see. And have you had this ability all your life?"

"No, just since December." Singh gave me a questioning look, and I found myself babbling, "I banged my head a few times, then drowned and apparently died. When I came back, I started experiencing things."

"Was there no medical explanation for your symptoms?"

His face remained blank and his manner polite, but I could tell he thought I was brain damaged.

"None that the doctors could find."

Giving up on getting any attention from Singh, both dogs wandered over to Ryan, who slipped them each an animal cracker.

"And what *impressions* did you get when you handled the rib bone that your dog found?" Singh asked me.

Now it was my turn to search for words. I tried to explain the suffocating darkness and fear and the sense of evil without sounding like a complete loon. Singh's eyebrows twitched once or twice, and he pressed his lips together as if to prevent himself from commenting.

When I petered out with, "And that's all," he grimaced and said, "I see," in a way that made me think he clearly didn't see at all.

Opening his briefcase, he removed four brown paper sacks with folded tops and placed them on the coffee table in front of me. Lizzie and Darcy immediately abandoned Ryan and came over to investigate, but Singh stretched out an arm and pointed a finger at the doorway.

"Kitchen," he said firmly, and they both sulked out.

"How do you *do* that?" I asked, amazed.

"These bags" — Singh indicated the collection with a sweep

of his hand — "each contain a single object. I would like you please to touch or handle the objects one by one and let me know what you … get." I didn't think I was imagining the note of cynicism in his voice.

"Okay, sure."

Feeling like a contestant in a game show, I unfolded the top of the nearest bag, stuck my hand inside and pulled out a man's wristwatch. I held it in one hand, then in both, but felt none of the sensations I associated with getting a reading. I closed my eyes and concentrated, sending my full attention to the timepiece in my hand.

I shrugged and dropped the watch back in the bag. "Sorry, nothing."

Singh nodded, as if this was exactly what he'd expected.

The next bag contained a small silver crucifix. Again, I held the object, closed my eyes, and concentrated. Again, I got nothing.

"Look, I don't always get a reading. In fact, most of the time I don't. I can't *make* it happen." Even to my own ears, it sounded like I was making excuses.

"Of course, I understand perfectly," Singh said, his lip just hooking in the beginnings of a sneer.

Scowling at Ryan for putting me in the position of feeling like a performing monkey, I tipped the contents of the second to last bag into my hand. It was a matchbook, pure black except for a silver exclamation mark embossed on the front and a New York address on the back. I held it tightly, shut my eyes and channeled my anger into my hands. My fingers prickled, my scalp tightened, and my breath caught at the image that flashed into my mind.

A young woman, early twenties, heavy makeup.
Topless.

Surprised, I looked up — just in time to catch the look Singh exchanged with Ryan. His expression was one of clear derision, and it pissed me off royally. I closed my eyes again and doubled down over the matchbook. It took me a couple of seconds, but I got it again, like re-entering a dream when you've just woken up but are still half-asleep.

A woman, topless, wearing a sequined G-string. She's in a box. No, a booth — a small booth with gold walls and a heavy red curtain across the doorway.
Music plays. She writhes and wriggles, rubbing her hand over her breasts and between her legs.
A man looks on, his expression caught between would-be cool and growing lust.
She dances across to him, straddles his thighs.

I opened my eyes and told Singh, "I got something on that one."

"Oh, yeah?"

"Yeah. A topless woman wearing a silver wig was giving a lap dance to a man." I smiled, savoring the moment. "To you."

Agent Singh kept his face impassive and said nothing, but he ran a finger under his collar as if it was suddenly too tight.

I shook out my tingling fingers and took a deep breath before tipping the last bag over the table. A button rolled out — round, made of light wood, with a raised rim and four central holes. I picked it up and at once felt like I'd been kicked in the gut. Heavy darkness closed in, and a suffocating sense of wrongness robbed me of breath. I teetered on the edge of an abyss of deep shadows. And fell.

The button, fused to my hand, was pulling me down, down, deeper down. *No!*

Wrenching my eyes open, I opened the tightly closed fingers of my right hand and dropped the button back onto the table. I rubbed the palm of my hand, which burned as though I'd been holding a red-hot coal.

"This is it? This is the thing the killer left with the bodies of his victims?" I said, my voice sounding breathy.

The agent shot Ryan a filthy look. "What the hell, Jackson — you told her? So much for this being an objective test!"

"I only told her the killer had left something with each of his victims, not what that something was," Ryan snapped back. "It could just as easily have been the cross or the matches."

Singh frowned at me and demanded, "What did you just see?"

"I didn't really see anything except darkness." A stygian gloom blacker than the darkest night. A darkness that was less the absence of light than the presence of something ancient and evil. "And I got a bad feeling, same as when I touched the bone the other day. But this time, I didn't feel fear. I mean, I was scared, but for me. It didn't feel like there was fear connected to the button."

"Darkness and a bad feeling. Fear but no fear," Singh repeated. "That's it?"

I nodded.

"I see. Well, I think we're done here."

Clearly, I hadn't won him over.

He dropped the button back into the bag and returned all the bags into his briefcase. "Thank you for your time, ma'am."

"You're most welcome," I said coldly.

"We'll take it from here and contact you if we have any further questions."

Translation: don't call us, we'll call you.

"What if I have more visions about this?" I asked.

Seeming reluctant, he handed me his business card. "You can call if you get something new."

I made no effort to see him out. As usual, after having a vision, I felt limp and drained. Sighing, I closed my eyes and relaxed back into the couch cushions.

That was when it happened.

A latex-gloved hand caresses a stubbled jaw and a bloodied lip, then trails down a throat, over a wire garrote. Pushes aside an open shirt to stroke a naked chest, circling bruises with a forefinger, on its way down lower. Opens the fly, slowly, one button at a time, kneading the flesh beneath with fingertips and knuckles. Rubs. Harder and harder.

Shuddering and swallowing down nausea, I opened my eyes and said, "He's white."

Agent Singh, who was almost out of the room, stopped and turned. "What's that?"

"Your perpetrator. He's white. Left-handed, I think. He

wears a ring." I tapped the third finger of my left hand. "So he's probably married."

Both men's attention was riveted on me now.

"The perp is definitely male?" Singh asked.

"Yes. That is, I didn't specifically see ... But yes, he's male."

"How do you know?"

"I just do." I raised a hand to my throat. "And he killed this victim by strangling him with a wire."

Singh and Ryan exchanged a glance.

"The victim wore a red-and-blue plaid shirt, and blue jeans with buttons, not a zipper. Levis, maybe," I said.

"Did you get anything else?" Singh asked.

I stared at my hands for a few moments, trying to recapture the feel of the vision.

"He likes them. Sexually, I mean," I said. "He wants to have them. And to know them. No, to *be* them." I nodded. That was it. "He wants to be them."

Ryan's mouth was open, and Singh's eyebrows were raised so high they almost merged with his hairline.

"Give me that button again," I said.

Wordlessly, Singh walked back over to me and tipped the button out of the bag and into my palm. As if readying myself for a dive into deep water, I took a deep breath and closed my eyes. Then I brought both palms together, holding the button between them. My eyelids fluttered as my vision went dark.

Two hands, wearing latex gloves now, thread the button with black twine. Secure it with a double knot. Thread the other end of twine through the eye of a large, curved needle. One hand pinches the bloodied lips together between finger and thumb, and the other begins stitching ...

With an involuntary cry, I opened my hands and dropped the button. Singh bent to retrieve it from the carpet while Ryan said, "You're as white as a sheet, Garnet! What did you see?"

I pushed the back of a hand against my mouth and swallowed down my nausea.

"You found that button on his mouth, on the victim's mouth."

Singh returned the button to the paper bag. "No, we didn't."

"The remains were skeletonized, and the bones were scattered, Ron," Ryan said. "You can't say for sure where the button was originally left."

"Neither can she."

"He sewed the boy's mouth closed, with the button and black twine," I said. "Excuse me."

As I rushed out of the room, I heard Ryan ask Singh, "The other victims — were the buttons on their mouths, too?"

I couldn't hear Singh's reply over the sound of me retching into the guest toilet. When I'd emptied my stomach, I washed my hands with hot water for several minutes, trying to scrub off the lingering sensation of darkness, wishing I could scour the images I'd seen off my corneas.

I walked to my front door, from where I watched Ryan and Singh talking animatedly by the fed's car. At a movement in my peripheral vision, I turned my head just in time to see my neighbor's curtain twitch. No doubt Nosy Ned would be

154

popping by soon to get the scoop on Chief Jackson's latest visit. I took several deep breaths, calming myself, and crouched down to hug Lizzie for comfort.

Ronil Singh's car started and pulled away, and the dogs — released from his inexplicable control — left me and bounded down the path to greet Ryan's return to the house. He studied my face as he approached.

"You okay?"

I nodded.

"Sure?"

"Yeah," I said, though I wasn't.

"Grab your coat," he replied. "We're going for a drive."

– 21 –

"Where are we going?" I asked Ryan as we climbed into his police cruiser.

"The quarry. I want to see if you can pick up anything else. You okay with that?"

"I guess."

I wasn't exactly keen to return there, but I was curious.

We pulled out of the Andersens' driveway, and Ryan drove slowly through the roads of the estate toward the entrance.

"Did you really see Singh getting a lap dance at a strip joint?" Ryan asked, breaking the silence.

"I really did. He was getting into it, too."

"Man, he looks like butter wouldn't melt in his mouth. Goes to show — you never can tell," Ryan said, flashing me a grin.

It was a very cute grin, especially with that single dimple on the right side of his mouth. It was the kind of grin that you couldn't help returning. It was the kind of grin that sparked a little flip in a girl's stomach and put her in danger of falling for a guy.

At the entrance to the estate, Doug the guard peered into the car and shot me a reproachful look before opening the gates.

As we turned left onto the route that headed away from town, I asked Ryan, "So, did I make things better or worse for you with the feds?"

"Singh wasn't happy, but judging by how rattled he was, I'm guessing you got more than a few things right. He might be back."

"I can hardly wait," I muttered.

I'd be happy never to cross paths with Agent Singh again, but I did want to know more about that killer, the man with the buttons. And at the same time, I also wanted, at a visceral level, to have nothing more to do with it ever again. But just in case, I fished his card out of my pocket and captured his number into my phone. Still irritated with his disbelieving attitude and his inexplicable authority over the dogs, I made his first name *Skeptical* and listed his company as *G-Man*. I doubted I'd ever hear from him again.

"It must have been hard for you — seeing that stuff," Ryan said, casting me a sideways glance.

"Yeah."

I stared out at the bleak winter scenery, seeing bruises and fondling and blood and a garrote. Seeing lips being sewn together, with a button in the middle. Buttoned up.

I pushed the disturbing images from my mind. "I was at the syrup factory yesterday, with Kennick Carter."

"You were? Why?"

"I'm kind of working for him now."

"Wait, what?"

"I, uh, I'm helping him investigate his sister's death."

"Garnet." Ryan's tone was equal parts exasperation and warning.

"There's no law against that, is there?"

His brow furrowed, as if he was trying to think of one.

"My mother kind of strong-armed me into it," I confessed. "I don't know if I can really help — and I did tell him that in case you think I'm ripping him off — but I'm nosy enough to want to try. Besides …"

"What?"

"It's wrong. If she was murdered, then that's just wrong. And the person who did it shouldn't get away with it."

"You have a real thing for justice, huh?"

Did I? I wouldn't have said it about myself. Colby had always been the one who was hot for law and order. *He* was the one who'd planned to become a cop. But, thinking back over the last week, I realized that I *was* feeling a slow, relentless burn to see justice done. Maybe this was another aspect of him that had now merged with me.

"I guess so," I said.

"Got any suspects?"

"Well, reluctant as I am to pile suspicion on my own client, I reckon you should probably investigate Carter's finances because I think he inherits everything."

"Follow the money trail — now there's a thought! They should've taught us cops that back in training."

"Sarcasm," I said pertly, "doesn't become you."

"Hmm."

I stared out at the road that arched and bowed through the

forests outside of Pitchford. "He's a gambler, too."

"Interesting."

"And not a very good one."

"I'll check it out," he promised. "Why were you at the syrup works?"

"I wanted to speak to Bethany Ford. Carl Mendez, too, when I saw he was there. But he skedaddled as soon as he met me, and she will only see me by appointment. And," I added, grumpily, "only next Friday."

A week was too long to wait; I needed to come up with a plan to see her sooner.

"What did you think of them? Get any …?" Ryan waved a hand between his temple and field of vision.

I opened my mouth to tell him about the vision I'd had of Laini confronting Denise, but instead I heard myself saying only, "No, I saw nothing about Mendez or Bethany."

It was the truth, and nothing but the truth, but not the whole truth. I knew I should tell him about Denise — as he'd said, follow the money — but that photograph of her cerebral palsied son had upset me. For now, I'd keep my suspicions to myself.

Just before the Brookford turnoff, Ryan pulled off into a dirt lane that curved behind a wall of hedges.

"How's *your* investigation going?" I asked. "Did you find out anything more?"

He said nothing as he parked the car near the trail that led up to the decommissioned stone works and killed the engine. On this cold winter afternoon, we were the only car in the lot.

"Come on, Ryan, I've given you a great lead. It's your turn to dish."

He turned in his seat to face me. "If I tell you this, it's off the record. I don't want you telling *anyone*. And that includes your client."

"Please, I'm a professional secret-keeper! Your confidences are safe with me," I said.

"Alright then, someone was sexually harassing Laini, sending dick pics to her phone from an unknown number. They tried to trace it, but it's an old burner not registered to anyone."

"Ah," I said.

"That mean something to you?"

"I might have an idea who the dick belongs to."

"*Who?*"

"Jim Lundy, the custodian at the syrup factory."

"And you know this because … you've had a vision of his dick?"

"God forbid! No, I just– I happened to find myself in his office in the sugar shack, and his locker just happened to be open."

"Oh, yeah?"

"And I couldn't help seeing what was at the back of it, hiding behind some coats."

"The coats just happened to part themselves so you could see, I suppose?"

"Exactly!"

"And what did you see?"

"I guess the best word for it would be a collage. Of photographs of Laini Carter."

He raised his eyebrows at that.

"Yeah, dozens and dozens of photographs stuck overlapping each other so there isn't a clear inch at the back of that locker. All kinds of pics, too — long-distance shots and grainy close-ups that I guess he'd enlarged. Taken at the factory, the syrup shop, in town, in her car and lying on a lounger beside a swimming pool. He must have been stalking her for ages. He was clearly obsessed."

Ryan gave a low whistle.

"Plus, he'd stuck cut-outs of her head and face over the naked bodies of other women — porn magazine pull-outs, by the look of them."

"Holy shit."

"And there was something else." I made a throaty sound of deep revulsion. "There was a dirty piece of string hanging from the coat rail inside the locker."

He cocked his head quizzically at me. "A piece of string?"

"And at the end of that piece of string," I continued, "was a lock of hair. Black hair."

"What the hell?"

"*Right?* And it was exactly long enough and hung at precisely the right spot so that if you stood outside and looked in, the hair hung where Laini's hair was in the biggest picture stuck directly behind it."

And at the exact point where it would touch the face and tickle the lips of a person of my height hiding crouched inside the locker. The thought of that still turned my stomach.

"I'll try to get a search warrant, though I don't know what I'll say to the judge as a basis. Or maybe the locker belongs to the business, rather than to Lundy, and I can get permission from Bethany. We'll have to check his employment contract and the company policies."

Ryan drummed his fingers on the steering wheel.

"What?" I asked.

"The thing is, if he's such a creep —"

"Oh, he's that alright."

"— then why would Laini have gone up to the quarry with him?"

I considered. "Good point. You wouldn't catch me going anywhere with him voluntarily."

"Is he a big strong guy?" Ryan asked.

"Nah, he's a runty little thing. Definitely not strong enough to carry an unconscious woman up that hill" — I pointed out of the window — "if that's what you're asking. In fact, Laini could probably have taken *him* in a fight."

Besides, in my vision of Laini at the top of the quarry, she'd been conscious.

"Hmmm," said Ryan.

"Was there anything else interesting on Laini's phone?"

When he didn't reply, I held the silence and his gaze. I'd done enough therapy role plays to learn the value of waiting until the pressure to respond made the other person speak.

Eventually Ryan broke eye contact and said, "Seventeen calls and thirty-one messages from Carl Mendez in the twenty-four hours preceding her death."

My jaw dropped. "What kind of calls and messages?"

"Angry, sad, humiliating. She'd ended their relationship on Saturday morning. In the messages he raged that she had no right to leave him like that, begged her to come back and give it another go. He promised that things would be better, that he'd try harder, give her anything she wanted."

"And her replies?"

"She begged him to stop contacting her and refused to meet him — said it would do no good because her mind was made up. Then from nine o'clock on Sunday morning, radio silence."

"So, she broke up with a man who was jealous, controlling, angry and humiliated? He's suddenly looking like *my* top suspect."

"We still don't know that she was murdered, Garnet."

"You might not, but I do."

"Come on," he said, opening his door. "Let's go up to the quarry."

– 22 –

Ryan led the way up the path to the old stone works. "Did you know that Laini was interested in taking a self-defense class?" I asked.

He glanced back at me, surprised. "How do you know that?"

"Hugo told me she took a flyer from his shop counter." My feet slipped on the mulchy pulp of leaves underfoot, and I grabbed a branch to steady myself. "I think you should check Carl Mendez out — see if he has a history of violence." Seeing the slight tightening of Ryan's shoulders, I said, "You already have, haven't you?"

"Yeah," he admitted.

"Does he have a criminal record?"

"No comment."

"I'll bet he has. And, psychologically speaking, the best predictor of future behavior is past behavior."

"You don't say."

"And I'm sure I don't have to tell a police officer that almost sixty percent of murders on women are committed by their intimate partners."

"Uh-huh."

"You could check at local doctors and hospitals to see if Laini was ever treated for injuries following an assault."

"You teach your grandmother to suck eggs, too?"

"Just trying to be helpful."

"Hmmm."

"I need to speak to him. Mendez, I mean. Can you get me in there?"

"In case I never made it plain before, you're a civilian, Garnet."

"Kennick Carter told Mendez I was a 'special consultant in victim analysis' who was assisting with the investigation."

"Did he now?"

"*Special consultant* — I thought it had a nice ring to it."

"Uh-huh."

"Mendez seemed to buy it, too. Didn't ask any inconvenient questions. I reckon I could just tag along with you."

"If you stop nagging me, I'll see what I can do. Just don't, for God's sake, let Ronnie find out."

We were nearing the quarry. In one narrow section of the trail, a tree had fallen across the path. Ryan lent me a hand to clamber over it. It was a nice hand, too — firm, warm, despite the chill of the air, and steady as I leaned down on it.

No!

The word inside my head felt like it hadn't originated there, but it could just as well have been a message from me to myself. Because I wasn't there to notice Ryan's warm hand or his charming grin or his fascinating dimple. I was supposed to be focusing on picking up messages and images from the site of at least one murder.

I followed Ryan to the spot by the big boulder where Jacob Wertheimer's body had been dumped almost a decade ago. A few strips of yellow police tape still dangled limply from trees around the wide area that had been excavated to a depth of about four feet. Beyond that, the brush had been cut back and tufted grass trampled flat.

Ryan paced the perimeter of the scene, pulling off the cordon tape and rolling it around his hand, while I slowly explored the area, touching the boulder, the tree, the dirt; standing beside the freshly turned earth; listening with my heart and my mind, and getting ...

"Nothing," I told Ryan. "Sorry."

His shoulders dropped in disappointment, but my chest lightened a little — I'd been dreading falling into that darkness again.

"I felt nothing here the first time, either," I said. "Maybe because it happened so long ago?"

"Can you try with this again?" From a jacket pocket, he pulled out the plastic evidence bag containing Laini's note. The blue paper was now covered in smudges of black powder.

"Did they get any prints off it?" I hadn't known that you could get fingerprints off non-glossy paper.

He shook his head. "Nothing usable. It was all too smudged."

As I opened the bag, he said, "Please touch just the tiniest bit."

I wasn't sure that would work. "You let me hold the necklace and driver's license," I pointed out.

"Those were just belongings at the scene. This is evidence of suicidal intention, and we may want to run more tests on it."

I touched a fingertip to the edge of a corner of the note and closed my eyes to concentrate.

A trembling hand holds a piece of paper scrawled with loopy handwriting. The paper is pale blue, the background a blur of pink and green.

It was the same image I'd seen before, but now I could see the hand was female and tell the person was distraught. I took a deep breath and pushed my mind down through my fingertip, into the point of contact with the paper.

Her hand is steadier, now. She folds the paper once and then again. Tucks it into the pocket of black denims. She's calmer, decided, determined.

The image swam out of focus and I blinked my eyes open. I hadn't seen much, but still, I'd seen *more* than I had the first time I got a flash of the note. Was this a skill I could develop and improve?

"Well?" Ryan asked.

"I saw Laini's hand holding the note, then folding it and putting it in her pocket."

From his expression, Ryan had clearly expected more.

"That's all I *saw*. Do you want to hear what I felt?"

"Of course."

"She was very upset at first, and then she felt resolute, like she'd made her mind up about something."

"That would fit with suicide."

"I guess. I'd like to try at the top of the quarry again. That's where I got the first sensations the day I found her."

Excited at the possibility that I might see more of Laini's death, possibly even the identity of her killer, I strode back up the path, climbed over the remains of the fence, walked to the lip of the quarry and peered over the edge.

"There's something on the ledge." I squinted my eyes to see better. "Flowers, I think. All different colors."

"Are you sensing anything?" Ryan asked from where he stood a few feet back.

"Give me a minute."

I closed my eyes and focused my attention. There was something there, prickling at the edge of my awareness, but it was elusive, and fading fast.

"Just faint words," I said. "*Crisis ... eat ... love.*" They were slipping away even as I tried to hear them. "Clee-something. *Cliché*, maybe, or *clingy*?"

"Feeling anything?"

I dropped my head on my chest, tried to tune in to any lingering emotions. "Anger. Contempt?" I held my breath, reaching with my mind into the fading sensations, but all I felt now was myself, swaying a little.

"Garnet?"

I opened my eyes to see Ryan staring at me, his face tight with concern.

"*I'm* feeling something now," he said.

"*Really?*" This was amazing. "What do you feel?"

"Hugely uneasy at you being so close to the edge of that drop. I so badly would not like it if you fell."

I took the hand he held out, and he tugged me a few steps back to relative safety.

No! Not him.

Okay, this time I was sure — the words were definitely inside my head, and also definitely not my own. They sounded and felt like they came from ... But that couldn't be. Even so, I released Ryan's hand.

"Let's go," I said. Then, catching a faint scent, I sniffed the air like one of the beagles. "Can you smell cola?" I asked Ryan.

"Like the drink? Or a candy?"

"Like the lip balm flavor."

He sampled the air. "Nope."

He turned to go, but I closed my eyes and leaned into the awareness of the scent. This time, the images that rippled into my mind's eye were from my own memories.

> *Colby, his skin golden in the warm summer light, stands in front of me on the edge of the ledge above the swimming hole. He's wearing a pair of cut-off denims that hang low on his hips, his hair is wet from previous leaps into the swimming hole, and he's smiling. His brown eyes are filled with love and mischief.*
>
> *"I can't!" I insist, my back pressed against the rough*

gray-green rock of the quarry wall.

"Sure you can. Just stop overthinking it."

"It's too high."

"That's what makes the falling fun."

"I can't."

"Okay, then, we'll do it together." When I hesitate, he steps closer. "Didn't you promise 'always and forever?'"

I nod, slip my hand into his and hold on tight. My heart hammers in my chest, and blood rushes in my ears.

"Always," I say, my voice hoarse with fear, because I'm sure I'm about to die.

We run the few steps to the edge and leap into the air in tandem, screaming, "Forever!" as we fall.

I opened my eyes. Once again, I was standing on the miserable hill, on a cold, cloudy day. *I haven't forgotten you, Colby.*

"What did you say?" A few yards away, Ryan had turned to face me.

Had I spoken aloud? I wiped my eyes and hunched my shoulders against the past.

"Nothing," I said, and headed back to the path.

– 23 –

At two minutes past ten on Saturday morning, I drove up the crushed stone driveway and parked outside the huge colonial-style house. A Virginia creeper clawed its way up the front walls, weaving through decorative black shutters, headed for the slate roof. In summer, this would be a shimmering wall of green, and in fall, a spectacular display of flame-colored leaves and purple berries, but now it was an intricate web of bare vines, tendrils and suckers gripping the wood and stone.

The front door was answered by a diminutive woman in a maid's uniform.

"Hi, I'm Garnet McGee. I have an appointment to see Bethany," I said, omitting the fact that the appointment was scheduled for the following Friday and at her office.

The maid looked unsure. "She didn't tell me about it."

"She must have forgotten to mention it."

"She's still doing exercises in the solarium."

"I'm a little early. Can I wait inside, please? It's wicked cold out here."

Reluctantly, she opened the door and led me through a vast

hallway with Persian rugs on hardwood floors, a vase of pink stargazer lilies well past their prime on a marble-topped half-moon table, and a huge sunburst mirror with radiating copper rays on the wall, to a front reception room.

"Please wait here," she said.

When she seemed inclined to remain in the doorway, keeping a watchful eye on me, I asked, "I could *really* use a cup of coffee. Any chance I could trouble you for one?"

As soon as she left the room, so did I. I tiptoed down a long hallway, peeping into rooms on either side. The interior of this mansion was elegantly decorated in a clean modern design that was the antithesis of the froufrou onslaught of the Andersen house. Hearing the clinking of china coming from one end of the hallway, I headed in the opposite direction, passing an informal living room with a flat-screen TV bigger than my parents' kitchen table and a study with shelf-lined walls bearing books that looked like they'd been arranged according to color. I peeped inside the last room. What on earth?

Blinking, I stepped inside and rotated on the spot, taking it all in. The shelves which covered one wall were stacked with dozens of glittering trophies and award shields of every size and shape. I stepped closer to read the inscriptions: *Baby Miss; Little Miss Beauty — first princess; Little Miss Sweet Potato — personality award; Little Miss Charleston — first princess; Georgia Junior Queen (1994), Miss Teen America — queen; Miss Southern Belle* and more. A glass cabinet against the opposite wall housed tiers of sparkling crowns and tiaras, and the remaining walls were covered with framed beauty pageant sashes and photographs.

There were pictures of what was surely Bethany Ford as a rosy-cheeked baby holding a plastic rattle in the shape of a jeweled scepter, and then a bunch of her as a toddler — blond curls piled high upon her head, face made up to resemble a grown woman, wearing sequined gowns and bathing suits and heels so high, *I'd* be afraid to walk in them. Then there were images of her as a teenager sitting on glitter-encrusted thrones or clutching enormous bouquets of flowers. And in every picture, she was smiling, smiling, smiling; my cheeks ached just to see it.

In the biggest picture on the wall, two preteen girls with their heads tilted against each other smiled sweetly for the camera. The one on the left, whose pretty face supported a towering cascade of blond curls, was easily recognizable as Bethany. The girl on the right was wearing a glittering crown, and with her straight black hair, pale skin, red lips and big cornflower-blue eyes, she looked a lot like a miniature version of Laini Carter.

Lipstick and sequins! Was this what Denise had meant about Bethany and Laini's past? When Kennick had said they'd been childhood friends, I'd imagined them growing up in the same neighborhood. This was something else entirely.

I went back to the pageant pictures and studied the images of tiny queens and princesses. It looked like Laini — if the dark-haired girl was indeed her — had kicked butt in the earlier pageants of the 1980s, but I couldn't find her in any of the later pictures. Had she dropped out of the pageant circuit? Put on a few pounds? Stopped smiling? The most recent photograph was a lineup of ten Miss America finalists from 2000, which included Bethany. She wore a sheath gown of glimmering silver and the widest smile of all of them.

Drawn by the sparkle of rhinestones and crystals, I walked over to admire the crowns that had once graced Bethany's head. I picked up the tawdriest of them all — a gold plastic tiara studded with pink and yellow "gems" — and placed it on top of my head. Turning to a mirror, I smiled wide enough to crack my cheeks and crooned sweetly, "If I am chosen as Miss Sweet Potato, I will work tirelessly for world peace. And I promise to end world hunger. With yams."

An impatient throat clearing startled a squeal out of me. I spun around, sending the crown flying off my head and rolling across the carpet, where it came to rest at the maid's feet.

"What are you doing in here?" she demanded.

"Sorry, I just– I was just admiring the bling."

"This is Miss Ford's trophy room." She picked up the crown, polished it carefully with a cloth to wipe off any smears I may have left, and restored it to its rightful place on the shelf. "I think I must take you to her now. She will soon be finished with the exercises."

The solarium had glass walls, a domed glass ceiling, and dozens of potted palms and hanging ferns. Bethany Ford — in knee-length yoga pants and a cropped top — balanced above an exercise mat, with all her weight resting on her forearms and the balls of her feet. The maid waited patiently while I admired the perfectly straight plank, the lean, hard body and the intense focus.

After a minute she pushed back to sit on her knees, eyes closed and hands resting palm-up on her thighs. If I was a pageant judge, I'd award her ten out of ten for grooming. Even though she'd just completed a serious workout, she still looked perfect — from her smooth, blonde bun to her perfectly manicured pink finger- and toenails.

Expelling a deep breath through her nostrils, Bethany Ford opened her eyes, checked the display on her Apple Watch and frowned up at us, taking in my odd eyes without comment.

"The lady says she has an appointment with you, Miss Ford," the maid said.

She turned to go, but Bethany halted her to reel off a list of instructions. "I'm ready for my smoothie — kale, pineapple and chia seeds. Please empty the paper-bin from the shredder in my office into the recycling bin, and don't forget to clean all the birdcages before you go."

"Yes, Miss Ford. And Miss Laini's flowers? Do you want me to leave them until Monday?"

Bethany stared bleakly at a corner for a few moments, then sighed deeply and said, "No. I suppose it's time to put them on the compost heap."

"Yes, Miss Ford."

The maid left, and Bethany turned her attention to me. Before she could ask what the heck I was doing in her house, I said, "That plank was a thing of beauty! I've never been able to hold one for longer than ten seconds."

Truth was, I'd never tried planking at all.

"It takes practice and discipline," she said, eyeing me like she doubted I had either. "Correct me if I'm wrong, but isn't your appointment with me next week?"

"You're absolutely right, but Kennick Carter suggested I try to chat with you sooner. He said you're a kind and generous woman, and would probably help me if I asked nicely," I said, wondering if my nose was growing from all the lies I was telling. "Poor guy, he's really suffering. As you must be, too."

Her erect posture slumped a little, and she sighed. "I can give you five minutes, I suppose."

"Thanks, I really appreciate it. I know you must be an exceptionally busy woman."

Was I laying the flattery on too thickly? I didn't think so. Maybe your average Joe would suspect an ulterior motive in my ass-kissing attitude, but I was talking to an ex-beauty queen. If anyone welcomed recognition, attention and appreciation, surely it would be one of them?

A phone buzzed on a nearby bench. Bethany grabbed it, checked the screen, and tossed it aside with an impatient sound before sliding her hands back down the mat, arching her back upwards and tilting her head backward in what looked like a seriously uncomfortable pose. Slinking tiger, stretching cat? I estimated the amount of body fat on her angular frame to be 0.0%. In clothes, she looked fabulous, but up close in exercise gear, she looked thin to the point of being bony, like if a bear took a bite out of her, he'd get mostly gristle and sinew.

"That looks like such hard work!" I said.

"A hard worker — that's me," she said in the direction of the glass dome above her. "One day, the inscription on my gravestone will be: *she tried harder.*"

I wondered what mine would be. *She doubted everything and trusted no one*, perhaps? Or, *here lies a woman who preferred hot peppers to most people.*

Bethany curled her spine the other way, like an angry cat, and with her nose almost touching the yoga mat, demanded, "Well, why did you want to talk to me?"

"Kennick thought you would have valuable insights on Laini. He said nobody knew her better than you." He'd said no such thing. "You were her best friend, is that right?"

With a final stretch, she finished and stood up, dabbing at the sheen of sweat on her neck and face with a small towel, being careful not to smudge the mascara, eyeliner and nude lipstick I now saw she wore. Wearing makeup for an early-morning yoga session in the privacy of her own home — was that vanity or insecurity?

"Yes, I was her best and oldest friend. We knew each other since we were little ladies."

Little ladies. That fit. I doubted Bethany had ever been a little girl. I couldn't imagine that bejeweled and bedazzled creature in the old photographs ever climbing a tree or making mud pies.

"Where was that?" I asked, even though I knew.

"In the South. I'm originally from Savannah."

"Right, I can just about hear it in your accent. So how did you two meet? Were you at school together?"

Bethany slipped into a long kimono and tied the sash. "We worked the Southern beauty pageant circuit together."

"Beauty pageants?" I said, like this was new to me. "The two of you must have been spectacular together — you with your tanned skin and golden hair, and Laini with her white skin and black hair."

"We were," she said and promptly burst into tears.

– 24 –

"Oh dear, I'm so sorry. Here, sit down," I said, guiding Bethany to a bench and patting her on the shoulder as she sobbed. I should've offered to leave her in peace, but I didn't. "Can I bring you anything?"

She shook her head, blotted her eyes on the kimono sleeves and, with a visible effort, regained control of herself.

"I'm so sorry, I don't usually —"

"Please don't apologize. You've suffered an enormous loss."

"It is," she said, staring at me earnestly. "It is enormous." She ran a hand over the midnight-blue silk of the kimono. "This was hers," she said. "It still carries the scent of her fragrance. I wear it because it helps me feel closer to her. Kennick has left all her clothes and things with me. He says I should keep what I want and give the rest away. But I won't. I won't get rid of any of it."

She smoothed her already-sleek hair and then got up and exited the solarium. I followed, hoping she wasn't taking me back to the front door.

"I'll have my smoothie in the living room, Sofia," she called in the direction of the kitchen, then led me into the same room I'd waited in earlier. Once we were seated, I tried to get the interview back on track.

"So, you and Laini were in beauty pageants together?"

"We both started when we were very young, and we did well, too, if I do say so myself. One or the other of us was always winning. Laini more often, if I'm honest. It was an extraordinary thing. We used to joke that she was the only contestant with black hair that ever won pageants. My mother said it was her talent that gave her the edge," Bethany said with a shrug. "When she was tiny, she had this amazing routine with a bunch of dancing poodles, and then when she grew older, she swallowed fire and juggled flaming torches. Playing with fire — literally." Bethany gave a small, sad laugh and traced a pink nail over the pattern of her upholstered chair. "It always wowed the judges."

"What was your act?" I asked, genuinely curious.

"You didn't come here to hear me reminisce about the old days, Miss McDonald. Can we get to business?"

Not correcting her on my name, I said, "Right, of course. Laini's brother has hired me to investigate his sister's death."

"I don't understand why. It was a suicide."

"That hasn't been fully established yet."

"But she left a note! The police showed me."

"Her brother doesn't believe she killed herself."

"I think he might be in denial. Isn't that a stage of the grieving process?"

I nodded, conceding the point. "It sounds like he and Laini didn't spend much time together in recent years, so I thought you might be able to tell me more about her," I said. "About the Laini you knew."

"Yes," Bethany said thoughtfully. "She *was* a different person with each of the people in her life."

"Who was she with you?"

"She was —" She paused, considering. Fully expecting her to say "beautiful" like everybody else had, I was surprised when she said, "Bright."

"Bright? As in clever?"

"No. Well, yes, that, too. Laini was no one's fool. But I meant bright like she had an inner glow. She could light up a room, you know? So much energy and laughter — when she was feeling good, that is."

The maid came in, bearing a tray with a tall glass of dark-green sludge.

"I should have offered you something," Bethany said. "Can I get Sofia to make you a smoothie?"

"No, thanks!" It came out sounding rude, so I smiled apologetically and added, "Really not my thing, kale smoothies."

Sofia gave me a narrow-eyed gaze. "I think you'd like a cup of coffee?"

"Yes, please," I said meekly. When she left, I asked Bethany, "Did you and Laini stay in contact all these years?"

"No. She dropped out of the pageant circuit before her teens, just gave up." She shrugged, as if Laini's decision still baffled her. "We lost contact. I connected with her online a couple of years back, and when I found out she was in marketing, I offered her the position here."

I watched, fascinated, as she swallowed down the entire glass of green gloop in one go. I would rather have stuck pins in my eyes.

"It must have been good to get to know each other again."

"It was. We had girls' nights together, watching old movies and painting each other's toenails, laughing and gossiping about the people in town." Her smiled faded, her lips trembled, and her eyes welled. "What will I do without her?" she asked, her voice bleak.

Hoping to avert more crying, I asked, "What was she like at work?"

She sniffed and dabbed at her eyes. "Gifted. She added such value to our organization — the business won't be the same without her."

No doubt Bethany would have to lean more on Denise's assistance. Denise might even get Laini's old job. Should I warn Bethany about my suspicions in that quarter? Probably. But not yet.

"Did Laini *like* her work?" I asked.

"Of course! She said she'd finally found her niche. Although ..."

"Yes?"

"She resisted taking extra responsibility. Don't get me wrong, Laini was excellent with innovative ideas and creativity, but she wasn't great at handling pressure. Sweet and Smoky had grown by leaps and bounds, and we were planning to expand further. I wanted her fully in on that. I even offered her half-shares in the business. That was a mistake, I see that now. I blame myself."

"For what?"

"I think it was all the stress and the prospect of taking on even more responsibility that broke her. It was too much pressure, on top of her rocky relationship with Carl. And her brother's problems, of course."

Struggling to keep up with the revelations, I asked, "Which problems were those?"

"Money. He borrowed a lot from her over the years, and I gather he hadn't repaid very much of it. Well, Laini was never good at setting boundaries or confronting others."

That was odd. In the vision I'd had of her and Denise, Laini hadn't seemed to have a problem confronting the employee, and she hadn't succumbed to Carl Mendez's pressure to marry her.

The maid came in then and set down a tray on the table in front of me — a demitasse of black coffee, a tiny jug of cream, and a side plate of almond biscotti. The look in her eye said, *"Waste this cup, too, and I'll tell the boss about the crown affair."*

I thanked her effusively.

Bethany said, "Once you've finished the kitchen, you may go, Sofia."

"Yes, Miss Ford. Have a good weekend."

Swallowing a bite of biscotti, I asked Bethany, "Did Kennick know about the shares?"

"Oh, yes. She said he was impressed, that he'd urged her to accept the offer."

I'll just bet he did. First loans and then shares — I wondered what else my sideways-smiling client had kept from me.

"But Laini wasn't sure. She knew it meant more stress, I suppose. And when she felt overwhelmed, she'd get very down. She suffered from depression, you know?"

"I didn't. Was she on medication?" People, I'd discovered, tossed terms like "depressed" around very loosely.

"I urged her to see a doctor or a therapist, but she refused. She said cycling out in nature was the best medicine for her." Bethany glanced at my biscotti and then looked away. Resisting temptation? "I often wondered if she had bipolar disorder because she had such wild ups and such bad lows. I think it caused problems in her relationship with Carl."

"You think that's what caused their breakup?"

"You know about that, do you?"

I nodded.

Bethany glanced out of the window, as if seeing past scenes of domestic unhappiness. "It was a stormy relationship. Laini with her moods, and Carl with his temper. Well, I know all about *that*. I used to date him years ago and let me tell you, the man has serious anger issues."

"Was he abusive?" I asked bluntly.

"To me? No."

"And with Laini?"

"She never actually said so in as many words, but ..." Bethany's voice trailed off.

"Did she tell you why they'd broken up?"

"She didn't give me any details, just said they'd called it quits. She arrived on my doorstep on Saturday morning with all her stuff — packed bags, coffee machine, camera — and asked if she could spend a few nights because she'd moved out of his place. She said Carl was taking it hard, and she didn't feel comfortable staying there for the night."

"'Comfortable' — is that the exact word she used?"

Bethany tilted her head, considering. "She may have said 'safe.'"

"She spent the rest of day with you? Slept here on Saturday night?"

"Yes. Look, I did tell the police all this already."

I could tell she was running out of patience.

"And how was she that night?" I asked.

"A little subdued, perhaps, but then she *had* just broken up with Carl. We shared a bottle of wine and spent the night chatting."

"About?"

"This and that. Life, men, traveling, future plans for the business. She seemed better the next morning, calmer, more settled, you know? She had more color in her cheeks and said she was more certain of her plans going forward." Bethany's face crumpled under the weight of her distress. "At the time, I thought she meant life without Carl. Now, I realize that she'd made up her mind about ending it all."

People who were planning to end their lives often did seem calmer and more settled just before they implemented their plans. For some, the hardest part was making the decision. Once that had been done, the follow-through was easier. When I'd seen her hand holding the note, I, too, had picked up on that growing sense of resolution and decision.

"When was the last time you saw her?" I said.

"Early Sunday morning, around eight o'clock. She said she was going for a drive into town to buy us a box of cider donuts for breakfast."

"Cider donuts? I wouldn't have said your body had ever

come within ten yards of one of those," I said.

"A rare seasonal treat." Bethany smoothed a hand over her flat stomach. "Then she hugged me and kissed me goodbye. I never dreamed that would be the last time I saw her. But I should have *known* when she kissed me!" She punched a fist into her thigh, hard. "I mean, you don't kiss a friend goodbye when you're just nipping into town, do you? I should have known, or guessed. But I had no inkling of what she planned, honestly!"

"So, you think it was planned?"

"Well, I don't think she just went for a stroll up to the quarry and on the spur of the moment decided to hurl herself off!" Bethany said acerbically. "Plus, she left a suicide note. And she sent me a text, you know, saying she was spending the day with Carl. And *he* got one from her, too, saying she was spending the day with *me*. That was deliberate."

Bethany stood up and walked to the door. "I've told you what I know, and now I really do need to get going with my day." Judging by the tears that were welling in her eyes again, she really needed to get going with a good crying jag.

"Right. Thanks so much, I really appreciate your insights." I followed her out of the room. "Can I just ask about Jim Lundy?"

"Jim? He's a funny little man — those ears! — but absolutely reliable and vital to our operation."

"How did he get on with Laini?" I asked as we walked into the entrance hall.

"He *adored* her. He was always bringing her odd gifts. I advised her to keep her distance so he didn't get the wrong idea, but I think she felt sorry for him. Always asking him how his arthritis was doing and giving him advice."

"What kind of advice?"

"He'd had some kind of trouble, and she was helping him with that, but I have no idea what it was about."

Bethany opened the front door and stood aside for me to leave. I stepped out, but before she could close the door, I squeezed in a final question.

"So, Laini wasn't afraid of Jim?"

Bethany blinked. "No. Should she have been?"

– 25 –

I drove directly home, mulling over the interview with Bethany Ford. I hadn't had any visions or intuitions while at her house — did that mean something? It occurred to me that I'd worn my smart coat to visit her, rather than my parka with the crystals in the pocket. Was that why I hadn't seen anything? No, that thought was just stupid. I was getting as superstitious as my mother.

At the Andersen house, I changed into sweatpants, an old sweater and thick socks, and stuffed my hair into a messy bun secured by a pencil. I found the local news on the TV — which had shifted channels again — and checked to see if there were any official updates on either the Laini Carter or Jacob Wertheimer cases. There weren't.

My phone pinged with a message from Professor Perry, asking whether I was ready to send him my completed thesis for review. When I was a teenager and grouching about homework and group projects, my father used to say, "Sometimes, kiddo, the only way out is through." I needed to apply that advice to my thesis now — just do the work, finish it and then I could be free. Free to … do whatever I finally figured out I wanted to do with my life.

I turned off the TV, determined to get stuck into the difficult task of integrating my conclusions on grief studies, but as I turned away from the screen, I noticed something odd. The porcelain clown was back at the front of the shelf and facing forward again. Had Agent Singh done that yesterday? He'd been standing right there, and he looked like the sort who liked things neat and tidy. It had to have been him. Unless the house really was haunted? Perhaps what the *Welcome to the nut-house* message on the front doormat referred to were the peculiarities within its walls, and especially its freaking attic, rather than the copse of hazelnut trees outside.

The clown grinned at me, slack-mouthed and silent. I shoved it out of sight behind a stack of gardening books, making a mental note to restore it to its proper spot before the Andersens returned.

Lizzie kept giving me beseeching glances and running to the front door.

"Sorry, Lizzie. I need to work. We'll go for a walk later."

When she got excited at hearing the magic word, I flung a handful of dog treats in each of their bowls, like a bad mother trying to buy a half-hour of peace by bribing a toddler with candy.

I was still thinking about toddlers and mothers when I fired up my laptop in the study. Those photographs in Bethany's trophy room of little girls in pageants had disturbed me. On a whim, and because procrastination had always been my middle name, I typed "child beauty pageants" into my browser's search bar. And got close to five million hits.

As I scrolled through the results, read articles and watched videos, my earlier unease solidified into a growing sense of horror, because this whole child beauty business was nothing short of batshit bonkers.

A few years back, I'd caught an episode or two of the *Toddlers and Tiaras* reality show and found it appalling. But I'd assumed the program was about an unusual competition on the fringes of a dying beauty pageant industry, a bizarre but passing fad. Between what I'd seen at Bethany's house and what I read now, I was learning that nothing could be further from the truth. Kiddy pageants with tiny little girls — some as young as two weeks old — who fiercely competed against each other were at the very heart of the industry. They were the nursery in which future beauty queens were sown and grown.

There were big prizes up for grabs, but I figured that competing must come at a high price. Surely girls taught to believe their tiny bodies and pretty faces were their most important assets were at a much higher risk of developing disorders such as anorexia, bulimia, body dysmorphia, depression and anxiety, and were destined to live under the lifelong whip of deeply ingrained perfectionism?

I rummaged in a desk drawer, trying to find a packet of Skittles — munching on the mouth-puckeringly sour candy usually helped keep my fingers out of my mouth. When I couldn't find any, I made myself a pot of ginger root tea and then, with Lizzie and Darcy dozing at my feet, settled in to watch a bunch of YouTube videos featuring reality programs of child beauty pageants. It was horrifying.

The way the little girls were prepared (waxed, spray-tanned, bleached and made to diet) and coached (drilled in their routines, endlessly rehearsed and trained), and then prepped on the day (with fake hair, eyelashes, nails and even breasts, and slathered in heavy makeup) was grotesque, if not downright abusive.

Backstage, the tots were squeezed into disturbingly sexy outfits, then they snapped on their savage smiles, pranced out onstage and strutted up and down for the judges, who marked them on beauty, personality, talent and a certain mysterious quality called "poise."

They sang, danced, juggled and tumbled. Occasionally, they tripped, fell, and forgot lines. It was a spectacle of glamor, bling and patriotism — every second song was God Bless America, and every other costume a dazzling confection of red, white and blue.

Backstage, the girls' high energy and smiles fizzled into slumped shoulders and exhausted tears until everyone was called back out front for the crowning ceremony. Trophies and bragging rights went to the winner, bitter disappointment and crushing blows to self-esteem went to the losers, who maintained their unwavering smiles even as the hope and joy drained out of their eyes.

The pageants set girl against girl and mother against mother. These kids lost their childhoods the minute they entered the pressurized, sexualized, competitive world where the only acceptable standard of both appearance and performance was perfection. What did the girls take away from this dog-eat-dog business, I wondered.

Laini had grown up to be a woman who ran away from commitment and problems. Bethany had started a business — so she could finally have something under her full control? Because these kids had no control. They were living dolls. They may have had more intact limbs than the doll in the attic upstairs, but in their own way, they were just as creepy.

– 26 –

Sickened, I took a break, letting the dogs out for a run around the yard while I made myself a ham and jalapeno sandwich, washing it down with a beer before returning to my research.

The various reality TV series on toddler beauty pageants were made after Bethany and Laini's time on the circuit, but after wading through pages of posts, newspaper archives and old photographs, I tumbled across an old documentary from 1986, called *Little Queens*. The program followed four girls through a single pageant, all the way from the face-painting, hair-teasing process backstage, through their rhinestone-studded, sequin-encrusted performances out front, and on to the final crowning of the winner.

One of the girls was Bethany Ford, and even at the age of around seven, it was easy to see the woman she'd one day become. Little Bethany was blond, beautiful and diligent. She sat still while her mother applied an inch-thick layer of makeup and tugged her hair into an intricate bouffant, nodding at last-minute instructions, rehearsing her pre-written lines over and over again.

In front of the judges, her posture was perfect, her routines flawless, and her smile relentless. She did indeed try harder.

My phone rang, startling me back into the present. It was Ryan, inviting me around to his place that evening.

"Come around seven o'clock, and we'll talk," he said. "I'll throw in a steak and a few beers."

"Okay." I could fill him in on what I'd discovered and pick his brain for new leads. And, if I was honest with myself, it would also be good to spend some time with him. "Do you have hot sauce?" I asked before he could end the call. "And I mean scorch-your-taste-buds, make-your-eyes-water, fire-your-endorphins, *hot* sauce."

"Does Tabasco count?"

"No. Tabasco falls so far short of the fire-inducing blazing red-hot hell I seek that it may as well be ketchup."

"I could buy you something this afternoon?" he offered.

"Don't worry your pretty little head about it, Chief. I'll come armed."

I returned to watching the documentary, catching glimpses of a girl who might have been Laini in the background of footage shot in the dressing room. Her mother was dragging a brush through her sleek black hair and fussing over her face. When all the girls were led out to wait by the stage for their turn out front, the camera panned across a boy sitting scrunched in a chair in the corridor, hunched over an old Nintendo device. When the black-haired girl passed by him, he glanced up, said something and then returned his attention to Mario Brothers or Donkey Kong. Could that be Kennick?

I paused the video and rewound, watched again, frame by

frame. It *was* him. The same black hair and the same mole high on his left cheek. He was onscreen for less than a second and then gone. Had it been that way generally in his life — with all the attention focused on Laini? Laini's beauty, Laini's performance, Laini's achievements. Poor kid. It couldn't have been easy.

The camera cut to show the girls doing their thing out front, under the scrutiny of a panel of five judges. As each contestant walked out, she said her name, age and ambition — "When I grow up, I want to be a ballerina. Miss America. A pop star like Tiffany. A ballerina. Miss America. The president. Miss America" — before sashaying down the runway.

Every time a new contestant came out, her mother would take up position behind the judges' table to cheerlead her kid through the rehearsed routine. They mimed the movements and mouthed the words along with their onstage performer — gesturing for bigger smiles, straighter posture, more pizzazz — like puppet-masters remotely controlling their robotic marionettes. When the routine ended, the mothers returned to their seats, either hysterical with joy or sour-faced that their kid had botched it.

Bethany Ford confidently stated her intention to be a TV star. She wore a frothy dress edged with a swatch of pink ostrich feathers for her evening wear and a sequined top hat and matching tuxedo jacket over a white leotard and silver fishnet tights for her talent section, performing a three-minute show of magic tricks. They were pretty good, too. I watched closely but couldn't see where she'd gotten the ace of spades from, or where the handkerchief had disappeared to.

When she finished with a graceful bow, the judges nodded

and smiled, and the camera cut to Bethany's mother in the audience.

"We're in it to win it!" she said, her face glowing with fierce triumph.

Laini hadn't been chosen as one of the four main girls followed in the documentary, which was a mistake, because she drew and held the eye like none of the other contestants did. When she stepped onstage, wearing a glittering dress the bloodred color of a ripe cherry, she lit up as though her inner glow couldn't be contained by mere skin.

She seemed somehow more real than the other girls, and harder to forget. Her hair was darker and straight, her smile more mysterious. Where the others radiated in-your-face confidence, her charm was more playful, a little elusive. Almost fey. Where their charisma exuded out from them to the judges and the audience beyond like the shock wave of an explosion, Laini's magnetism sucked you in, captivating you. You got a sense that she was playing at a fun game, not grimly determined to win a competition, and it was instantly more appealing.

She didn't *need* to win. And so, of course, she did. Because we all secretly despise those who crave our approval and want to bathe in the light of those with true self-assurance.

Bethany placed second. Her high-wattage smile undimmed, she graciously congratulated Laini. Perhaps I only imagined the flash of emotion in her eyes as she met her mother's disappointed gaze over the heads of the judges.

I tracked what I could of Bethany and Laini's progress after that competition. Laini had won many more pageants but disappeared from the circuit before she became a teenager. Was that because her mother had died, or did she simply drop out because she was bored or burned out? Bethany continued competing, winning more pageants once her chief competitor had quit, until the Miss America competition which must have been the pinnacle of her beauty career. She failed to place in the top five.

She surfaced a year later as a weather girl on a local television station and then progressed to news anchor, where she stayed for several years before being swept aside for a younger woman. I felt a sharp pang of anger at the injustice, because The Hair was forty-five if he was a day. Such a double standard. Then again, maybe it had been Bethany's choice to leave and start her own business.

I closed the search pages and videos. It was time to work. Truthfully, it was about four hours *past* time to work. The morning had slipped away in a dazzling blur of glitz and glamor. I spent the afternoon working so hard that for the first time, I began to see light at the end of my academic tunnel.

My parents popped over for a visit at around five, though I didn't remember inviting them. Lizzie and Darcy went insane with excitement at seeing new faces — barking, baying, and running up and down the hallway until they'd rippled up the rug in a concertina-style pile.

"Sorry," I yelled above the noise. "They've got too much pent-up energy."

"Show me where the leads are, and I'll take them out for a nice long walk," Dad said.

The dogs' excitement rose to fever pitch when they saw my father holding the leads, but the moment the front door closed behind them, all was blissful silence. Until my mother spoke.

"My, my. They sure do have a lot of stuff in this house," she said, taking in the ornaments that covered every surface. "Trotskys, they're called in Yiddish."

"Tchotchkes," I said.

"Yes, dear," she said, on a long-suffering sigh. "And have you experienced any more strangenesses here?"

Since denying everything never seemed to succeed in getting her off my back, I decided to go to the other extreme.

"Oh, yes! I often hear funny noises."

"Where?"

"In the ceiling."

"Ooh! What kind of noises?"

"No rattling of chains," I told her. "But loads of creaks and rustles."

"That sounds like mice, dear. Any scratches in the walls?"

"Not in the walls, no."

"That's what you usually get when a house is haunted."

"You live and learn. How about smells? Because I've noticed some odd ones."

"Not sulphur, I hope! The smell of sulphur means a demon is about."

"No, just mint and cola."

My mother sniffed the air experimentally, then looked disappointed. "Maybe it's just your toothpaste or candy. Anything else?"

"Lots! There's a dismembered doll in the attic that spooked the crap out of me, and a child's dressing table with an old hairbrush which still has hairs in it. There's a clown figurine on a shelf in the living room which turns around by itself, and a mermaid statue in the bathroom that watches me while I bathe and shower. I had a moment when I thought the radio was playing a song especially for me. And sometimes the faucets drip."

My mother blinked at me several times, while I waited for her latest wild theory. Pixies, maybe, or poltergeists.

Instead, she said, "Well, I suppose that could all be the work of an overactive imagination and absent-mindedness. Never mind, dear" — she patted the back of my hand — "at least you still have your visions."

"Mom," I said, shaking my head, "you never cease to amaze me."

"How about a nice cup of tea? I'll make it while you fix that carpet."

I straightened the rug and went to the study to back up my documents. Mom stuck her head in the door while I was shutting down my laptop.

"Any cake or cookies to go with our tea?" she asked.

"There are some animal crackers in a bag in the pantry."

She bustled off back to the kitchen, where I joined her a few minutes later.

"This is all that was left." She gestured to the solitary cracker — a camel, my least favorite — on a plate on the table.

"No way, I couldn't have eaten all of those."

Could I? There'd still been lots left when I'd served some up to Agent Singh and Ryan. Singh hadn't touched them, but Ryan had enjoyed them. Could he possibly have stolen my snacks? It was more likely that I'd been on autopilot when working last night and this afternoon, munching while I worked without being aware of it. Mushy brain syndrome — that's what I had, probably due to being increasingly more in the *then* than the *now*. Or maybe finding Laini's body had affected me more than I'd assumed, because problems with short-term memory were a typical symptom of post-traumatic stress.

"Perhaps next time you should buy a smaller packet," my mother said. "It's all too easy to fall into comfort-eating, and we all know what happens to our figures then."

"Are you saying I'm putting on weight?"

"Of course not!" she said, though she gave my sweatpants a critical glance. "But, on the other hand of the coin, I will repeat Elizabeth Taylor's words of wisdom: beware of pants with elasticated waistbands."

– 27 –

I poured us each a cup of the Earl Grey tea Mom had made and nestled into the couch with my feet up on the ottoman.

"So," my mother asked, "how is your assignment coming on?"

"Very well, actually. Another day or two's work should get it to the stage where I can send it to my supervisor for review."

"I meant your private eye assignment."

"Oh. Well, you know." I sipped my tea.

"No, dear, I don't know. That's why I asked."

"Well" — I piped my bottom lip and puffed hair out of my face — "I don't know either. I have no clue what I'm supposed to be doing. I'm just driving around talking to people who knew Laini Carter and seeing if anything clicks."

"Talking to people?" my mother repeated in the tone of one who considered this to be a bizarre thing to do in a murder investigation. "Use your powers!"

"I don't know *how* to. They come when they come and aren't always there when I need them. I can't figure out a pattern to it. Look, I'll show you!" I fetched the printed copy of my vision spreadsheet, which I hadn't yet updated with the flashes of the serial killer, and handed it to my mother. "See? Sometimes I get a vision or a feeling when I concentrate, and sometimes I don't. Sometimes," I said, thinking of the flash about the killer touching the corpse, "they come when I relax and I'm *not* consciously trying. The only common denominator is that they always make my head hurt afterwards. Other than that, it's all a mystery."

My mother puzzled over the grid for long minutes, muttering to herself and tilting her head as if viewing it sideways might help. At last she sighed and handed it back to me.

"I'm afraid I don't see a pattern, either. But maybe you're chasing a wild goose, here, dear."

"What do you mean?"

"All this logical analyzation — no doubt it's the normal way to figure things out."

I nodded.

"But," she said with a rueful smile, "what if the paranormal *can't* be studied with normal methods?"

I tried to follow her thought to its logical — or more accurately, *illogical* — conclusion. "So, I'm supposed to wait for intuitions about my intuitions?"

She raised her eyebrows. "I hadn't thought of that. I suppose it could work, though it's not what I meant."

"What did you mean then?" I snapped, frustrated that this conversation, like most exchanges with my dippy mother, was wandering around in circles.

"What you need is paranormal help. And I came prepared!"

My mother extracted her deck of tarot cards and accompanying pocket guide from her handbag and began shuffling.

I groaned. "Mom, you know I don't believe in those things."

"The question is, do they believe in you?"

"Huh?" I said, bewildered.

"The last time I was at the Tuppenny Tavern, I needed to use the ladies' restroom. Disgustingly dirty, by the way, avoid those toilets at all costs! But there was some interesting graffiti."

"Oh, yeah?"

"Written on the door of my stall was this: *God is dead.* And then there was a dash and *Nietzsche.*" She pronounced it Neetzercher. "You know, like she had written it."

"He," I said. "Nietzsche was a man."

"Well, I don't know what he was even doing in the ladies' room, then, let alone defacing the doors with his nonsense!"

"Does this story have a point?" I asked.

"If you give me a chance, I'll tell you. Well, under that *God is dead, Nietzsche* bit, someone else had written, *Nietzsche is dead – God.*" She sat back and smiled at me triumphantly.

"I have no idea what you're trying to say, Mom."

"Some things exist and are true even if people like you, Garnet McGee, don't believe in them."

"Smartass," I mumbled.

"Here you go." She thrust the deck into my hands. "Shuffle eight times, please."

Deciding it would be quicker to just go along with this, I did as she'd instructed.

"Now, while you shuffle, you need to meditate on what you

want the cards to tell you. So, are you thinking of the need for future guidance?"

"Oh, yeah. Definitely," I said sarcastically.

"That's seven times. Once more ... Good! Now cut the cards wherever it feels right."

None of it felt right. But I cut the deck in half. My mother took the top half and set it aside.

"Now draw the top card off the ones you're holding and place it face down here." She tapped a spot on the table. "Good. Now the next three cards in a line beneath it. Wonderful! And turn over the first card sideways, so we see it just as you dealt it. That will be your overall guiding card."

"The Lovers," I read off the card depicting a naked man and woman, with an angel hovering above them and what looked like an erupting volcano in the background. "I suppose this means I'm going to fall in love?"

She tutted at my simplistic interpretation before launching into her own. "The male figure, on the right, represents your mind, your conscious self that gathers information and uses logic. The woman stands for your heart, your subconscious self — feelings, intuitions, memory."

"Well, that's not sexist at all."

"And the angel above them — Raphael, I think, or perhaps it's Michael? — is the super-conscious mind."

"Super or supra?" I asked. "Is it *very* conscious? Or is it *above* consciousness?"

"Are you mocking me, Garnet?"

"Never!"

"The point is, it's your conception of yourself, who you

think you are. And it's also there to remind you of your connection to the world of the divine."

"Clear as mud," I said.

"And your card is reversed, see? It's upside down."

"That means something, too, does it?"

My mother was already consulting her well-thumbed guide. "Oh dear. Disharmony, imbalance, misalignment of values, failure," she read out.

"I'm feeling better already."

"Perhaps it means you should try to unite these parts of yourself?"

"Sure, Mom. I'll get right on it."

"Now turn over the other cards, left to right. Not all at once, Garnet! You're supposed to do them one by one."

"I couldn't stand the suspense."

"The first card represents the material plane, what's happening for you in the earthly physical world."

"Let me guess — I've been eating too many cookies?"

"You've drawn the Ace of Wands, and it's reversed, which means" — she checked her booklet — "emerging ideas, lack of direction, delays and distractions."

"*I* could've told you *that*," I scoffed. "In fact, I think I did."

"That just goes to show you how accurate the tarot is! Now the middle card represents the mental realm, what's brewing in your mind, or what's unspoken and perhaps holding you back. And you've drawn the Five of Cups."

"Cups … for too much drinking? Hangovers?"

"For shame!"

"Just kidding, Mom. Go on."

"No, I mean the card symbolizes shame. See how this poor fellow is hanging his head? It means he — and you — feel regret and remorse. To move forward, you'll have to make amends and ask for forgiveness."

"This just keeps getting better," I said. "Am I supposed to be feeling ashamed of something I've already done, or is this still going to happen?"

"Hmmm." She flipped furiously through the guide but came up empty. "Either, I suppose. Or both?"

"And does it definitely refer to me, or could it be about someone associated with this investigation?" I asked, despite myself.

I was thinking of Kennick Carter, who'd trained as a professional liar and cheat when he was just a little kid. He'd borrowed money from Laini and possibly lost it all. That would have caused him shame, as might the relief of inheriting much-needed moola when it came at the cost of his sister's life. Then again, *whoever* had killed Laini — and I couldn't yet exclude Kennick — would surely be feeling shame.

"Probably mostly you," my mother said. "But the cards don't like to have their meanings narrowed down too specifically."

"I'd noticed that."

The final card featured a frowny-faced moon glowering down at a howling dog and a wolf who reminded me irresistibly of Darcy and Lizzie, with a pair of high watchtowers on either side in the distance. In the foreground, a crayfish was crawling out of a pool of water.

"Now the third card governs the spiritual plane, and you've

drawn The Moon," my mother said. "And in the upright position."

"That's good, isn't it?"

She pursed her lips and made a seesaw motion with her hands. "It means all is not as it seems. There is double-dealing and deception. Secrets! This card speaks of illusions — either in the form of self-deception, or trickery and deceit from another. Lots of confusion."

"No kidding."

"You feel the lure of the unknown, of hidden knowledge and obscured truth."

"I'm trying to investigate a murder, so yeah."

"And, I'm sorry to say, it's also a red flag of sorts, warning of danger, fear, risk and enemies."

"Lovely."

"According to this booklet, the Moon card can also signify mental health issues."

"Awesome."

"And if you're awaiting a decision on something, the answer will either be delayed or be so ambiguous it will add to your confusion rather than clarifying your course."

"Rather like a tarot reading then?"

It seemed to me that the cards could mean anything and everything, or nothing at all. They were so vague as to be useless.

Ignoring this, my mother gave a little squirm of excitement and said, "Ooh, I forgot to tell you about the lobster!"

"I thought it was a crayfish."

"Tomayto, tomahto. Sometimes it's even represented as a crab."

"Is *anything* precise and specific in tarot?" I asked, irritated.

"No, dear. Because nothing's precise and specific in *life*. Now, the lobster symbolizes emerging intuition, your unfolding and expanding consciousness. And if that isn't a fit for your life at the moment, I don't know what is!"

"Anything else? Because my intuition is telling me Dad is on his way back and it's time to wrap this up." I could hear the dogs barking and the squeak of the front gate.

"It says here in my guide that the Moon reminds you to pay attention to dreams, because they might be messages from the divine or the beyond."

The night before, I'd dreamed I'd been washing dishes, scrubbing to get dried egg yolk off a plate. If the spirits were trying to tell me something other than to put my eggy plates in to soak as soon as I finished eating, they'd have to get a lot more specific.

Dad and the dogs came inside then. He complained about the bitter cold outside, and Darcy and Lizzie, judging by the sound of them pushing their food bowls around in the kitchen, were complaining about their empty stomachs. I checked my watch and saw that it was half-past six already.

"Crap, I'm late!"

I jumped up and ran to feed the dogs. Why had I wasted so much time on indecipherable idiocy with my mother?

She followed me into the kitchen. "Late for what?"

"I'm supposed to be at Ryan's at seven, and I still have to shower."

Her face split into a delighted smile. "You have a date with Ryan Jackson?"

"Don't get excited, Mom. It's to talk about the case. Do I have to shower, or can I get away with this hair?" I asked, releasing it from its bun.

"Go shower and wash your hair," she said firmly. "Better late than lank."

– 28 –

Ryan welcomed me to his house in town with a dimpled smile and a kiss on my cheek.

"Come on in," he said, taking my coat.

He wore khaki chinos and a blue button-up under a gray sweater which brought out the color of his eyes. I immediately felt underdressed in my jeans and Patriots sweatshirt, especially when I caught sight of the dining room table. It was set for two, complete with white tablecloth, wine glasses and candles in crystal holders. It was saved from being an undeniably romantic tableau only by the floral arrangement — a fistful of berries and dead leaves shoved into a coffee mug with *I see guilty people* printed on the side.

"Nice vase," I said.

He shrugged. "Hey, I'm a bachelor, what do you expect?"

"These from your garden?"

"It's slim pickings this time of year. What can I get you to drink?"

My inner Colby was rooting for beer, but seeing the thick steaks laid out on a plate in the kitchen, I asked, "Do you have red wine?"

"Sure. pinot noir or merlot?"

"Honestly, I couldn't tell the difference."

"Coming up."

He poured me a glass and then set to work making a salad.

"Can I help?" I asked.

"Can you cook?" he replied, looking doubtful.

"I can slice a freaking cucumber."

He handed me a sharp chef's knife and stepped away from the chopping board, hands raised in surrender.

"How do you like your steak?" he asked.

"Medium rare."

He nodded his approval, fired up the burner under a heavy grill pan on the stove and spiced the meat.

"Damn!" I said.

Ryan looked up, concerned. "Amputate a finger?"

"No, worse! I forgot the hot sauce."

"At least you'll be able to taste the meat," he said, searing the steaks on the grill.

I sliced a tomato and chopped the cucumber into blocks, remembering too late that my mother always halved cucumbers and scraped the seeds out first. Was there a reason why she did that? Ryan finished the steaks and removed baked potatoes from the oven. Ten minutes later we were at the table, digging in.

"Great steaks," I told him. "And delicious *vino*."

I'd been tempted to ask for ice for my wine — I liked hot things very hot and cold things very cold — but was glad I'd resisted.

"Can you taste the undertone of black currant and hints of

cinnamon?" he asked, grinning.

"No, but I'm catching a strong whiff of BS. How's your salad?"

He gave me an enthusiastic thumbs-up, even though I could now see I'd put in way too much cucumber, and that the tomato and onion slices were somehow way too big for the torn bits of lettuce. The whole thing looked unbalanced. A little like me.

"Eh," I said. "Cooking's not one of my gifts."

"You have many of those?"

"So many. Too many to count, really." I added extra butter to my baked potato. "I even have the lobster of intuition."

"You lost me at 'lobster of intuition.'"

"My mother," I said. He'd met her, so that ought to be explanation enough.

"Ah, say no more."

He finished his wine, and while he went to the kitchen to fetch the bottle, I glanced around, taking in his home. Leather, a few interesting paintings on the walls, a big-screen TV, and a real fire crackling in the living room. It had that slightly random, uncoordinated look of a bachelor pad — nothing matched, but everything looked lived-in and comfortable. I liked it.

He returned and topped up our glasses. Before we could return to lobsters or any other subject, I cut to the chase.

"Heard anything from the G-Man?"

Ryan shook his head.

"Me either," I said. "What do you think he'll do with what I told him?"

"You want the truth?"

"No, Ryan, I want you to tell me sweet, sweet lies to make me feel good."

He grinned. That grin did things to my insides. Melted some hard places.

"Then, yes, Garnet, I expect him to call you soon with an update that he's told his colleagues and boss all about you and is getting stuck into chasing up new leads based on your invaluable assistance. And you should expect delivery of a big bunch of thank-you flowers any day now."

I gave a huff of disgust and swallowed a slug of wine. "How's the Laini Carter investigation going? Any new leads?"

"We're not talking about the case tonight," he said.

"We're not? I thought that's why you invited me."

"Then you thought wrong."

I eyed him suspiciously, confused about what was happening between us and frustrated that I couldn't crack open a door to his skull and excavate what he knew about the case. Perhaps I could tempt it out of him.

"*I* learned a couple of interesting things today," I said, with what I hoped was a mysterious smile.

"Great! I want to hear all about them." I opened my mouth to speak, but he added, "Just not tonight."

"What are we going to talk about then?"

"Ourselves."

"Oh." I ate a forkful of salad. It was weirdly watery. Really, it was beyond time I learned how to cook. Looking up, I saw Ryan was staring at me expectantly. Deciding attack was the best form of defense, I said in the dulcet tones of an empathic therapist, "So, Ryan, tell me about your *childhood*."

"Oh no, you don't." He said it lightly enough, but there was an underlying tension in the speed with which he closed off that avenue of discussion, and a sudden tightness in his face which piqued my interest.

"Sure?"

"Yes." There was no accompanying smile this time. That subject was out of bounds.

"Fine." Since he wouldn't talk about two of the subjects I wanted to know about, I picked another. "Tell me about your marriage."

He ate a slice of steak before responding. "Her name was Desirae, and she was a lovely lady." He returned his attention to his meal.

"That's it?" I challenged. "You were the one who wanted to get personal, Bud-dy."

He opened his hands as though to indicate he was an open book, ready for the reading. "What do you want to know?"

"How long were you married?"

"Four years before we separated. The divorce was settled about a year later."

"Which was ... when?"

"Four years ago." Before I could ask, he added, "When I was thirty. How old are *you* now?"

"Twenty-eight, but we're still talking about you." I did some rapid mental calculations. "So, if you were twenty-five when you got married, then it must have been pretty soon after your relationship with Vanessa Beaumont came to an end."

He'd been dating Colby's sister back when we'd been

seniors, but they'd called it quits sometime after Colby died.

"It was an entirely decent eighteen months later."

"But how soon after the breakup did you start *dating* Desirae?"

"You know," he said, putting down his knife and fork, "if this psychologist thing doesn't work out, you should consider law. I think you'd be a natural at grilling a witness in the stand."

"The witness will answer the question," I said.

"Around six months."

"Wow," I said. "Was it a rebound relationship?"

"No."

"Was your heart still broken, maybe?"

He pinned me with a look. "Broken hearts can mend, Garnet. We don't have to give up on love when the first time around doesn't work out."

I knew he was taking a dig at the way my life, especially my love life, had gone on hold after I lost Colby. I finished my steak and gave up on the salad.

Leaning back in my chair, I asked him, "So, what went wrong if your wife was such a 'lovely lady?'"

"Nothing dramatic or tragic, we just drifted apart. I think — I *know* — that we were way too young when we got married. I was only twenty-five, and she was just twenty-two. At that age, you aren't the person you're going to be. You're too young to commit to forever." He shot me another meaningful glance. "You haven't finished developing."

"You *never* finish developing," I replied.

"Sure, but there's a big change in your personality and maturity between when you leave school and about twenty-five, don't you think?"

Don't ask me, friend, I hardly changed between eighteen and twenty-eight. I took a gulp of wine.

"Well, it was too young for us in any event," Ryan continued. "She clearly wanted more than I could give her, and it just kind of … fizzled out?"

"What did she want? Big city, big life?"

"No," he said, gathering the plates and heading to the kitchen.

I followed, eager to hear his reply.

"What Desirae wanted more than anything was attention. Loads of it, all the time. I couldn't pay her enough compliments, or spend enough time with her, or reassure her enough to fill the hole of insecurity that ran through the core of her."

He scraped the plates and put them into the dishwasher.

"In the end," he continued, "I got tired of being a perpetual cheerleader. And she got tired of me withdrawing into myself and my career. Well, that's my side of the story, anyway. If you spoke to her, she'd probably tell you I was a boring fart who prioritized his work over his wife, dragged my heels on starting a family, and never put the toilet seat down after I peed."

Ryan extracted a tub of ice cream from the freezer, handed it to me, and got us a couple of bowls and spoons.

Back at the table, I asked, "So, you don't have kids?"

"Not a one."

"Are you still in contact with your ex?"

"We send each other texts on our birthdays." He placed two large scoops of ice-cream into a bowl and handed it to me.

215

"They didn't have a jalapeno-flavored one. Hope Rocky Road's okay."

"Sure," I said, although I despised Rocky Road. All those bits of nut and marshmallow spoiling the creamy smoothness. "Hugo from the hardware store told me your wife left you because she was from the South and her blood was too thin to stand the northern winters."

Ryan laughed. "She sure did hate the winters!"

"He also said that she ran away with a Texan."

"That part he got wrong. She ran away *to* Texas. Got an impressive position as a sous chef at a fancy restaurant in Austin."

"Your wife's a chef?"

"Ex-wife. And yes."

"That's how you learned to cook?"

"She taught me a thing or two. Now," he said, pointing a spoon loaded with ice cream at me, "it's your turn to spill the beans."

– 29 –

Knowing that Ryan was asking for details on my love life, I instead gave him a long, detailed answer about my thesis, telling him more than he surely ever wanted to know about theories of grief, while I smashed my ice cream into a paste with the back of my spoon.

"It's almost finished," I concluded.

"What's next?" he asked. "Are you going to do your doctorate?"

Steering my spoon between the offensive bits pocking my ice cream, I spooned up a mouthful of frozen chocolatey goodness. "Nope. I don't know much about my future, but I'm fairly sure that being a shrink isn't in it."

Ryan pointed at my bowl. "What do you have against nuts and marshmallows?"

"Nothing. I like them, just separately."

"Okayyy. So, what will you do then?"

Too embarrassed to admit that I'd been contemplating my mother's suggestion of becoming a private investigator, I fobbed him off with a joke about becoming a barista at Starbucks.

He laughed, but asked, "Seriously, though?"

"Seriously, though, I don't know. Look for a job, I guess."

"Here or in Boston?"

"Are there many jobs going here?" I asked.

"Fair point."

"How about you? What's it like being Police Chief of Pitchford?"

"Mostly good. Not very eventful, usually. Though things do seem to get more interesting every time you breeze into town."

I made an indeterminate noise and held up my empty glass. "Can I have a refill?"

"I'll open another bottle. Unless you'd prefer something else? A brandy?"

"Do you have whiskey?"

He nodded.

"Lots of ice."

We took our drinks into the living room, where I sat at one end of a long couch, with my feet curled under me, nibbling on a nail. He added a log to the fire in the grate before sitting down at the other end, facing me.

"Why did you become a cop?" I asked.

Ryan leaned across to brush my fingers away from my mouth, saying, "If you're still hungry, I can make you something more to eat."

He said it gently, but it still got my back up. Why did my condition bother people so much? It wasn't like I was chewing on *them*.

"I have a condition, okay?"

He cocked his head in interest.

"An anxiety disorder. The nail-biting is part of it. And I know I have it — I don't need reminding."

"Noted" he said, in the tone of someone closing a subject, but then he asked, "So, are you seeing anyone back in Boston?"

"I'm not in therapy."

"I meant in the romantic sense."

"No." I took a swig of whiskey, enjoying the burn as it went down. "I don't really date."

Ryan drew back his chin in surprise. "Come again?"

"It's complicated."

"I'll try to keep up."

"I mean, I do go on dates. I just don't, you know, do *relationships.*"

"Why not?"

In reply, I downed the rest of my whiskey. He topped me up, even though I was fairly certain I'd already had too much to drink. My cheeks were getting numb, and my eyes felt like they wanted to focus in different directions. As heavy as I'd seemed to be hitting the bottle lately, you'd think I'd have built up more of a tolerance by now.

Ryan was still watching me, waiting for an answer. It seemed like cops also knew about the holding-a-silence trick.

"What were we talking about?" I asked.

"Romantic relationships. Why you don't have them."

"Oh, right." I took another sip. "Well, I don't have relationships for good reasons. For fine reasons. Several of 'em."

"Such as?"

"*First* of all, all the best men are gone. They're dead. Or gay.

Or" — I gestured at him with my glass, sloshing a little of the amber liquid over the side — "married!"

"I'm divorced. Though I'm glad you rank me with the best men."

Wait, what?

"What's another reason?" he asked.

"For what?"

"Not having romantic relationships."

"Oh. Are we still talking about that?"

"We are," he said.

"Fine, I'll tell you! And don't blame me if I overshare because I'm jingled. *You're* the one that keeps filling up my glass."

"I take full responsibility," he replied.

"I don't do relationships because my heart won't survive another break. There! Happy now?"

"How can you know for sure it will end in heartbreak?"

"Because it does."

"Garnet, you can't make a decision that rules the rest of your life based on one experience you had years and years ago."

"Oh, can't I?" I replied and was surprised to hear how belligerent I sounded. I took a breath and said in what I hoped was a more reasonable tone, "It wasn't just 'an experience.' Colby and I were totally in love. It was perfect."

"No relationship is perfect."

"That may be true, over time. But we didn't *get* time. We weren't together long enough for things to cool down, to get pissed off at each other's quarks." That didn't sound right. "Quarks?"

"Quirks," Ryan said.

"Yes, them. It just ended abruptly, right in the middle of *wunnerful*. We never said goodbye, so it kinda felt like we were still together. Or that he was still in Pitchford, waiting for me. And then, in December, it felt like he was back, and we were together again. Can you understand that?" I sent him a pleading glance.

He was sitting very still, his full attention on me. "Does it still feel that way?" he asked.

I set my empty glass on the table and hugged my legs to my chest, bouncing my chin on my knees while I considered.

"I don't think so. I think finding his killer and being there when his ashes were scattered helped settle something. Like maybe I finished some unfinished business."

Ryan moved closer, took one of my hands and began playing with my fingers. I smiled at him. What I'd told him had been true. I *did* feel like I'd reached some kind of conclusion with Colby. But I wasn't sure *he'd* reached the same kind of closure with *me*, because it was also true that sometimes I sensed him. I imagined I could feel him nearby, at times. Like right now.

"Cola," I murmured.

"You want a soda?" he asked, surprised.

"No. No, thanks."

I wondered what he would say if I told him that I thought Colby was right beside me at that very moment, jealously guarding my left side and probably unhappy about the fact that Ryan was holding my hand. And that far from wanting him finally gone, I liked the occasional sense of his presence.

"So, you said you were going to speak to Carl wassisname tomorrow?"

"Did I?"

"I have a clear recollection of it," I said, nodding firmly and enunciating each word so I didn't slur. "I think your special consultant should tag along to see if she picks up anything. Tha's what I think."

"You do, do you?"

"Uh-huh. And also, I found out some *verrry* interesting stuff about him, but I'm not telling you now because you said we couldn't talk about the case tonight." And then, in case he hadn't gotten it, I spelled it out. "But I could tell you about it tomorrow. I could meet you there, at his place. Nine o'clock." I contemplated this plan for a moment. "If you tell me where it is."

"I'll collect you from your place tomorrow morning," he said, sounding resigned. "And I'll come in your car because we've both been drinking, and I reckon I should call you a taxi."

"A *taxi*?"

"Would you rather sleep over?"

I narrowed my eyes at him.

"In the guest room, of course." He gave me a slow, sexy smile. "Unless …"

"If I'm too drunk to drive, I'm too drunk to …" What had Hugo called it? "Nug-a-nug."

"Agreed. Let's hope you're not a regular heavy drinker."

I nearly fell asleep with my head on his shoulder, waiting for my ride. Some date I was. At the door, Ryan gave me a soft kiss. On the mouth this time. At the touch of his lips — warm and firm — something lightened in my chest. I felt a small ballooning of hope, of expectation, even. But Ryan ended the contact right there.

And I could tell that if this was to go any further, the next move would have to come from me.

– 30 –

Ryan arrived at the Andersen house in my car at nine the next morning, which was too early for someone who felt — and probably looked — as rough as I did that day. Ned Lipton, who was hanging a wind chime on his porch, gave me a friendly wave as I slid behind the wheel.

"If a crime is ever committed in this estate," I told Ryan, "check with my neighbor because I swear, he sees everything that happens here."

"Good morning, Garnet," Ryan said.

"Speak for yourself."

I searched the dash and glove compartment for my polaroid sunglasses, then discovered I was already wearing them. They were doing a piss-poor job of screening out the sunlight.

"Here" — he handed me a cup of coffee — "I thought you might need this."

"God bless you, Chief Jackson," I said, and took several sips before starting my car and backing out the drive.

"I had a good time last night," he said.

"So did I."

Fact was, I'd had too good a night. I'd woken up this morning to a pounding headache and whining dogs standing beside my bed, pawing at me and licking my face. I must've forgotten to lock them in the kitchen the previous night before I flopped on my bed and passed out.

"So," Ryan said, "sometime after your first whiskey last night —"

"My first? How much leprechaun juice did I have?"

"— you began tempting me."

Shit. What had I done?

"I don't recall any ... *tempting*," I said, avoiding meeting his gaze.

"You said you had some interesting things to tell me. Verrrry interesting, you said."

"Oh, right," I said, relieved. "That I do. I met with Bethany Ford yesterday."

"And?"

"I feel sorry for her, but I don't much like her." I waved a thank-you to Doug when he opened the gates for us. He glowered back. "Left, or right?" I asked Ryan.

"Right. Why didn't you like her?"

"For one thing, she has a maid. And she keeps birds in cages. I don't approve of keeping wild things trapped."

"They were wild birds? Not, like, parakeets or canaries?"

"I didn't actually see them," I admitted. "And she has a paper-shredder, which surely only people who want to destroy evidence have."

"Or sensible people who want to protect themselves against identity theft and industrial espionage."

"I suppose," I conceded, grudgingly. "But she's one of those people who makes the rest of us look inadequate. She has a killer body with a rock-hard eight-pack. She composts and recycles. She even enjoys kale smoothies. I mean, who does that? And she works insanely hard and knows exactly what she wants from life. She's scarily disciplined."

"So, basically, you don't like her because she's the opposite of you," Ryan said.

I was seriously tempted to punch him. I settled for giving him a dirty look and drinking more coffee.

"In the interests of peaceful cooperation between police and civilians, I am going to pretend I never heard that," I said tartly.

Ryan merely chuckled.

"Did you see her house?" I said. "She has a whole trophy room dedicated to her time as a beauty queen! That's where she met Laini — they were both contestants in kiddy beauty pageants together. And *that* industry, let me tell you, is a whole other level of disturbing. Did you know that they make the kids wear fake teeth? They're called flippers, don't ask me why. And some of them get Botox injections!"

"The *kids*?"

"Yup. For those pesky toddler frown lines. It's insane! And on pageant days, they're given this cocktail of Red Bull and Mountain Dew to drink. It's called 'gogo-juice.' Or else they're fed something called *pageant crack*, which is a mixture of sugar, caffeine and who knows what other stimulants."

"What for?"

"It pumps them up for their performance onstage. I mean, that can't be legal, can it?" Without waiting for an answer, I added, "And the way they dress these kids – like little hookers — and teach them to pout and twerk and grind their hips, it's nauseating. Especially when you just know there have *got* to be pedophiles in the audience getting their rocks off."

"It sounds obscene."

"That's the perfect word for it."

I'd caught up with the vehicle ahead of us, an oversize-load truck carrying a monster section of concrete piping. It was traveling super-slowly, and I was glad of it because it would give me more time to talk with Ryan.

We sat in silence for a minute, then he asked, "So, you like Bethany Ford for Laini's murder?"

I pulled a face. "No. Much as I would like to, I don't. No motive. You don't find and recruit an old friend, benefit enormously from her skills, and then push her off a cliff because she beat you in a few beauty pageants thirty years ago. Besides, she seemed sincerely distraught over the loss of her bestie, and no two ways about it, the business is going to suffer without Laini."

"Did you learn anything, you know, *factual* from your chat with her?" Ryan asked.

I wagged an admonitory finger at him. "Never underestimate the character stuff, Chief."

"Spoken like a true shrink."

"I learned lots. For instance, Laini spent the Saturday night before her death at Bethany's house."

"Yeah, we already knew that from her statement."

"According to Bethany, Laini went into town the next morning, kissing her goodbye on the way out, and a little later sent texts to Bethany and Carl, telling each of them she'd be spending the day with the other. Was that in their statements, too?"

"Uh-huh."

"Those texts, though … They puzzle me," I said.

"They're not puzzling if you assume it was a suicide. She was buying time to kill herself."

"Why not just send a goodbye message? She could still jump before they could possibly find her and try to stop her."

"Maybe she was still undecided. She wanted to think about it first — alone and in a quiet spot, without being disturbed by either of them."

"Hmmm." I downed the last of my coffee, even though I was beginning to suspect that strong coffee on an empty morning-after stomach was probably a bad idea. "Bethany said that Jim Lundy was infatuated with Laini, but we knew that already. Did you check his locker?"

"Yeah, but we found none of that stuff you mentioned."

"I didn't imagine it."

I could still feel that tickle of the lock of hair on my face, still see that crazy collage of photos.

"I didn't say you did."

"He must've cleaned it out. Maybe I didn't put the coats back right, and he could tell someone had seen it."

"And his record is clean apart from an altercation with a woman on the street last year."

Up ahead, the truck driver stuck an arm out his window and signaled that it was safe to overtake. I ignored him.

"Altercation?"

"Jim said the woman — a known heroin addict who was panhandling in town last summer — accosted him, and when he refused to give her money, she got violent. Jim wound up with a black eye and a bruised ego, but the junkie ran off and then skipped town before we could catch her."

"Or get her side of the story. Did Jim have an alibi for the time of Laini's death?"

"Nope."

"And Denise, Bethany's assistant?"

"Denise? Why are you asking about her?"

That was the moment I ought to have come clean on Denise's dipping into the company cookie jar. My inner detective advised me to tell Ryan. My inner therapist begged to disagree.

"Just dotting i's and crossing t's," I said, trying to sound casual. "I mean, she'll probably get Laini's job — that could be seen as a motive."

"I didn't peg a small syrup company as that cutthroat," he replied. "But yes, as it happens, she had an impeccable alibi — me."

"You were with Denise early on Sunday morning?" I asked, running through the possible permutations of how this could have happened. Even so, his next words surprised me.

"I was watching her perform in the Bethel United Methodist Church choir, at the eight-thirty service."

"You go to church?" I asked, studying his face.

"Sometimes. Watch out!" he yelled.

I snapped my eyes forward and slammed on brakes, bringing the car to a halt with just a hair's breadth of space between my fender and the back of the huge truck, which had stopped at the intersection.

"Sorry," I said, meekly.

Ryan blew out a breath. "Take a left here. We'll go around via Fifth, it'll still be quicker than staying stuck behind this guy."

I grabbed my coffee from the cupholder to take a sip, discovered it was empty, and shoved it back, sending an assessing glance at Ryan's coffee.

"No, you can't," he said, clutching his cup close to his chest.

"If you know what time to alibi Denise, that must mean you've got some clarity on the time of death."

"Laini Carter died at eight fifty-seven AM."

"That's very specific."

"She had a fitness-tracker app on her phone, which was in her pocket. It stopped updating to the cloud at that time, because presumably that's when it got crushed in the impact."

The impact.

The words triggered a flashback to the sight of Laini's body at the quarry. Black clothes, white snow, red blood. I shook my head to clear it and resumed my summary of what I'd learned from Bethany.

"Bethany said Laini suffered from depression, that she didn't handle pressure well and felt overwhelmed at the prospect of being made a shareholder in the business. And, for the record, that shareholder plan surely gets my client off the hook even though, according to Bethany, he borrowed money from his sister and hadn't paid it back —"

"Is that so?"

"— because if he *was* planning to off her, surely he would've waited until she owned a chunk of the company? And, yes, before you ask, Bethany says Kennick did know about the plan to make Laini a shareholder. She also said there were problems in Laini and Carl Mendez's relationship. By the way, did you know that Bethany dated Mendez before Laini did?"

He shook his head. "What kind of problems?"

"Bethany said Mendez is a guy with a temper, kind of implied he might have been abusive toward Laini." I gave Ryan an I-told-you-so look. He didn't respond. "Look, are you going to drink your coffee or just fondle it?" I demanded.

Ryan smiled and took several long sips, smacking his lips afterwards. I picked up my empty cup, flicked off the lid and bit around the rim, flattening the curled cardboard lip with my teeth.

"Slow down a bit," Ryan said.

I took my foot off the gas, even though we were cruising at a sedate pace.

"Slower," he said, studying a battered blue sedan parked on the verge of the road as we pulled alongside it.

A man in faded jeans and a black hoodie was leaning with his elbows on the rim of the open driver's window, talking to someone inside. As we crawled past, he glanced our way and then resumed his conversation with the driver.

Ryan pulled out his phone and thumbed through a call. "Ronnie? I need you to check a vehicle for me."

He gave her our position and rattled off details of the car, including its license plate number, then listened while Officer Capshaw spoke.

"Right, right …" His eyebrows lifted, and he cut me a glance. "Is that so?"

"*What*?" I whispered.

"And the phone records? Uh-huh, right. So that checks out. Right, I'm on my way to interview Carl Mendez. Call me if you pick up anything on that Toyota." He ended the call and then said to me, "Guess whose client is back on the hook?"

"Judging by the smug look on your face, that would be mine?"

"Right in one. Laini Carter had a one-million-dollar life insurance policy, and Kennick is the sole beneficiary. Did he share that interesting bit of information with you?"

"Sure," I lied.

"Why didn't you tell me?"

"I didn't get a chance yet," I protested feebly. "Also, client confidentiality, ethics!"

"You're not a priest, Garnet, or a psychologist."

I wasn't much of an investigator, either. It felt like the rug had just been pulled out from under me. With the news of the insurance policy, Kennick was once again looking like a fine suspect.

To change the subject I asked, "Any more news on the Button Man?"

"You mean the serial killer?"

"Yeah."

"No. Though it's not likely they'd share it with me even if they *did* have something, the territorial bastards," he muttered. "Take a left here. Mendez's place is number 1103 on the right."

I hadn't realized we were almost there. "So, what's the plan for interrogating this suspect, Chief? Are we going to play good cop, bad cop?"

"The plan is that this will be an interview, not an interrogation," he said. "I'm going to play good cop, and you're going to play silent sidekick."

"That doesn't sound like much fun."

"Seriously, Garnet." He gave me a warning look as I pulled up outside Mendez's house. "You have no official standing here. I shouldn't be taking you along and will get into deep shit if you screw up and it gets out."

"I'll be on my best behavior," I promised. "Scout's honor."

"But maybe …"

"Yeah?"

"You could try to touch something of his and let me know — afterwards — if you picked up any cosmic transmissions."

I grinned. "Aye, aye, Cap'n."

– 31 –

Carl Mendez's house was the epitome of suburban blandness, from the white picket fence out front to the generic Ikea furniture and uninspired art inside. I couldn't imagine the colorful butterfly that was Laini being trapped in the middle of all that beige and oatmeal dullness. Then again, maybe that had been the plan — to provide a lackluster canvas against which she could radiate life and loveliness. The only element of the décor that popped was a series of enlarged photographs of her which hung on a wall in the living room.

I'd been hoping for another cup of coffee, but Carl Mendez merely settled his bulk into the largest chair and rubbed a hand across his stubbled cheeks when Ryan introduced me as a special consultant. I stared at the brass buttons on the leather jacket Mendez was wearing and then looked away, pushing back the flashbacks of that other button. The wooden one.

"… just wanted to clarify a few things," Ryan was saying when I tuned in to the conversation. "Such as the reason for the breakup in your relationship with Laini Carter?"

"Don't ask *me*," Mendez replied, as though we could still

ask her. "It wasn't my idea. And Laini didn't give me a reason. Not a real one, anyway. She just said our time together had run its course, and that nothing lasts forever."

"Was there someone else?"

"She swore not."

"And for you?" Ryan pressed.

"No! I loved her, I wanted to marry her."

"We've been told that there was a lot of conflict in the relationship."

"Who said that?" Mendez demanded, gripping the arms of his chair.

"Is it true?"

"No! We were happy! I still can't believe she did it. That she didn't even leave me a note. How could she do that — leave one for Bethany and not one for me? I loved her! I thought —" He pinched a thumb and forefinger across the bridge of his nose, as if trying to push back a headache. Or tears. "I thought she'd just take a few days and then come back. I never dreamed ..." His voice petered out.

Ryan gave him a moment, then pointed to something I hadn't noticed — a fist-sized dent in one of the walls. "What happened there?"

Mendez shifted uncomfortably in his chair. "When Laini left, I got mad, you know? I lost it for a moment."

"Ever lose it with her?"

"*Never.* I never laid a hand on her in anger. I would never have hurt her. That's not who I am."

"And yet, you have a criminal record for assault," Ryan pointed out.

Aha! I'd *known* there was something hinky in this guy's past.

Mendez sneered. "I had a fight in a bar when I was a student twenty-something years ago. That's a very different thing from assaulting a woman."

Ryan consulted his notes — more, I suspected, for effect than actually to jog his memory — and said, "The fight was over a woman."

Double aha. Mendez with his hot temper and aggressive attitude was rising in my suspect stakes by the moment.

Mendez stared incredulously at Ryan. "Yeah, but I didn't hit *her*, did I? I've never hit a woman. What has this got to do with Laini's suicide, anyway? Are you thinking that having ditched me, she was so sad we were over that she threw herself off that cliff? Because I can assure you, she hardly seemed devastated," he said bitterly. "There must have been another reason for why she … why she did what she did."

"In an unnatural death, we're obliged to investigate all possible options, Mr. Mendez," Ryan said. "Including that her death was not suicide."

"What do you mean? Do you think it was an accident? Or" — he looked from Ryan to me and then back again — "*Murder*?"

"We haven't yet established the manner of her death conclusively," Ryan said smoothly. "We were hoping you could help us with our enquiries."

Mendez thrust his jaw forward and glared at Ryan. "Are you trying to pin this on me? Do I need a lawyer?"

"If you feel you *need* a lawyer, please go ahead and call one."

"But if I call one, I look guilty, right?"

I leaned forward in my chair. "Mr. Mendez, may I ask — did you throw flowers into the quarry where Laini died sometime in the last few days?"

"Who are you exactly? And why are you here?" he demanded belligerently.

"*Was* it you?" Ryan asked.

"No. Now you're going to read something into that, too, I suppose? You should check with that creep she works with. Sounds like the kind of thing he'd do."

"What creep?"

"Jim. He was always bugging Laini, giving her shit she didn't want. One time he gave her a dried spring hare's tail. Said he'd chopped it off one he hunted himself. And last month — yeah, get this! — last month he gave her a bra in her exact size."

Gross. I couldn't decide what part of that was most disturbing.

"Guy's a freak, man," Mendez said, bunching his hands into fists.

"Did she confront him about it?" Ryan asked.

"Sure. But she wasn't tough enough with him; she felt sorry for him. Said he cried when she returned the bra and told him no more gifts. I wanted to go and sort him out myself, but she begged me not to. With what you're telling me today — I should've. If you think this is murder, you should be talking to him, not me."

"We'll certainly interview him again, Mr. Mendez, but right now there are a couple of things I'd like to check with you." Ryan glanced down at his notes. "You told us you last saw Laini Carter on Saturday the tenth at around nine o'clock in the morning, correct?"

"Yes."

"And the next day, on that Sunday morning when she died, you were here at home. Alone."

Mendez nodded.

"Make any calls? Send any texts?"

"No, Laini had begged me to stop, and there was no one else I wanted to talk to."

"Work on your PC maybe?"

"I was watching golf on ESPN. The World Championship in Mexico."

"Who won?" I asked, feeling all Sherlock Homey.

"Phil Mickelson, in a playoff over Justin Capshaw," he snapped.

"Oh."

"So, there's no way to validate you were actually here?" Ryan asked.

"I didn't know I'd need an alibi. I wasn't planning on murdering anyone. *I didn't* murder anyone."

I glanced at Ryan. If Mendez had been home when he received the text from Laini, surely that could be established from cell phone records? Admittedly, my knowledge of this came from episodes of *CSI* and *Law and Order* rather than any clear understanding of how things worked, but I thought there was a way to plot location using cell phone towers and signals. Then again, maybe that only applied to calls, not text messages. Or maybe Ryan was just trying to rile or unsettle Mendez in the hope of getting him to spill more details. I could help him with that.

"How did you meet Laini?" I asked.

But Mendez was clearly pissed off and had decided to clam up. Lucky for me, I'd been knee-deep in the work of psychiatrist Elizabeth Kübler-Ross the previous afternoon, watching an old interview in which she'd laughingly discussed how to get terminally ill children to talk to therapists. The trick, she'd said, was to keep guessing wrong until the kid's frustration overcame their reserve, prompting them to correct the therapist. I reckoned it was worth a shot with this sullen lover-boy.

"Maybe you met at the market or at the syrup emporium?"

Mendez crossed his arms across his wide chest and scowled down at the biscuit-colored carpet.

"No wait, maybe you were both in the same cycling club?"

No response.

"A blind date set up by a friend?"

Mendez rolled his shoulders like he had a pain in the neck, and Ryan gave me a disapproving glance. I guessed my questions didn't fall under the definitions of either "silent sidekick" or "best behavior." I gave him a look of my own, one that said I-know-what-I'm-doing-just-give-me-a-little-leeway-okay?

"Oh, dear," I said to Mendez, "don't tell me you two met on Grinder?"

That got a response out of him.

Balling his hands into fists, he growled, "I'm not gay!"

"Tinder, then? Or Match.com?"

"For your information, I met Laini via Bethany."

"You dumped Bethany for Laini?"

"That's not how it happened," Mendez said. "I'd had a few

dates with Bethany, but we weren't in an exclusive relationship, though I guess she was keen for one. Anyway, she threw a party to welcome Laini to Pitchford, and I was invited. I walked out into the backyard, and there she was, standing in the sunshine, in this crazy blue dress. And that was it. She was so …"

"Beautiful?" I guessed.

Mendez looked from one of my mismatched eyes to the other and scowled.

"Poor Bethany," I said. "I bet she was heartbroken."

Mendez made a scoffing sound.

"Or maybe she was really mad and wanted revenge."

He rolled his eyes. "She was *happy* for us, okay? She told me so. She was glad Laini had found someone 'cos she wanted her to be happy. She loved her."

"Why weren't you and Bethany a good fit?" Ryan asked.

Mendez stared back mutely.

"Sexual problems, am I right?" I said. "Bethany's kind of sinewy. And bony — a man could hurt himself on those pointy hips. Maybe it put you off enough that you couldn't … you know?"

"Garnet, that's enough!" Ryan said.

Mendez shot me a filthy look and then, to Ryan, said, "We just didn't click. Bethany was too driven and ambitious. She worked insanely hard at that business of hers — I could see it would always come first with her. Like, it's her everything. I just wanted a woman who could … be my wife, someone to share my life and grow old with. I thought I'd found her at last. But Laini wouldn't marry me. She said she'd feel trapped. *Trapped* — by me! I just wanted to love her."

Mendez covered his face with his hands. His shoulders were shaking, and he was making soft, guttural noises, but I couldn't tell if he was truly crying, or just faking it. I opened my handbag, found an only slightly crumpled tissue and walked over to hand it to him. Laying an ostensibly comforting hand on his shoulder, I closed my eyes and concentrated.

Immediately, an image coalesced in my mind.

Laini laughs and shakes her head at Carl Mendez. "Don't be silly — I'd be a terrible mother. I'd forget to feed the baby and sleep right through its nighttime cries."

"They're not babies forever. They grow up. It gets easier," Carl says, with a smile that looks more like a grimace.

"I wouldn't be better with an older kid. I'd encourage it to play hooky, or to run away and join the circus."

"If you just —"

"And it would make me miserable, darling. It would … squash me. I know what I need to do, and that's to —"

Carl shrugged my hand off his shoulder, ending the vision and leaving me wondering what Laini had thought she needed to do. I returned to my seat.

"You wanted kids, but she didn't," I said softly. "Not ever."

Shaking his head, Mendez stood up and stalked across the room to stand by the window with his back to us. His hands were once again curled into fists, crushing the tissue between his powerful fingers.

Had Laini possibly already been pregnant and contemplating a termination? I got the sense that Mendez would *not* have been okay with that. It was infuriating that my visions didn't come with a helpful, orienting context. Had the two of them merely been discussing a hypothetical possibility of having children one day, or had they been talking about a choice they had to make immediately? And when had that conversation taken place — last week, last month, a year ago?

"Was Laini —" I began, but Mendez interrupted me.

"Losing her — it's killing me. I can't eat, can't sleep. The doctor's given me tranquilizers and told me not to go back to work before Wednesday. But what am I supposed to do here, alone?"

Neither Ryan nor I said anything.

"I'd like you to leave now," Mendez said, and I could tell that we'd get nothing more out of him.

Outside, on our way to my car, Ryan said, "What part of silent sidekick did you not understand?"

"I got him to open up, didn't I?"

I was about to tell him about the vision when a police cruiser pulled up in front of my car and Officer Ronnie Capshaw got out.

"Ah shit," Ryan said softly.

Greeting him, Capshaw said she'd been in the area to check out the Toyota he'd called in and had decided to drop in on the Mendez interview. "Though I see I arrived too late."

Her shrewd gaze slid to me and then took in the single car — mine. I could see her putting two and two together and assuming the worst. Her face tightened with anger.

"Are you freaking kidding me?" she said to Ryan. "I don't care how cozy you are with this– this *person*" — she shot me a look that clearly conveyed she thought any man who cozied up to someone like me needed getting his head read — "but she's got no business being here."

"I'm not —" I stuttered. "We didn't —"

"She's a *civilian*," she said to Ryan, completely ignoring me. "And she's a kook."

"Hey!" I protested, and shot Ryan a dirty look. What had he told her about me?

"Don't tell me you buy into all this nonsense, Chief?" Capshaw said.

"Give us a minute?" Ryan asked me, his expression tense and unhappy.

"Yeah, give us a minute, Miss McGee," Ronnie said. "I'm just dying to hear why my boss included *you* on an interview, instead of his own officer!"

I left them arguing on the sidewalk and strolled back to the house. There wasn't much to see in the yard apart from a few leafless shrubs with mushy snow around their muddy bottoms and an empty birdfeeder stuck in the ground near the porch. It seemed Carl Mendez wasn't as concerned about feeding wild animals as Laini had been.

Glancing back, I saw Capshaw with her hands on her hips, still giving Ryan a piece of her mind, so I kept walking. At the side of the house, a double garage was set well back from the front of the property. When the garage doors resisted my best efforts to lift them, I turned my attention to the trash cans screened by a wooden lattice.

Judging by the mound of recyclables in the green trash can, Mendez preferred his Corona in bottles and his Buds in cans, and he'd been hitting both hard in the last week. I lifted the lid of the black trash can and was hit by an overpowering odor of fish. Gagging, I pinched my nose closed and was just lifting the top trash bag when I heard a car door slamming and the sound of an engine starting.

"Garnet?" Ryan called from out front.

I untied the drawstrings of the trash bag and peeped inside — ready-meal containers, chip packets, empty toilet rolls, a couple of crumpled, moldy oranges, an empty deodorant can. I set the bag aside and, bending over the trash can, reached deeper inside to pull out the next bag. It was clearly the source of the heave-worthy smell, but I wasn't tempted to open it, because my gaze was fixed on the item that lay in the bottom of the bin.

"Garnet!" Ryan sounded angry.

I quickly replaced the trash bags and scampered around the house, eager to tell Ryan what I'd seen. But one look at his fuming face and I knew that he wasn't in the mood to hear another word from me — the source of his disagreement with Capshaw.

I opened the car and slid inside, uneasily aware that my hands were dirty and might well be contaminating my handbag, car keys and steering wheel with disgusting microbes. Ryan flung himself into the passenger seat, slammed his door shut and fought with the seatbelt, which locked every time he tried to yank it.

I said nothing and, miraculously, managed to stay silent for the entire uncomfortable drive to drop him back at his house, but all the while, I was thinking about what Laini had been about to say in my vision, and about what I'd seen in Mendez's trash can — a mangled frame holding a large photograph of Laini Carter, with shards of broken glass radiating out from a central point of impact located directly over her winsome face.

— 32 —

After I dropped Ryan off, my mind was still buzzing with what we'd learned from Mendez. Setting aside his relationship with Laini, the new information about Jim Lundy was unsettling. It didn't seem like Laini had ever told Mendez about the dick pics — was that because she feared he might react violently? And what else might she have held back about Jim from a possibly misguided sense of pity or compassion?

Instead of turning off at the Beaumont Estate, I kept going in the direction of the Sweet 'n Smoky factory. Even though it was a Sunday, I guessed that I'd still find Jim on duty; syrup-makers tended to keep production going throughout the sugaring season.

While I drove, I decided to tick another item off my list. Yeah, it was a Sunday morning, but FBI agents surely didn't keep strict office hours, and I wanted answers. The bone, that murder and the images I'd seen were all haunting me.

Ronil Singh answered the call with a curt, "Yes?"

"This is Garnet McGee," I said.

"Who?"

"Garnet McGee. On the Jacob Wertheimer case?"

Silence on the other end of the call.

"I'm the ... psychic." I squeezed the last word out past reluctant lips.

"I know who you are. Do you have more information for me?"

"No. No, unfortunately not. I was hoping you had more information for *me*."

"Excuse me?"

"I wondered if you'd taken what I told you any further?"

"There wasn't much further to take it, Ms. McGee. Your feedback wasn't very specific and doesn't constitute evidence."

"I could come to your field office in Rutland? Maybe there's something else I could touch?"

"Thank you, but that won't be necessary. Now, if that's all, I —"

"Are you blowing me off?" I asked.

"What would you like me to do with the unverified conjecture that our unsub might be a white, married man with sexual issues — interview half the male population of the United States?"

"I thought maybe you could share it with your colleagues, a profiler maybe?"

"I came to hear you out because Jackson is a good cop and he asked me to, and because I was curious. But I won't be spreading the news of our meeting far and wide at the agency. Working with a psychic is more likely to amuse my colleagues than intrigue them."

"You're scared they'll laugh at you," I accused. "You want

to save face — even if that comes at the cost of endangering lives!"

"Endangering what lives? We have no proof the killer is still operating."

"You have no proof he *isn't*, either."

"Goodbye, Ms. McGee," Singh said, and the line went dead.

So much for trying to help the authorities.

A metal sign stating that the factory would open to visitors at noon stood in the middle of the dirt road turnoff. I drove around it and headed through the gloomy woods with their endless sap lines to the parking lot. I couldn't make out anyone inside the factory store, and the lot was empty, but the door to the sugar shack was open, which surely meant that Jim was on site.

As I walked toward the red shed, a shout from behind drew my attention. It took me a moment to locate its source. Jim Lundy was halfway up a short ladder leaning against one of the roadside trees near the entrance to the parking lot, waving a finger at me.

"Hi, Jim," I said when I reached his tree.

"You're not allowed in the sugar shack," he said. "You can only go in on one of the tours this afternoon."

"That's okay, I really wanted to talk to you."

"To me?" His already-wrinkled face scrunched up even more. "What for?"

Figuring I should ease slowly into what I really wanted to know, I said in a casual, friendly tone, "Well, I'm working for Laini Carter's brother. We're trying to figure out exactly how she died. That's why I'm talking to the people who knew her best, like you and the others who worked with her here."

Jim turned back to face the tree. Unhitching one of the quaint tin buckets hanging from a nail in the trunk, he tossed it down into a big plastic bin on the ground below.

"Can you tell me about Bethany Ford?"

He tapped one of his gloved fingers against the metal spile protruding from the trunk of the soft maple. "She's the boss."

"Yeah, I know. What's she like?"

"I don't got a problem with her. She's fair. You just gotta do your job right."

"How about Denise?"

He tapped the spile again, harder. "She's not as nice as she pretends to be."

"Can you tell me more about that?"

Jim shook his head vigorously.

"And Laini? What was she like?" I asked.

Twisting and turning the spile, Jim eased it out of the trunk and then held it up to one eye to inspect it.

"Jim?"

"She was pretty. And kind," he said, his voice rough with emotion. "She was always kind to me."

"When was the last time you saw her?"

"Are you a cop?"

He climbed down the ladder, scowling at me. I took an involuntary step back, but he merely tossed the metal spigot into the bin with the buckets. From another plastic tub a few yards away, he fetched a new spile and a buttercup-yellow pail with pastel bunnies and baby chickens painted on the side.

Easter was coming, and the trees near the sugar works were getting spruced up for spring visitors.

As he climbed up the ladder to hang the colorful bucket on the nail, I asked Jim, "Was it Friday before last — Friday the ninth — when you saw her last?"

His hands stilled, but he said nothing.

"Or did you see her on the Sunday she died?"

"I saw her the day before, when she brought her bike. She waved at me."

"Did you talk to her?"

"No, she hung her bike up in the office, then she left. It was Saturday morning, not Sunday."

"But *did* you see her on Sunday?"

"No. I came in on Sunday afternoon to clean the boilers, but she wasn't here. Just her bike was. It was muddy, so I cleaned it for her." He twisted the sharp end of the new spile through the bark and into the trunk of the tree at a downwards angle. "I thought she would be happy to see it clean on Monday. But she didn't come in Monday. She was already dead."

"Did you ever go with Laini to the quarry?"

"No."

"Did you leave flowers there, after she died?"

"No." He gave the spile three taps with the head of the hammer, driving it deeper into the tree.

"Did Laini like you?"

My only answer was the sound of Jim flicking the new metal tube a few times.

"Because you liked her, didn't you? You liked her a lot," I prompted.

"There's going to be a cold snap soon," he said, coming back to ground level. "It's going to freeze and snow."

"You liked to watch her, to take pictures of her, to imagine the two of you together."

Jim's lips clamped together, and his brows lowered. Hoisting the ladder onto his shoulder, he pushed past me and walked to the next tree, grabbing a pink bunny-bucket on the way.

I trailed after him. "You were her stalker, Jim. You spied on her and followed her around, taking lots of photographs."

He slammed the ladder against the tree and spun to face me. "Get lost!"

"And you also sent her pictures, didn't you? Naughty pictures of yourself," I said, pointing at his groin. "Was it exciting to think of her looking at those?"

"Go! You're not allowed to be here."

"I know what you had in your locker. You knew someone had been in there, so you took it all down before the cops came calling. But I saw, Jim, I know the pictures you had, the pictures you made."

Clearly eager to get away from me, he scrambled up the unsteady ladder, going higher than necessary to swap the buckets. I stepped closer and cricked my neck to look up at him.

"You'd better get out of here right now!" he shouted in his gruff voice.

"Or what?"

"Or I'll make you!"

"Did you make Laini go away, Jim? Because she didn't want

your gifts, didn't want to be with you? Maybe she confronted you and made you angry. Did you push her into the quarry?"

"No! I never hurt her!"

His face was scrunched into a tight, wrinkled grimace. Any moment now, he'd break down, and maybe I'd find out something important. I needed to keep up the pressure.

"I saw the lock of her hair, Jim. How did you get it? Why did you keep it? What did you do with it — sniff it, maybe? Did you rub it against your cheek, or maybe other parts of you?"

Jim made a sudden hard swipe at me with the Easter bucket. I leapt back, only just managing not to fall over, but Jim lost his balance and tumbled off the ladder. I heard a sharp sickening crack as he landed, and then he began to scream.

"Jim!" I scurried over to where he sat clutching his shoulder. "Are you okay?"

"It hurts! Something's broken."

"Shit, shit, shit!" I groaned, taking in the pallor of his face and the odd angle of his wrist. "Here, let me help you up. I'll take you to the hospital, it'll be quicker than calling an ambulance."

He was reluctant to trust me, but I managed to coax him into my car. Figuring he'd need x-rays and possibly even surgery, I sped directly to the hospital in Randolph. Jim, white-lipped with pain, rambled all the way — insisting he'd loved Laini and never hurt her, that she was a nice lady who'd always been kind to him and tried to help him, and how I was a mean bitch and it was my fault he'd fallen.

No argument from me on the guilty-as-charged front. He was clearly in considerable pain, and I felt awful that he'd gotten hurt. But feeling bad about what had happened didn't stop me having doubts about Jim. I hadn't felt safe with him in amongst the maple trees, and his obsession with and behavior toward Laini had been sinister. Now he seemed merely pathetic, like the sort of runty dog that barks loudly and bares its teeth, then turns tail and runs away when confronted.

But even cowardly dogs can bite when challenged.

– 33 –

The devil makes work for idle hands — that was one of my mother's favorite maxims. And my hands were idle that Monday morning.

I stared at my computer screen and tried to cudgel my brain into creating a perfect conclusion for my thesis, but my mind kept straying back to the embarrassments and disasters of the previous day.

Ryan being chewed out by Ronnie Capshaw, taking the heat for my involvement in a case on which I'd shone little — if any — light, with my unreliable "talent."

That deeply uncomfortable ride back to Ryan's place, the silence reverberating with unspoken regrets and misgivings — a stark contrast to our friendly banter over dinner the night before.

Being dismissed like a pesky kid by Agent Singh.

The horrible confrontation with Jim, dealing with him clumsily. I'd scared him and was ultimately the cause of him falling and getting hurt.

The ear-singeing phone call from Bethany Ford last night,

in which she'd called me a menace, blasted me for entering her property without permission, ordered me to keep well clear of her staff, and threatened to lay charges against me for damaging her business, because just how was she supposed to do the next boil without Jim? Did I comprehend what a setback I'd caused? Did I know how hard it was to find good staff for maple production at the height of the sugaring season? She had a serious mind to lay a complaint with the police.

A restless night's sleep hadn't helped. I still felt ashamed, guilty and stupid. Helpless and frustrated, too. Then the phone rang, and things got worse.

It was Hugo from the hardware store, calling to tell me he'd found the stack of pamphlets about self-defense classes under a box of paint scrapers. They were run by a local resident, Mark Bolton, who I'd find behind the counter in the post office.

"How are your varmints doing?" Hugo asked.

"I haven't checked the traps in the attic, but I still sometimes hear sounds."

He gave a knowing chuckle. "You shoulda gone with the poison."

"I'll pop by sometime and get your most deadly bait," I vowed. "Bye, Hugo."

"Before you go, did ya see the newspaper this morning?"

"No," I said, wondering if it had a feature on pest extermination.

"You're in it, did ya know that?"

Fetching the copy of that day's *Bugle* from the front path, I opened it on the kitchen table and groaned as I read the article printed beneath a glamorous photograph of Laini Carter and an unflattering old picture of me lifted from my high school yearbook.

Stumped cops consult psychic

Pitchford Police Department appears to be relying on crystal balls and tea leaves rather than forensic evidence in its enquiry into the recent death of Laini Carter.

While all signs appear to point to suicide being the cause of her death, Police Chief Ryan Jackson has, according to a confidential source, involved former Pitchford resident, psychology student and self-proclaimed "psychic detective" Garnet McGee in the ongoing investigation, going so far as to include her in witness interviews.

When approached for comment on this unorthodox approach, Chief Jackson stated only, "This initiative was done of my own volition and does not reflect the policy of the Pitchford Police Department."

It has yet to be seen if Jackson will face sanctions for employing eccentric and unproven methods, particularly after McGee's involvement in the injury of Sweet 'n Smoky factory custodian Jim Lundy yesterday. A confrontation between the so-called clairvoyant and Lundy ended with the latter being admitted to Randolph County Hospital and treated for both a fractured wrist and a broken collarbone. Lundy did not choose to give details about the clash, except to say that McGee is "a nasty woman."

The investigation into Laini Carter's death continues.

Rubbing Darcy's fuzzy belly with my toe, I thought about who the *Bugle*'s confidential informant could be. Bethany Ford, and possibly her assistant, as well as Carl Mendez, knew I was a special consultant hired by Kennick Carter, but as far as I knew they were ignorant of my supposed abilities. Kennick knew, of course, but surely he wouldn't have spoken to a reporter about our arrangement. Which left only one person.

Determined to confront her and to apologize to Ryan in person, I drove directly to the police station and hurried inside. Ryan Jackson stood at the front counter, talking to Ronnie Capshaw.

"Can I talk to you in private?" I asked him.

"I don't have time for this now," he replied, his face grim.

Capshaw shot me a filthy look. "Don't let the door hit you on the way out."

"Please, Ryan, it'll only take a minute," I said.

He opened his mouth to reply, but just then the door was flung open, banging into the wall with a crash that startled all of us, and in came the one person guaranteed to exacerbate the situation.

Michelle Armstrong, town clerk and all-round Pitchford big cheese, marched in on a blast of cold air and freezing disapproval, clutching a copy of *The Bugle*. Her baleful gaze immediately locked on me and in a voice that thrummed with hostility, she declared, "*You!*"

"Good morning," I said.

"If it is, it's no thanks to you! How dare you show your face in here? Why are you even in Pitchford at all? Haven't you done enough to damage the reputation and ruin the economy of our town without this latest fiasco?"

"I —" I began, but Michelle Armstrong cut me short.

"Ryan" — she slammed the newspaper down on the counter — "your office. Now."

A muscle pulsing in his jaw, Ryan followed her down the hall to his office, and I heard his door bang shut.

Face hot with embarrassment, I spun around to face Capshaw. "How could you do this? Look what's happened now because you couldn't keep your prejudices to yourself and your mouth shut."

Capshaw's face tightened with anger. "How *dare* you? I would never leak information to the press. *I'm*," she said with heavy emphasis on the word, "a professional! More likely the leak came from *you*. Were you trying to get some extra publicity to drum up business for your ridiculous racket?"

"It wasn't me! I would never do anything that would hurt Ryan, or cause him problems."

"Lady, where have you been the last five minutes? You already did."

Face hot and tears burning behind my eyes, I snatched up the paper, marched outside and strode down the sidewalk to the offices of *The Bugle* several blocks down from the police station, eager for someone to kick. Capshaw was right. I *had* hurt Ryan, certainly professionally and probably personally, too. And he was one of the few people in this town I cared about. He was a good guy — smart, funny, attractive. I liked him. A lot. And he'd seemed to like me in spite of my uncensored mouth and prickly defenses. Plus, he'd been the only person who was open to believing me about my strange experiences. Well, except for my mother, and *she* was open to believing anything and everything.

The *Bugle* reporter who'd written the piece on me was a short woman with close-cut black hair and the stained fingers and wrinkled mouth of a career smoker. In defiance of regulations, she had a lit cigarette tucked in one corner of her mouth.

"I can't tell you that," she said when I asked who her informant was. "I protect my sources."

"This isn't Watergate," I snarled. "National security doesn't rest on the gossip your piddling rag prints."

In response, she merely narrowed her eyes. Smoky tendrils curled around the cigarette clenched between her teeth and eased their way out of her mouth. Out of her pores, too, probably. She reminded me of a devil in one of Hieronymus Bosch's depictions of hell.

"When it comes to the bit about tagging along on interviews," I said, "it could only have been Carl Mendez who told you that. Or Bethany Ford," I added, realizing Mendez might have told her about that.

The cigarette dipped briefly.

"Aha! I knew it," I said, pointing the rolled-up newspaper at her, seriously tempted to swat her upside the head with it. "And who told you about the psychic angle?"

"Oh," she said, deflating a little. "That's no big secret. It was your mother."

My jaw dropped. "*What?*"

"I called the number listed for McGee and had a chat with your mother. Funny lady, your mom, has quite the way with words. And she's really sold on your abilities, so at least you've got one person fooled."

My *mother*. My idiotic, foolish, brainless nitwit of a mother was the one who'd sold me out.

At my horrified reaction, the reporter subsided into a guttural, phlegmy bout of laughter. Without another word, I spun on my heel and left. Her unpleasant cackle and the stink of smoke followed me all the way out onto the street.

Cursing violently under my breath, I called my mother and gave her an uncensored piece of my mind that ended with a stern instruction never to talk to any member of the media about me ever again. And not to mention the phrase "psychic detective" in my or anyone else's earshot unless she truly desired to witness me utterly losing my shit.

Storming back through town to my car, my gaze was caught by a sign a few doors down: *Post Office*. Not wanting to scare anyone inside with a face that must've been flushed with fury and contorted with the murderous impulses roiling inside me, I forced myself to wait outside until the heat of my temper had come off the boil before going inside to find Mark Bolton, postmaster and part-time self-defense instructor.

He was a man of medium build, mild expression and friendly manner. He didn't seem like the sort to be teaching anyone blocks and tackles, but what, I thought savagely, did I know about anything?

"Oh, yeah, I remember her," Bolton said when I showed him the photo of Laini in the newspaper. "I was sorry to read she went over the edge at the quarry. Was she a friend of yours?"

"Did she do one of your self-defense classes?" I asked.

"Nope, not her."

"Oh," I said, disappointed.

"She brought someone else along to do the course."

"*Oh?*"

"She told me he'd been assaulted by a crazy junkie and needed to learn how to protect himself."

With a sinking feeling in my stomach, I recalled Ryan telling me about an assault committed by a heroin addict.

"But I got the sense he'd only agreed to the course to please her," Bolton continued. "Because the guy couldn't take his eyes off her. Neither could I, come to that, she was *hot*. Crazy beautiful."

"This guy, who was he?"

"Dunno. He only came the once."

"What did he look like?"

"Little guy." Bolton cupped his hands on either side of his jaw. "Big ears."

– 34 –

The migraine hit as I was pulling into the Andersen driveway.

I blinked hard as spots of white speckled my vision. A jagged crescent of flickering light shimmered at the corner of my left eye and already the pain was tightening its vise around my head, dulling my brain.

Wincing at Darcy and Lizzie's loud excitement when I entered the kitchen, I filled their food and water bowls, then shut them inside and trudged upstairs, holding tight onto the balustrade because the scintillating arc of light had flared as it crept across my field of vision, leaving me all but sightless to the outer world.

Swallowing a serious dose of painkillers, I made myself drink a full glass of water before drawing the drapes and inching carefully into my bed. I wanted to weep, but knew it would only worsen the headache; wanted to throw up, even though my stomach was empty; wanted to be under the covers, warming away the shivers which raised gooseflesh on my arms and legs, even though it hurt to have anything touch my skin.

My phone rang, loud as a claxon, jangling my brain. I

fumbled on the screen, trying to kill the call, but wound up answering it instead. It was Kennick Carter, asking for an update on my investigation. For a brief second, I considered giving him details of who I'd interviewed and telling him I was planning to follow up on some good leads, but my head hurt too much to talk, and my pride was too bruised to spin stories.

"Bottom line, Kennick? I've got nothing solid to tell you."

"I'm sorry to hear that," he said, though he sounded more relieved than disappointed.

"Tell me where I can find you, and I'll pay you back your hundred bucks."

"I'm going home on Wednesday morning, but you can catch me tomorrow at Dillon's — that's where I have breakfast."

"What time?"

"Between eight-thirty and nine-thirty."

"Will do. And, again, I'm really sorry."

"That's okay. Maybe it's for the best."

A corner of my mind wondered why he was suddenly keen to let the investigation slide, but the rest of my brain demanded a cessation of all mental exertion. I slowly lowered my head back onto the pillow, trying to breathe against the pain, pinching the tender spot between thumb and palm on my left hand hard, hoping the counter-pain on the pressure point would distract from the migraine.

I woke up in the late afternoon to the third call of the day. This time, it was the Andersens' landline ringing. My head still aching dully, and muzzy with sleep, I stumbled into the main bedroom, but before I could reach the phone, it cut off. As I turned to leave, it started ringing again.

"Hullo?" I answered, stifling a yawn.

Mrs. Andersen apologized for calling, said her husband had called her a worrywart, but could she just ask whether the dogs were fine? And check I'd given them their weekly vitamins? And that I'd watered the plants and had been keeping an eye on the thermostat because, as she'd explained in her list of instructions, it tended to go on the blink from time to time. And had the utilities bill arrived yet? No? When it did, please would I scan it and email it to her so she could pay it? And yes, they were having a fabulous time, and Easter Island was next!

As I ran around, watering plants, checking the mailbox and thermostat, and feeding the dogs vitamin drops, I reflected that not only was I an unreliable psychic and useless private eye, but that I hadn't even managed to house-sit very well.

"I've been a bad mommy. I'm going to make it up to you, I promise," I told Lizzie and Darcy, fetching the cannister of dog treats from the kitchen.

They yipped excitedly at the sight, but when I opened it, there was only one treat left. I snapped it in two and gave each dog one half. They swallowed my meager offering and stared at me expectantly.

"Okay, let's go for a walk. A long one."

That, at least, I could do well. I was even willing to bet that I could do it without tumbling over another corpse.

As I fastened the leads onto the wriggling dogs, my phone pinged an alert for an incoming message. Checking it, I discovered my mother had sent three convoluted and confused texts over the course of the day, both apologizing for and defending her disclosures to the *Bugle* reporter. I had less than zero desire to speak to her; somehow it felt like this whole mess — even down to being in Pitchford at all — was due to her.

I deliberately left my phone behind on the dresser as I opened the front door, but the juxtaposition of my phone and my mother in my mind kindled a memory. I switched on my phone, found the recording function and activated it, then replaced my cell on the dresser.

"Ghoulies and ghosties, if you're here, announce yourselves by making some noise or leaving me a message while I'm gone," I said to the house, feeling like a complete fool.

Then I grabbed my jacket, gloves and beanie and set off with Darcy and Lizzie, locking the door behind us.

Jim had been right in his weather forecast — the temperature *was* dropping. But at least the bracing cold helped to clear my head. Walking at a brisk pace, I led the beagles — or rather, they led me — around the full perimeter of the estate, until all their excess energy was burned off, and I was a little breathless. When we passed the guardhouse, Doug tried to stop me for a chat.

When I refused to engage, he gave me a mean look and said, "You'll regret it."

"What's that supposed to mean?" I challenged.

He mumbled something about there being plenty of women who would be falling over themselves to spend time with him.

"Have at it, dude."

By the time the dogs and I wound up back at the park in front of the house, my headache had mostly cleared. The sun had set, and the deserted park was lit an eerie yellow by the street lights. Since even the ducks had retreated to the shelter in their enclosure, I let the dogs off the leash to mosey around freely while I sat on one of the swings, lost in a funk of contemplation.

I'd tried my best to figure out what had happened to Laini, but I'd failed. I'd uncovered nothing useful with my visions. Sleeping off much of the day and cancelling the deal with Kennick hadn't changed anything; I was still stuck somewhere between try harder and give up.

Giving up my "investigation" would come with the upside of causing no further embarrassment to Ryan, while trying harder might merely involve more banging of my malfunctioning head against a brick wall.

But the idea of quitting rankled. It would let what I believed to be a murder go unsolved. But if I pushed on, I risked alienating everyone without any guarantee that I'd ultimately be able to help *anyone*.

And it was so tempting to just give up. After all, I'd only come to Pitchford to finish my thesis, and I was almost there — *would* be there by the time the Andersens came back home. If I paid back Kennick's advance and just kept my head down and my nose in my own academic business until the end of March, then I could escape back to Boston. Hopefully, I'd leave all the crazy stuff behind, too.

"That's it," I said into the dark emptiness of the park. "I quit."

I'd expected that coming to a decision would make me feel relieved. Instead, I felt dissatisfied and empty. And cold —

suddenly I felt icy cold, as though I was enveloped in a pool of glacial air. I shivered violently. Time to go.

"Dar-cy! Liz-zie!" I called, my breath coming in puffs of white which hung in the still, frigid air.

Silent and obedient for once, the dogs trotted over to me, but they slowed as they came closer, and halted a good five feet away. Lizzie whined and Darcy growled. Their eyes flicked from me to the empty swing seat on the left of me and back again. The hairs on the back of my neck lifted, and my eyes began to water. I turned to face the empty swing.

"You there, Colby?" I whispered.

Slightly but undeniably, the swing moved.

– 35 –

The world went silent as I stretched out a hand to the empty space where Colby was. I closed my eyes and leaned into the sense of him, the almost-presence.

"Hi," I murmured.

My mind blossomed, not with a word or an image, but with a comforting sense of union, of touching and merging with the bright essence of him in some ineffable way. My heart warmed and expanded. Tears trickled down my face.

"After all this time, I still miss you," I whispered.

We sat like that, moving gently to and fro on the swings, suspended in a bubble of us, while in the space outside, the dogs watched, and time ticked by.

"Colby?" I said at last. "Do you know anything about this crime, about Laini's death?"

Silence, inside and out.

"You got nothing, huh?"

Of course he didn't. He'd only known the details of his own life and his death. He wasn't wandering about on the other side interviewing deceased souls, which was a damn shame because

I could have used the help.

I wiped gloved hands across my eyes. "How does it work over there, anyway? Do you souls all hang out together, or only the ones with unfinished business? Is there a special waiting room for the lingering spirits of murdered people?" I could feel him smiling with me. "And why are you hanging around anyway? I solved your murder; we got the baddies."

The words, "You can go now" raced to the tip of my tongue and hovered, waiting to be spoken, ready to set him free. But I could not utter them. Would not.

His words came then, three of them, loud in my mind.

Always and forever.

A sharp bark startled me out of my fugue. A car — my father's — was driving past. Without hesitation, the dogs took off after it.

Standing up, I glanced back at the empty swing, but Colby was gone.

For now.

I caught up with my father at the Andersens' front door where he was alternately ringing the bell and begging the dogs to sit.

"Hey, kiddo," he said.

"You saw the *Bugle*?"

"I saw the *Bugle*."

Unlocking the door, I asked, "And did Mom send you to come speak to me?"

"No, but you need to call her. And be nice, will you? She's very upset."

"*She's* upset? I —"

"She meant well."

"Yeah, well, she did harm," I said, hanging up our coats. "And I know I did harm, too. So, if you've come to tell me to end this whole colossal screw-up before more people get hurt, there's no need. I'm throwing in the towel."

"Ah, kiddo," he said pulling me into a long hug.

Blinking away tears, I freed the dogs from their leashes. They made a beeline for their water bowls in the kitchen while we went to the living room.

"Want something to drink?" I asked.

He shook his head and I plonked on the couch with a deep sigh.

"So, you're quitting? Just like that?" he said.

I'd expected him to console me, to agree that ending this mess would be for the best. I hadn't expected a challenge. Dad didn't even believe in the paranormal, let alone approve of my investigation.

"No, not 'just like that,'" I replied, feeling defensive. "I tried hard, okay? I gave it my all."

In reply, he merely raised an eyebrow.

"I did! I interviewed a bunch of people, I weaseled information out of Ryan Jackson, I investigated online and got nada. And then I did the whole woo-woo thing, trying to get readings from objects and people, staying open to messages from the beyond. I even allowed Mom to read my cards. And where did my so-called psychic abilities get me? Nowhere. Plus, I've done damage with my meddling. I'm hopeless at this — out to sea in a chicken-wire canoe."

"You're just out of your comfort zone."

I snorted at this tactful understatement. "You bet I am. I have no idea what I'm doing. I didn't study for this. Hell, I didn't even go looking for it — I just sort of *fell* into it. And I'm useless at both logical investigations and *psychic detecting*," I said, with bitter emphasis on the last words.

"Maybe that's because you're trying them separately."

"Huh?"

"Perhaps it's not a case of *either-or*. Maybe it's supposed to be *both-and*."

I fiddled with a fingernail, tugging on a cuticle. "Both-and what?"

"It seems to me that you have abilities in two areas. On the one hand, you're a scientist with expert knowledge in psychology and excellent analytical skills when it comes to understanding and evaluating information, testing hypotheses, building logical arguments, that sort of thing."

"Okay." That much I agreed with.

"And on the other hand, you have these new abilities — ones which, admittedly, you're not yet expert in using —"

I nodded fervently.

"— of receiving intuitions and perhaps even ... visions."

I could tell it was hard for Dad to talk about this stuff as if it was real.

"And what I'm suggesting," he continued, "is that you use your scientific methods to study and analyze your psychic data, that you try to integrate the two approaches."

I considered his suggestion for a moment. It was sort of what I'd tried to do with the grid I'd created to study my visions, but ...

"They *don't* integrate — they're polar opposites, as different as night and day, black and white, oil and water. They just don't mix."

"What about twilight and gray and salad dressing?"

"Dad, you're starting to sound a lot like Mom," I said.

"There are overlaps between supposed opposites. And there are ways to blend and combine them which result in something more than the sum of the separate parts." Reading the skepticism which must have been plain on my face, he continued, "The logical and the intuitive approaches *must* integrate somehow, because they're both in you. You may not understand how just yet, but *you* are the integration. You aren't who you were, Garnet. You came up out of that pond, back from wherever or however you were when your heart stopped beating, a changed person. You aren't who you were," he repeated. "Not physically and not psychologically. You've accepted the physical changes," he said, gently touching the sides of my face beside my mismatched eyes. "Why are you kicking so hard against the changes in here?" He tapped my temple.

Good question. And how to answer it? How to explain, without sounding melodramatic, that it felt like a death to let go of my old, sure sense of self and fall into something new?

My father finished his drink and stood up to go.

"Did you know that to become a butterfly, a caterpillar must first digest itself inside that dead-looking chrysalis? I read up on it. It dissolves into a soupy, enzymatic mess, but some bits and pieces survive the digestive process and adapt themselves to be reused in the next life stage. And there are these clumps of specialized cells called imaginal discs that grow into the new parts it will need. Turns out that those cells were inside the caterpillar all along, lying dormant, like genetic blueprints waiting to be activated. Some species even walk around with rudimentary wings tucked up inside them — invisible, inactive, but there all the same, waiting to be called into use. In the process of eating itself up, the caterpillar unlocks the information in its cells, and metamorphosis happens."

At the front door, he shrugged into his coat and patted the dogs goodbye.

"And when the butterfly emerges, wet-winged and no doubt more than a little shell-shocked, it can't yet fly. But it doesn't throw in the towel and stay stuck on the branch as if it was still a caterpillar. It takes a moment to expand its wings and exercise its flight muscles, to take in all the crazy changes to itself. And then" — Dad opened the front door — "it puts all its trust in its wings, and takes flight, a miraculous integration of the old and new."

He kissed me on the forehead and left.

For several long minutes, I stood staring at the door, lost in thought. *Integration*. Was it possible? To my chagrin, I realized that this was what my mother had been getting at, too, albeit in her muddled and mystical way. She'd thought the Lovers card meant I should unite my mind and heart, my conscious and subconscious minds, my logic and my intuition.

Well, it couldn't hurt to try.

On my laptop, I created a new spreadsheet. This one would contain the information I'd gleaned from both my visions *and* my more regular investigations, and once I'd captured it all, I'd use my academic skills to analyze it, in the hope of wresting meaningful information from the raw data.

First, I listed everything I'd learned about Laini Carter, organizing it according to who I'd learned it from.

Next, I listed what I'd seen with my own eyes and research — Laini's broken body at the quarry, the blue note creased with fold lines, the car in the quarry lot, the placement of her desk in the office, the globe on her shelf, the broken photograph in Carl Mendez's trash.

I filled more rows with what I'd learned about the other players in this case — heart-broken Bethany, sneaky Denise, creepy Jim, inscrutable Kennick and angry Carl — listing their possible motives for murder, and their alibis where any existed. Thinking about Carl sparked an idea. I switched over to my search engine and checked the date of the World Golf Championship in Mexico, punching the air when I discovered that the final playoff had occurred several days *before* the Sunday of Laini's death. Then again, Mendez hadn't said he'd watched the action *live*.

I switched back over to my spreadsheet and thought for a moment, chewing on a thumb. Then I entered what I knew of Laini's last twenty-four hours, cutting and pasting details until I had what I thought was the most likely timeline, although there was still one item I couldn't make fit.

Finally, I listed all my visions, flashes and intuitions related to the case. I color-coded those items red because, although I was learning to trust my abilities a bit more, I still wasn't entirely convinced of their reliability. Like a good academic, I wrote down the exact details of what I'd actually seen and heard, rather than my interpretation of them. I left off the flashes I figured weren't connected to the case — my sense of being watched, the oddities in the Andersen house, the bone and button, my encounters with Colby and guessing Jessica's pregnancy. I racked my brain for any other intuition I might have forgotten, any other "message" I might have received or recorded in my abnormal brain.

Recorded. My phone was presumably still recording from its spot on the hallway dresser.

I fetched it and settled into my favorite spot on the couch in the living room, Lizzie and Darcy at my feet.

"Here goes nothing," I said, hitting the playback button.

I heard myself addressing the ghoulies and ghosties in the house — did my voice sound that high to other people? — and leaving with the dogs. There were several long minutes of silence, and I was back to thinking how ridiculous this whole EVP business was when I heard a definite sound, like a muffled click. And then a soft creak.

The hair on the back of my neck rose, and my scalp tightened. The recording played on, showing the raised graph of a series of soft noises. Could those be footsteps? Was a freaking ghost walking around the house? My eyes filled with water as they always did when I was seriously spooked. Was I about to hear audio evidence of a visitation?

Then I heard music — the radio in the kitchen was playing — and I also thought I heard a strange, non-musical droning. I pushed the volume on my phone to the maximum, and held it up against my ear, closing my eyes to try to hear better. The music played and the odd buzzing which almost sounded like an off-key tune continued. Then I heard a series of sounds that were easily identifiable.

"What the actual fuck?" I said out loud.

I listened to more of the recording, gasping, swearing and yelling at my phone as I heard more of what the recording had captured. Then I pressed pause and, for once grateful for my mother's crazy ideas, dialed the familiar number.

"Hi," I said. "I'm sure you don't feel like talking to me, but I need help."

– 36 –

I listened through to the end of the recording while I
waited, and I was a hot mess of emotions by the time I
opened the door for Ryan Jackson. He must've been able
to tell I was seriously freaked out, because he'd come over at
once. He really was a good guy, I thought, bitterly regretting
how I'd made his life more difficult.

I led him through to the living room, explaining that I
wanted him to listen to a recording I'd made while I was out of
the house.

His brows drew together. "And you did this, why?"

"Strange things were happening in the house, and my
mother thought I could record some ghostly activity."

I hit the playback button on the recording and handed him
my cellphone. He listened to the click, the creak, the radio and
the humming sound, frowning, but not saying anything. Then
he sat up straight and gaped at me.

"Is that– Was that the refrigerator opening? And glass
clinking? That sounds like a bottle of beer being opened!"

"Right? And not even my mother would claim a ghost was

visiting my kitchen to guzzle my liquor!" Honestly, I was relieved to discover that it hadn't been me polishing off all the wine and beer. "He ate my animal crackers, too, I'll bet!" I added.

"A felony misdemeanor, at least," Ryan said with just the hint of a smile.

"I thought maybe you'd taken them," I confessed.

"Oh, yeah, I always fill my pockets with snacks from the houses of witnesses and suspects. It's a perk of the job."

On the recording, we both now heard the sound of the television, channels changing until it settled on one — ESPN, judging by the station identification jingle. The TV hadn't been changing channels by itself, after all.

"Do you know who it is?" Ryan asked.

"You bet I do," I said and told him. "I think he's done this regularly. And the dogs wouldn't kick up a fuss or be a deterrent, because they know him. Besides," I said, remembering the nearly empty dog-biscuit tin, "I think he feeds them treats when he comes over."

"How does he get in?"

"He has keys! Or he *had* them and made a duplicate set. I think he's been coming in and out of here since I arrived. Helping himself to my booze, going through my stuff, stealing my underwear!" I said, recalling the missing pair of panties. "Listen — now he's wandering around the house." Probably rearranging statuettes and going to the toilet, leaving the basin faucet dripping, making me think I was losing my marbles. "And that's the sound of him going upstairs, no doubt to rifle through my personal things and lie on my bed like some perverted Goldilocks."

We listened through to the part where the doorbell rang, hearing footsteps running down the stairs, into the kitchen and the sound of the back door opening and closing.

"That's it," I told Ryan. "That's when I came back and he hightailed it."

Ryan puffed out a breath and placed my phone on the coffee table. Before I could grab it and turn off the playback, he got to hear my angry comment about my mother, and me telling my dad I intended to throw in the towel before more people got hurt.

Feeling my cheeks grow hot, I met his assessing gaze and said, "The worst part is that I think he may have been watching me when I've been upstairs. I've heard sounds from the attic, but I assumed it was rats. And I had a feeling of being watched, but I figured I was either imagining it or that there was some kind of ... paranormal presence." I rolled my eyes. "I feel like such an idiot! The most simple and logical explanation was that there's been an intruder."

I'd been so brain-dead from the academic work and so emotionally exhausted from the Laini Carter drama that I'd let all the woo-woo stuff — my visions, my mother's crazy ideas, the nightmarish doll — get to me, and I'd overlooked the obvious. I'd exposed myself to the real danger of a peeping Tom because I'd gotten stuck in a web of superstition and confusion.

"I'd better check up there," Ryan said.

I fetched him a flashlight, and we went upstairs together. Ryan pulled down the attic trapdoor and climbed up.

"Be careful — I set a bunch of mousetraps up there," I warned him.

He disappeared into the dark space, and a moment later I heard him mutter a low oath. He'd found the doll. I stayed below, tearing strips off my nails, putting two and two together. I recalled how I'd woken up with "I'll be watching you" playing in my head, and how the kitchen radio had gotten stuck on the Rockwell song. I'd squirmed at the lyrics about being a little crazy, but the main refrain of the song was "Somebody's watching me." Had those been messages from Colby, trying to warn me about the intruder?

Ryan emerged from the attic and stepped down the ladder, looking rueful.

"Find anything bad?" I asked.

"You mean apart from the doll?"

"I know, right? And the dressing table and the brush with the hair?"

"They probably belonged to the Andersens' daughter."

"Is she dead?"

Ryan gave me a perplexed look. "No, why would you think that?"

"Because I'm upset and creeped out, okay?"

"Sorry to tell you this, but there's more up there to be upset about than creepy old toys."

"Tell me," I said, heart sinking.

He handed me a plastic evidence baggie containing an empty Skittles packet.

"Son of a bitch!" I said at this new evidence of the trespasser's larceny. "So that's where they all went."

"There's more. And you are *really* not going to be happy about it."

"*What?*" I demanded.

"Two neat little holes have been drilled through the ceiling — one directly over your bed and one over the bathroom."

The asshole had been spying on me when I was dressing in my bedroom and naked in the bathroom. Watching me while I slept.

"And there's a mattress right by them with a pile of porn magazines," Ryan said. "It looks like he's been ... enjoying himself ... while watching you."

I shuddered with revulsion and swallowed down the bile that rose in my throat. "What now?"

Ryan closed the trapdoor and dusted his hands on his jeans.

"Let's pay the perv a visit."

– 37 –

The pervert's face lit up when he opened his door to find me standing there but fell when he caught sight of my police escort.

I leaned forward to sniff my neighbor's neck. "Nice minty aftershave you've got there, Ned."

"Can we come in?" Ryan said, stepping forward so that Ned had to back up.

Ryan walked through to the living room and sat down on one of a matching pair of wingback chairs. I took the other.

"What's this about?" Ned asked, perching his butt on the arm of a sofa.

"I have some questions to ask you about your trespassing inside the Andersen house," Ryan said.

"What? I never! I just swept the path sometimes."

"I've got you on tape, asshole!" I said, holding up my phone. "Drinking my beer, cheering while you watch women's volleyball, talking to yourself about which player has the best tits."

"Oh," said Ned.

"Yeah, *oh*!"

Ryan held up the evidence baggie with the Skittles wrapper inside. "And in the attic, right by two strategically placed spyholes, we found this. I'm guessing we'll find your fingerprints on it. On the porn magazines, too."

Ned looked from Ryan to me, took a deep breath and then shrugged.

A hot wave of fury washed through me.

"You are a pig and a pervert," I yelled at him. "You drank my wine, you ate my candy and crackers, you stole my underwear! You spied on me when I was sleeping, when I was naked!"

Ned's lips curved in a sly smile, which enraged me even further. How had I ever pegged him as Nosey Ned — a friendly, helpful, harmless neighbor? I jumped out of my seat and marched over to him, wagging a finger.

"*Annnnd*, you left my faucets running and moved the clown statue around."

"No, I didn't."

"Yes. You. Did." I poked him in the chest. "You despicable peckerhead!"

"I never did that. Not with the faucets or the statue. Why would I do that?"

"To gaslight me — to mess with my head."

"I didn't do it. Just because you say it doesn't make it true," he said, pushing his lip out in a sulky pout.

"Garnet, come sit down," Ryan said, and he waited until I took my seat again before asking, "Mr. Lipton, do you deny accessing the Andersen house without permission?"

"I won't be interrogated by the police without my lawyer being present," Ned said.

"Do you have a set of keys to their house?"

Ned started humming.

When Ryan merely nodded, I scowled at him. He was being inexcusably calm about this. Where was a good dose of police brutality when you wanted it?

"Hey!" I said, clicking my fingers to reclaim Ned's attention. "That telescope on your porch — it's not for stargazing, is it? You use it for watching women." That explained why he was so often out on freezingly cold nights. Cloudy ones, too, now I came to think of it. "You probably used it to spy on Laini Carter when she lived here in the estate. And, according to Hugo in the hardware store, you also have a pair of powerful binoculars."

"I like bird-watching," Ned said with a smirk.

I leapt to my feet and lunged at him. Ryan seized my jacket and tugged me back.

"Let me at him!" I cried, struggling against Ryan's restraining hold. "I want to kill him!"

"No," Ryan said evenly, dragging me back to the door. "I can't allow you to do that."

"Maybe it was *him* who sent Laini the dick pics!"

"We'll find out," he promised. "You go home, now. Try not to touch anything he might have touched. Tomorrow, I'll send forensics to your place to take fingerprints. I'm going to arrest Mr. Lipton now, and then tomorrow Ronnie and I will be back with a search warrant for this house and the contents of his phone, computer and any photographic or recording equipment we find."

The implications of that hit me as I walked back home, and I groaned. Could it get any worse?

I knew exactly how to deal with the kind of day I'd had — one cry and two alcohols. Feeling dirty and contaminated by Lipton's filthy gaze, I took a long, almost painfully hot shower, taking a glass of wine with me into the bathroom. I was desperate to bite, scratch, pick, and peel at my skin, but I ordered myself not to let Ned have any more power over me and managed to restrict my urges to merely scrubbing my entire body with a loofah until I smarted all over. Afterwards, I rubbed vitamin E oil into my stinging red skin, drank a cup of chamomile tea made with three teabags, and climbed into bed wearing my woolen mittens in case I scratched at myself in my sleep, which tended to happen when I was distressed.

I dropped into a restless doze, dreaming of Ned peering at me from the other side of a bright-red door, his eye magnified by the peephole. As he turned his face from side to side, angling for a better view, he whispered over and over again, "I like bird-watching."

The next morning was freezing. The temperature had plummeted overnight, and a late-season snowfall had covered the ground in a pristine layer of white. Heavy clouds hung low in the sky, threatening more bad weather. Even the dogs were reluctant to step out of the warmth of the house; I had to shove them outside the front door into the crisp air to do the necessary.

I scowled at Ned's house. Its windows were dark in the still-murky light, and I hoped that meant he'd spent the night in a cell at the police station, the scum-sucking, vile, voyeuristic, deviant excuse for a rancid baboon anus. His unrepentant attitude to getting caught still burned my biscuit.

I dropped two slices of bread in the toaster and, being careful to open cupboards by the edges of their doors rather than their handles, rummaged for peanut butter. I was unable to think about anything but Ned. His forays into this kitchen, his raids on my supplies, his occupation of my attic. I put an extra spoonful of coffee into the machine and switched it on. That irritating humming, those damn bowties, his voyeurism. My vulnerability. I was still spitting mad and glad of it, because I suspected tears were waiting in the wings.

I fed the dogs, realizing too late that Ned's hands had probably touched the bag of kibble. I wanted a glass of orange juice but couldn't figure out how to open the refrigerator without touching the handle, where Ned's prints would be. I ate my breakfast and washed the dishes, remembering how I'd liked the minty smell before I knew its source. I wanted to watch the news on TV, but he'd handled the remote control. Everything in this house reminded me of him. The whole place felt tainted.

I glowered at the clown on the shelf. Ned's petulant denials about moving it and leaving the faucets running still niggled.

Just because you say it doesn't make it true. The phrase looped through my mind. *Just because you say it doesn't make it true.*

A lightbulb went off in my head. A lot of that information about Laini and the others had been based on what people had *said*, rather than on verifiable fact. I'd been willing to question my own intuitions as a good scientist should, but I should have brought the same skepticism to other people's opinions, because surely what they said was no more objective or reliable than my visions and hunches?

I fired up my laptop, opened the spreadsheet and began color-coding — green for facts that had been confirmed and orange for what I'd merely been told about Laini or any of the others. Poring over the rows and columns with a more critical eye, I compared information, looked for patterns, underlined commonalities and highlighted inconsistencies, just as I would when reading and collating a bunch of academic sources.

Then I scrutinized the information from another perspective. If I let go of my self-doubts, if I started with the conviction that Laini had *definitely* been murdered and took all my visions as literal truth, then some things — the bicycle, the note, the flowers, the donuts — simply didn't fit. I saw now that I'd made assumptions and could almost hear one of my father's favorite witticisms: "When you assume, you make an *ass* out of *u* and *me*."

Had I made other wrong assumptions?

Reading through the details of my visions once more, I noticed another place where I'd leapt to a conclusion — quite possibly the wrong one. I also had gaps in my information that needed filling, a couple of which were probably not important.

Snatching up my phone, I called Ryan.

"A couple of quick questions, Chief. According to the autopsy, was Laini pregnant at the time of her death, or had she recently undergone an abortion? Does Kennick Carter have a solid alibi? What exactly was Laini wearing when she died? And what color was her nail polish?"

I nodded at his answers. "That fits."

I was mad at myself. I'd been sloppy. I'd jumped to conclusions about what I *thought* I'd seen, rather than examining what I actually had. I'd been careless instead of precise, and I'd shared general impressions with Ryan, rather than specific details. I'd succumbed to confirmation bias — interpreting data according to my expectations. In short, when it came to the data analysis of my crazy, I'd been a bad scientist.

"What fits?" Ryan asked.

"I'll tell you everything later. I just need to confirm a couple of things."

A pattern was emerging from the information. A possible motive — or motives — and even a method. The facts and visions clicked together, more or less, but it was still just a theory. I needed more information to confirm my hypothesis, so I went online to research the average lifespan of cut flowers, to compare the various features of fitness trackers, and to check distances on Google Maps. It all made sense.

I glanced at my wristwatch. At nine-thirty on this Tuesday morning, I knew where I'd find the person I needed to speak to. Should I call Ryan back and ask him to go with me? No. For one thing, he couldn't be seen doing any more investigating with Kooky-pants McGee, and for another, if I was wrong — again — I'd just be wasting more of his time. I needed to be sure before I troubled him. I needed *evidence*.

Besides, there'd be people around. I'd be perfectly safe.

− 38 −

Far from being full of people, the parking lot of the Sweet 'n Smoky sugar works was deserted except for one black Lexus SUV. Where was everybody?

I was about to ring the bell of the office block when the door opened.

"You!" Bethany Ford said, glaring at me.

This was how people reacted to me these days, it seemed. To know me was to loathe me.

Bethany locked the door to the office block behind her. The keys she held looked like the same bunch that Denise had fidgeted with, but Bethany's fingernails were painted pink, not turquoise.

"I thought I told you to keep off my property," she said.

"Well, technically, you told me to keep away from your staff."

She gave an exasperated "Tchah!" then pulled a red beanie over her soft blond curls and yanked on her gray leather gloves.

My own head and hands were bare. Expecting to talk to her in the warmth of her office, I'd left my hat and mittens in the car, and my ears were already beginning to hurt from the cold. I thrust my hands into my pockets.

"Can we go inside?"

"No," she said, pushing past me and zipping up her North Face winter jacket — ruby red to match her beanie — as she stalked off to the sugar shack.

"I just wanted to talk to you."

"And I just wanted you arrested for assaulting Jim, but we don't always get what we want."

"I didn't assault Jim!" I said, struggling to keep up with the pace of her long legs.

"So you say. And yet, *he* has broken bones and *you* are" — she shot a disparaging glance my way, and I had the sense that a number of unflattering descriptions hovered on the tip of her tongue — "fully in one piece."

"Well, okay, that's true, but —"

"Look at it!" She flung an arm out to indicate the sugar shack with its closed door and cold chimney. "The height of sugaring season, and I've got a shutdown."

"Is that why no one's here?"

"I've given the staff time off. My new custodian starts on Thursday, and we'll run the boilers flat-out from then, so I told the others to take their 'weekend' now."

When we reached the shed, I said, "Here, let me help you."

Grabbing the icy handle of the red sliding door, I tugged it open, and Bethany strode inside. I lagged behind a moment to activate the recording function on my cell phone. Then, tucking it microphone side up into my outer jacket pocket, I followed her into the sugar shack, rubbing my hands together for warmth.

"Why are you still here?" she demanded.

"Like I said, I just wanted to clarify a few things, check if you could help me reconcile some inconsistencies about Laini's death."

And, of course, I wanted to provoke her into telling me what she hadn't told anyone yet, and to get it recorded.

"What inconsistencies?" she asked, removing a clipboard from a hook on the wall, pushing down the wrist of her glove to check her Apple Watch, and writing the time on the form.

"The thing that bothers me most is how the different people I spoke to described Laini. For example, Kennick Carter, Carl Mendez, Denise who works here, even Hugo from the Hardware store — everyone described her as being happy. But you said she was moody, that she suffered from depression. You believed she committed suicide."

"That's because she did."

Bethany turned her back on me and walked over to a stainless-steel vat as long as a bathtub and much deeper.

"In some way or other," I continued, "everyone else said or implied that Laini hated being stuck in one place or occupation for long. She was too frivolous or too restless, or she just liked exploring more of life than any one place or person or line of work could offer her. Her brother called her a butterfly. Mendez said she was scared of being trapped. Jessica Armstrong —"

"What's she got to do with anything?"

"She said Laini didn't want more stakes in the ground."

Bethany lifted the lid of the tank, and I saw it was filled with clear liquid — raw sap sucked down from the trees in the woods surrounding us.

"But you," I continued, "you told me that Laini loved this job, that she'd finally found her niche, though you conceded that extra responsibilities tended to stress her out."

Bethany said nothing, merely sniffed the liquid in the tank, tutted, and made another note on her clipboard.

"And you were the only one who never described her as beautiful."

Bethany stilled for a moment, then she turned and went to the reverse osmosis machine and checked some readings on its display panel.

I followed her, wanting to see her face. "When you realized the cops might not be sold on suicide, you cast suspicion on other people. You said Carl Mendez' relationship with Laini was rocky, implied there might even be abuse. But he said they were happy, that he never laid a finger on her in anger."

"Well, he *would* say that, wouldn't he?" she snapped.

"You told me you'd warned Laini about Jim and made sure I knew all about Kennick's financial woes."

"I was trying to be helpful!"

"I didn't see it immediately, didn't notice that you were doing a magician's trick, something you'd learned as a kid in those awful pageants. You were making sure I looked in one place" — I twirled my right hand in the air — "while you executed your sleight of hand somewhere else." I hid my left hand behind my back.

"This is gibberish," Bethany said. "I have no idea what you're trying to say."

"You were distracting focus from yourself by directing attention to others."

She ignored this and marched across the factory floor to inspect a boiler and a few more tanks. I trailed behind her, tucking my hands back into my pockets. Without the boiler fires running, it was almost as cold inside the shed as it was outside.

"And I fell for it. I fell for your story and your tears and your distractions. I just assumed your version of Laini was different because you were closest to her. You saw more, or deeper, because you knew her best."

Bethany spun around to face me. "I did!" she said fiercely. "I knew her better than she knew herself — she admitted as much in her goodbye note."

"But then I wondered if you were the only one lying."

"Why would I lie?"

"I know, right? It made no sense, because you didn't stand to gain anything from her death. On the face of it, everyone looked like a better suspect than you. But murder isn't always sensible or logical. Sometimes, people are driven more by rage and pain than by gain. And so I wondered if I'd been looking at things from the wrong viewpoint, doubting what *everyone* said, even doubting myself."

"Is there a point to this rambling?"

"Because if only one specific person was lying, and that person was you, then everything slotted into place. And you'd committed murder."

"*Murder?*" Bethany scoffed. "Why would I want to kill the woman who was my best friend and the most valuable asset in my business? I was going to make her a full partner."

"Ah, yes."

"'Ah, yes' — what?"

"That's what spooked Laini, wasn't it? Another stake in the ground. She'd been in one place too long and had been growing twitchy for a while. Mendez was getting clingy. He wanted to trap her behind a picket fence with babies and a wedding ring, pinning her down like a butterfly on a board. And you wanted to hang onto her with golden handcuffs — more money and shares in the business. She felt crowded and claustrophobic and bored. She wanted out. She wanted to be free again."

Bethany pursed her lips and crossed her arms, holding the clipboard like a shield over her chest. "You've spoken to her friends for all of five minutes and you think you *know* her?"

"I know that she was kind and honest," I continued. "She had integrity, so she felt bad because you were making these plans and she had no intention of being here to help you see them through. And if she was planning to leave, she might as well go immediately. That would allow Carl to find someone else, too, which was only fair since she would never give him what he truly wanted. So, she ended it with him and arrived on your doorstep, with all her bags and a head full of exciting plans."

Bethany gripped the clipboard tightly, as though to keep herself from hitting me with it as I continued with my version of events.

"She tells you she's off on her next great adventure — one that doesn't involve you. She's quitting her job and leaving cold, snowy, suffocating Vermont to start again somewhere new, preferably on the other side of the globe. She's sorry to do this to you, so sorry she's even brought you a massive bunch of flowers. Pink lilies, I'm guessing," I said, recalling the pink and green background of my visions with the note, and the dying flowers in Bethany's hall that she'd instructed her maid to toss onto the compost heap.

Bethany narrowed her eyes. "She brought me flowers because she was a houseguest. *You* wouldn't know, but that's something well-mannered people do."

I shook my head slowly. "Nah, then she would have given you thank-you flowers when she left, not when she arrived. They were an apology, as was her note written on that pretty blue paper, telling you how sorry she was to leave you in a mess. The mess of losing a vital person in your business. The mess of trying to find someone new to take her place. Not the mess of suicide, as everyone assumed."

"You're delusional," Bethany said. "I read in the newspaper that you're a psychology student, but you should be a patient instead. I think someone should inform the university authorities that you're unstable and not fit to help anyone."

"Like you informed *The Bugle* about my assisting the police?"

She merely shrugged.

"Bitch! You were clouding the water again, so anything I came up with would be doubted."

She marched past me, back toward the entrance of the sugar shack, saying, "I'll be telling my contact there about this visit, too. Your wild theories and crazed accusations. Your threatening demeanor. How I didn't feel safe until you left — which I'd like you to do right now."

– 39 –

I had no intention of leaving until I got what I came for, so I continued to dog Bethany's footsteps, talking as I went.

"You and Laini spent Saturday night together at your house, like you said, discussing life, love, men, work, the future. You probably tried to persuade her to stay, but Laini Carter wasn't a stayer — not for her brother or the man she loved in Colorado, not for Carl Mendez or *any* job. Not even for you."

Bethany tried to hang the clipboard back in its place near the door, cursing as she missed the small hook several times. Her hands were unsteady; I had her rattled.

I stepped around to block the way out of the shed. "Maybe you urged her to think on it that night. You hoped she'd change her mind. But the next morning, you saw she was determined to leave. She was going to ruin everything on a selfish whim. How dare she? And thinking a bunch of flowers could compensate for ruining your business, your 'everything' Carl called it, and leaving you without your right hand and best friend? Maybe your only friend? It was an insult. She'd even snatched Carl out from under you, and now she was just ditching him. And you doubted he'd want you back — who wants first princess when they've had the pageant queen?"

At that, Bethany struck me across the face, hard enough to make my ears ring.

"Ow!" I gasped, outraged.

"You had it coming."

"Is that your life philosophy? Giving people what they have coming, especially when they cross you?" I demanded, pressing my cold hand against my stinging cheek and ear. A muscle worked in Bethany's pale cheek. "You were angry that morning, too. Your rage must have been building all night. Hell, you'd been seething for decades — since you were tiny tots, and she kept breaking your little girl's heart, trampling on your dreams. Over and over, she kept winning the crown, stealing the attention, enchanting everyone. And doing it so effortlessly! While you had to work for it. You sweated and trained and *tried harder*. And lost."

Bethany's breaths were coming faster now. I pressed my advantage.

"You were so jealous of her, so deeply envious in so many ways, that you couldn't even bear to face it consciously. She was prettier, freer, less needy and more lovable. She'd beaten you in every way that counted. The envy and the anger and all the wounds had been accumulating for years and years, collecting emotional interest, turning what you felt for her into something bitter and dangerous. Only two things mattered in your life — your business and your relationship with her, and now she was going to jeopardize the first and abandon the second. Abandon *you*. Her decision to flit away was the straw that broke the camel's back."

I took a step closer to Bethany.

"Laini was going to ruin your hopes once again. And once again you were feeling like that little girl you once were — furious, jealous, inadequate, rejected. And so alone. If you could've, you would have caged Laini like one of your birds, kept her by your side. But you couldn't, and if you couldn't have her, no one would."

I took another step closer, and Bethany backed up a few paces, her ice-blue eyes fixed on me and filled with hatred.

"That Sunday morning," I said, "Laini didn't volunteer to go buy you cider donuts — I'll bet a pastry hasn't crossed your lips since you were a little girl. No, you came up with a ruse to get her to the quarry. Maybe you told her the magnificent view would change her mind. Or maybe," I said, thinking of the black Lycra cycling pants Ryan had said Laini was wearing when she died, "she wanted to go for a bike ride, and you volunteered to drive her out to the quarry so she could take a pretty route back through the woods."

Bethany's mouth was a tight white line. She said nothing.

"You suggested going in Laini's car because hers had a bike rack, and yours didn't. You left, with no one to see you go — you live alone, your maid doesn't work Sundays — and you swung past the factory to collect Laini's bike and helmet from the hallway in the office before driving out to the serpentine quarry. And when you got there, you begged her to hike to the top with you — *one last time, Laini, for me, please?*" I mimicked a cajoling tone.

"Nonsense! This is all nonsense," Bethany spat.

"And at the top of the quarry, you tried one last time to convince her to stay. You argued, and she laughed, confused. She said you couldn't be serious."

"Wha– How do you …?"

"I *saw* it. I *heard* it."

"That's not possible," Bethany cried, backing away from me until she came up against the huge tank of sap.

"She hadn't even seen it coming. It never occurred to her carefree, gypsy mind that every time she upped sticks and moved on, she left broken hearts and damaged lives behind, and that one day it might catch up with her. But she'd hurt the wrong person one too many times. You thrust out your hands and pushed her over the edge."

"No!"

"You hurried back down the hill, took her bike off her Jeep and put on the helmet, hiding your face. Then you cycled all the way home, put the bike in the back of your SUV and returned it to its rack at the factory before driving back home to wait. I'm guessing you didn't expect her body to be found so soon. You'd probably planned on waiting until the next day before checking in with Carl and raising the alarm with the cops. Still, it worked out well enough anyway, didn't it?"

"This is all wild speculation. You have absolutely no proof," Bethany said.

"Not true. You made a mistake with the bike. Jim saw Laini bringing it to the office that Saturday morning. She was on her way to you but left it there in case anyone from the company wanted it once she left town — she wasn't planning on taking it with her, and she knew you weren't a cyclist. Then, when

Jim came in on Sunday afternoon to clean the boilers, he saw it again, but this time it was muddy, because it had been ridden. Thing is, Bethany, you made no mention in your statement to the cops about Laini going for a ride."

"I forgot. She went out on Saturday afternoon."

"There's a witness who saw someone cycling on a mountain bike — while wearing a blue helmet — near the Brookford turnoff on Sunday morning."

"I mean Sunday," Bethany said. "It was on Sunday morning when she went cycling. I remember now."

"At a time when she was already dead? They know the exact time from her phone."

"Then your witness — if there even is one — must have seen another cyclist. It could have been anyone."

"And that hi-tech watch you always wear?"

"What about it?"

"It has a fitness tracker on it, too. And I'll bet that when the cops check it, they'll find an intense period of activity after eight fifty-seven on that Sunday morning that corresponds with a five-mile cycle between the quarry and your house."

"If it does, that's because I was exercising at home."

"The tracker can tell the difference between yoga and cycling — your heart rate would be different. Besides, it's got a built-in GPS tracker that will show exactly where you were."

Bethany's mouth fell open, then snapped shut. She stared down at the watch on her left wrist for a moment and then, quick as a flash, unfastened it and tossed it into the vat of sap behind her.

I dashed over to the tank and stuck my arm inside, trying

to grab the watch as it sank through the clear liquid, but it slipped through my fingers and dropped to the bottom. Cursing, I leaned over, stretching my arm and fingers to their limit.

Then solid ground disappeared beneath me as Bethany lifted my feet into the air, tipping me face-down into the tank. Keeping my head deep in the sap.

– 40 –

The rim of the tank dug painfully into my midriff as I thrashed around in the sap, trying to wriggle my feet loose of Bethany's tight grip. I kept my mouth clamped shut so I didn't accidentally gasp in the thin liquid, but already I was desperate for a breath of air. *Think!*

Relaxing my muscles, I slid deeper into the sap, braced my hands against the base of the vat, and pumped both feet back in a vicious kick, feeling the satisfying thud of impact beneath my heels. Immediately, my feet were released. I spun around in the tank and thrust my head up toward the surface, but hands covered my face and pushed down.

My lungs were burning. I needed to breathe.

I tried to peel the fingers off my face, but my short nails and the slippery liquid gave me no purchase. I flailed at the arms above me, banging at them, grabbing for her head, but her arms were longer than mine. I was running out of time. Black dots speckled my vision.

No! I was not going to drown again. I refused.

Opening my mouth wide, I bit down hard on the fingers

spread across my face. And was free. I broke the surface, coughing and gasping, sucking in deep breaths of air.

Soaked through with the sap, I climbed out of the tank like a monster emerging from the deep, dripping and trying to wipe my eyes clear. There was no sign of Bethany. I fished my phone out of my pocket and switched it on. A few wavy lines appeared on the screen, then it went dark.

Shit. So much for my plan to get hard evidence. I needed to turn this over to the cops and get myself someplace warm and dry.

Knowing the main office outside was locked, I checked the sugar shed for a phone but found nothing. Jim's office door was padlocked and didn't budge when I gave it a hard kick that sent pain reverberating into my knee. Fine. If I couldn't call for help, I'd go fetch it.

I trudged out of the shed, gasping as the arctic air hit the wet skin of my face and hands. I trotted over to my car and yanked on the door handle, but it didn't budge. I tried again, then cupped a hand around my eyes to peer inside. Vermont-style, I'd left the door unlocked and the keys in the ignition. Now the door was locked, and there was no sign of the keys.

Cursing Bethany hotly through cold lips, I rotated on the spot, wondering what to do. Her huge SUV was still in the lot, but a quick check revealed it, too, was locked, as was the door of the office block when I double-checked it. Where *was* she?

A movement in my peripheral vision caught my attention. There! A flash of red moved between the trees just beyond the lot. I set off at a run after her, needing to get my keys. Needing to get her phone.

Racing past the trees decked out for tourists, I ducked under the brightly colored buckets hanging from their trunks and sped deeper into the woods, stumbling over protruding roots and felled logs, weaving my way under and over the obstructing tapestry of plastic tubing and supporting rebar rods.

The woods were misty, silent and cold. Within minutes, I was freezing, my wet clothes no protection against the icy chill as I chased the patch of red moving always just ahead of me.

Go back.

Had Bethany shouted the words at me?

Go back!

No, they were inside my mind.

"Bethany, *Bethany*! Stop!" I shouted.

The figure ahead paused as though considering my words or waiting for me to catch up. But as I drew near, she took off again, darting between the trees.

Where did she think she was going? It was too far, surely, for her to run all the way through the woods to the highway beyond. Or was it? It was too far for *me* — would have been so even without the sodden clothes that weighed me down and would ensure I died of exposure before I ever reached help. But Bethany was fit and strong and wearing dry all-weather gear. Only her wrists and hands might be wet. When drowning me in the tank had failed, she'd come up with a plan B — to lure me into the woods because she knew that here she could outwit, outlast and outlive me. We were in our very own game of Survivor, and I'd played right into her hands. *Stupid!*

No doubt as soon as I was deep enough in the woods to lose any sense of direction, she'd pick up the pace and disappear from view, circle back to the office and wait until she was sure I'd frozen to death before summoning the cops with some cock-and-bull story about my car in the lot. Then again, she had my keys. She could simply drive my Honda somewhere else and abandon it there, distance herself from my disappearance. The strategy had worked for her before.

Go back.

The words were in my brain again, and this time, I understood. They were a warning — from Colby.

Shivering uncontrollably, eyes and nose streaming from the cold, I turned on the spot, gazing desperately at the trees and gossamer mist that surrounded me on all sides. I could see no sign of the sugar works and had no idea which way to walk. I had an idea that we'd moved in a circular path through the woods and were now near the top of one of the many hills that studded the forest, so I needed to go downhill, but on which side of this knoll?

My brain felt dull and slow with cold, like the wheels and cogs of my mind were freezing up and grinding to a standstill. My fingers ached, and my lungs — as I stood panting, doubled over with my hands on my knees — felt raw. I could taste blood.

And I was just so tired. Tired of running and of thinking.

What I needed more than anything was to rest, just for a minute or two. That would help me catch my breath and gather my wits. I slumped against a tree, slid down the trunk and sat on the soft mulch beneath. I yawned, and the juddering of my arms and legs subsided for a few precious seconds. There — I was feeling better already.

Go back!

"Sure. Just gimme a few minutes," I told Colby.
And then I closed my eyes.

– 41 –

The voice in my head wouldn't shut up.

Go back.

"Gimme a break, Colby."

Gobackgobackgoback!

"I don't know which way, okay?"

I struggled to open my eyes and look around, just in case the specter of Colby had appeared to guide me down to warmth and safety. The mist was closing in, clouding the trees in a shroud of white. Or was it my mind that was fading and blurring as it slid into the sleep that beckoned?

Lines. Lines.

I yawned deeply, then yawned again. "What lines?"

Go back … lines!

I snuggled into a ball against the base of the trunk, then shot up straight as the meaning of the words penetrated the confused fog of my mind. The lines. I could follow the lines of plastic tubing down the hill — they would all ultimately lead to the sugar shack.

Using my last reserves of willpower, I forced myself to my knees. Then, hanging onto the tree trunk, I dragged myself up onto my feet. I staggered to the nearest length of tubing and began walking downhill beside it, holding the line and letting my hand ride over the forked iron supports.

When my sore knee buckled beneath me, I tortured myself with pitiful images of my parents weeping over my frozen body. I couldn't do that to them. When I tripped and fell face-first into a bank of snow and longed to stay there, I lured myself back to my feet with promises of hot coffee and log fires and steaming baths. And all the way down the slope, I talked to myself, aloud or inside my head, I hardly knew the difference by then.

"Do you want Ryan Jackson to know how stupid you are? Well, do ya, punk? And Capshaw — think of how she'll react."

I could imagine Capshaw shaking her head over my frosty corpse, muttering sagely about things being bound to end badly when kooky-ass amateurs stuck their noses into police business, and telling Ryan he'd been a fool ever to involve me.

"Keep walking!" I told myself and added the promise of a giant Johnny Walker to the rewards that waited for me back at the sugar works.

I imagined what that smoky imp of a reporter at *The Bugle* would write about my fate and whether they'd publish a photo of my body. By now, I probably resembled a Sasquatch what with all the bark, dead leaves, twigs and dirt that clung to my wet, sticky clothes. I kept plodding.

"And Bethany, do you want her to get away with murder again? Think of lovely Laini. Do it for the Lanes." I laughed, more than a little hysterical now.

I pictured Darcy and Lizzie, hungry and alone, and took another step. And another.

Strangely, what gave me the most motivation was the thought of Michelle Armstrong's reaction. Until that very moment, half-dead and crazed with cold, bouncing off trees like a pinball off bumpers and cursing at the showers of snow that fell on top of me, I hadn't realized how much I despised her. My faltering mind painted a hazy vision of Pitchford's Town Clerk holding forth at my funeral, delivering a regretful address to the gathered handful of mourners, her face an appropriate mask of sadness, while on the inside her black, hypocritical heart danced a gleeful jig of triumph. She'd be able to get back to spin-doctoring the virtues of Pitchford without me inconveniently dredging up murders.

Fury, I now discovered — as Bethany had ten days ago — could be the most powerful motivator of all. Over my dead body, literally, would I cede the field to the likes of Michelle Armstrong.

But that was likely to happen unless I got to a shelter soon. Watching where I placed my feet and focusing on moving them faster, I walked headfirst into a bucket. Looking up, I saw I'd reached the pretty section of the forest that Bethany — or had it been Laini? — had set up for tourists. Beaded with dew, the pastel buckets and metal spiles glimmered in the dull light, and I could see the vague shadows of buildings hulking in the shifting mist beyond.

Almost there. I was *almost* there.

A thrashing in the undergrowth behind me made me spin around. Eyes mad with fury, Bethany Ford was racing toward me, one of the heavy rebar stakes in her grasp. I threw my arms up in front of my face as she raised her weapon to bring it down on my head and cried out in pain as the rod glanced off my arm and crashed into my shoulder.

Hoisting the rod, Bethany came at me again. But I lunged forward and grabbed the bar with both hands. We wrestled for possession, twisting and tugging, grunting with exertion. Then Bethany wrenched it toward her, yanking me off-balance, before immediately thrusting it back at me, sending me sprawling backward. With my arms flung wide for balance, I slammed into the unyielding bulk of an enormous tree, the splayed fingers of my right hand landing on the steel spile lodged in the trunk.

Bethany rushed at me, holding the rod like a spear she intended to drive through my chest, and pin me to the tree. I dodged sideways. My fingers closed around the metal tap. Twisted it free. Dropping my left shoulder, I turned and thrust the sharp end of the steel spile into the side of her neck.

Her momentum carried her forward a few paces, then she folded, sagging to her knees, letting the rod fall from her hands. She reached a hand up to the left side of her neck, where a line of blood trickled out of the tap, stippling the snow beside her with flecks of red.

"No, don't!" I cried, reaching to bat away her hand, struggling to comprehend that it was me who'd stuck the thing into her. "If you pull it out, you'll bleed to death."

She might well bleed to death anyway.

"Wait!" I crouched down beside her, pulled off one of her gloves and with trembling fingers, stuffed a finger of leather into the spout, packing it closed as best I could. Then I placed her hand against the spile, pushing gently. "Hold it there. Keep the pressure."

I patted her pockets, found her phone and dialed 911. Bethany's face drained of color as she swayed on her knees and then crumpled, slumping sideways into my lap, her mouth opening and closing soundlessly as her wide blue eyes stared up at me.

– 42 –

Bethany's face, as she lay in the hospital bed, was bare of its usual makeup, and pale apart from the shadows — dark as plums — beneath her eyes. Once again, she was wearing Laini's midnight-blue kimono. Her neck was bandaged and protected by a brace that prevented her from turning her neck. With a little luck, she'd still be able to move it once the brace came off.

According to her attending physician, the spile had "penetrated the sternocleidomastoid muscle, posterior to both the jugular vein and carotid artery, missing the trachea, hyoid and larynx to the front and approaching but not impacting any of the cervical vertebrae or spinous processes toward the rear. Very neatly done," he'd added, looking impressed at my handiwork.

Ryan Jackson and Ronnie Capshaw had been considerably less impressed. Ryan, infuriated, had called me reckless, stupid and a danger to society before insisting I get myself checked out at the Randolph County Hospital ER. But he'd also hugged me tightly, and I could've sworn his eyes were moist when he threatened to murder me if I ever got myself killed. Capshaw had merely lifted one eyebrow, turned down one corner of her mouth, and directed a scathing look at me.

"Message received," I told her, punctuating my words with a smart salute. She didn't smile.

My parents hadn't smiled either, even though I'd given them a highly edited version of my adventure, making it sound like I'd clumsily tumbled into a vat of sap and Bethany had accidentally obstructed my path to air before she and I had gone for a stroll in the pretty woods on a balmy day, during which, by sheer chance, she'd fallen onto a sharp object I'd happened to be holding.

I'd said nothing — to anybody — about how Colby's messages had saved my life. It would have thoroughly overexcited my mother, and Capshaw or the medical staff would've called for a psych consult. I wasn't sure how Ryan would've reacted.

"For God's sake, kiddo, this has to stop!" my father said, when he and Mom came to get me from the ER. His hair was standing in different directions and his shirt was buttoned up wrong.

"I did tell you," was my mother's reaction, after she'd squeezed me hard enough to make me wince, forced a gemstone into my hand — "Seraphinite, for healing!" — and slipped a bottle of homeopathic arnica into my pocket, glancing around nervously, like a dealer slipping me some weed.

"Tell me what?"

"Deceit, danger, enemies and expanding consciousness! The Moon card, remember?"

We were back to the lobster of intuition.

Now, two days after I'd confronted Bethany and stabbed

her, the dust was settling. I'd given a brief preliminary statement to the police, Bethany's surgery had gone well, *The Bugle* had published one article on her arrest which made zero mention of me, and another on the arrest of Ned Lipton which speculated pruriently about just what he'd seen and done as he lolled around in my attic, making it sound more like a sexy peep-show than a criminal violation.

The impulse to visit Bethany that morning was motivated more from a desire to assuage my unwarranted guilt by checking she was okay, rather than an altruistic urge to delight her with my company. Still, I'd brought grapes.

When I found Ryan and Ronnie Capshaw already in her room, I offered to return later, but Ryan said, "Stay. Maybe you can fill in some of the gaps."

Capshaw directed an incredulous look his way.

He ignored it.

I grinned.

"So …" Ryan said, glancing down at his notebook. "Where were we?"

"Laini was leaving," Bethany said, her voice tired and resigned.

She knew she was nailed. The cops had obtained search warrants for her house, business and technology, including any data stored in the cloud. It turned out that her Apple Watch would have been syncing regularly with an app on her phone and automatically updating to the cloud. So, basically, my swim in the sap and subsequent adventures in the woods had been entirely unnecessary.

I hadn't known, but cops are allowed to lie to suspects in

order to get a confession, and they'd lied to Bethany. First, they'd told her that my phone's recording of the conversation between her and me in the sugar shack had been updating to the cloud in real time, and that the recording still existed. Next, they'd told her that, using a new hi-tech method, forensics had succeeded in lifting her prints off the note. And finally they'd said that the lab in Burlington had confirmed the presence of her DNA on it, too. That last bit might still turn out to be true, but the results weren't in yet. In any event, confronted with the "evidence," Bethany had confessed.

Of course, they also had her for the assault and attempted murder of me.

"Leaving Pitchford? Or Vermont?" Ryan asked.

"She was planning on buying the earliest ticket out of the States."

"Where to?"

Again, I saw that image of olive groves glittering silver in the golden sun.

"To Spain," I said.

Bethany flashed me a sharp glance.

"How did you know that?"

"Lucky guess," I said. "It was one of the places she'd marked on the globe in her office."

Bethany seemed satisfied by my explanation, but I was aware of Capshaw's shrewd gaze fixed on me.

"Laini said she'd had enough of fir trees and maple syrup and snow. She wanted sunshine, oranges and olives. It was laughable!" Bethany rolled her eyes and twisted her mouth in contempt. "She turns thirty-nine and immediately has a midlife crisis. So pathetically predictable. She wanted to chuck it all and do what — go eat, pray and love Spaniards?"

"Such a cliché," I murmured, remembering the words spoken at the top of the quarry in my vision.

"Yes, a ridiculous cliché," Bethany said, seeming surprised that I understood so well.

"You tried to persuade her to stay?" Ryan asked.

"Of course. I spent that night trying to reason with her, telling her she was being a fool, because despite her promises, I knew she wouldn't come back. After Andalusia, she'd go on to Turkey or Thailand or Timbuktu. She never went back to any place she'd lived. She used to say that you can't step in the same river twice. So, I begged her to reconsider, to sleep on it and we'd chat again the next day."

The machine beside me, which was connected to a pulse meter on Bethany's finger, gave off a series of rapid beeps. I moved to the other side of the room, and it resumed normal functioning.

"You were saying about asking Laini to reconsider," I prompted Bethany.

"Yes. Well, the next morning, she said that I was right. I was so relieved, so *happy*. I thought she meant I was right about choosing to stay, but she only meant that a night's rest had done her good and helped her realize her decision to go was the right one. She'd book her ticket immediately and be out of my hair within a day. 'Out of my hair' — those were the actual words she used," Bethany said, sounding like she still couldn't believe it.

"You suggested the two of you go for a drive early that morning?" Ryan said.

"To town, for breakfast. She said it would be her treat."

"So that's why she took her handbag," I said. "And you encouraged her to cycle back?"

"That was her idea. She wanted a last cycle to say goodbye to Vermont before she kicked it in the teeth." Bethany's face twisted into a sour grimace.

"You took the note of apology she'd given you with the flowers. Rereading it, you realized it could work as a suicide note," Ryan said.

Bethany rubbed at her temple with a knuckle as if to ease away an inner ache. She was still wearing the pink nail polish I'd seen in my visions of the hand holding the blue paper. Laini, as Ryan had told me in my call to him on Tuesday, hadn't been wearing any nail polish on the day of her death.

"So, you folded the note, then folded it again and tucked it into the pocket of your black denims," I said.

In my visions, I'd seen a woman's hand tucking the blue note into the pocket of black pants, and wrongly assumed it was Laini. But she, planning on cycling back to Bethany's house, had been wearing black Lycra pants, with no pockets.

Bethany frowned at me. "How do you know what I was wearing?"

"And then you drove her to the quarry?" Ryan interjected quickly.

"*She* drove."

"How did you persuade her to hike up to the top?"

"For a look at the view. I told her she just *had* to see it before she left, because it was the best viewpoint in Pitchford. She'd never been, so she didn't know any different."

"And on the way up, you asked to borrow her phone, saying you'd forgotten yours at home? You sent yourself and Carl those texts, making it look like Laini was buying time to decide whether she really wanted to die. But you were actually buying time for yourself, time to cycle home and provide a reason why you didn't immediately alert anyone when Laini failed to return from a quick drive into town to buy donuts," Ryan said. "You'd deliberately left your phone at home so that it looked like you were there if we checked cellphone tower records afterwards. After sending the texts, you put on your gloves, wiped your fingerprints off the phone and handed it back to her. And when you got home, you sent Laini a reply to 'her' text to you."

"What did the reply say?" I asked.

"I can't remember the exact words," Ryan said. "Ronnie?"

Without consulting any notes, Capshaw quoted the message. "Do you think that's wise, Laini? You know how Carl gets. Leave at once if he gets violent."

More muddying of the waters, more redirection of suspicion. If Bethany had known about Denise's theft of company funds, she'd no doubt have pointed investigations in that direction, too. I'd decided against telling anyone about Denise's actions, but I *had* sent her a text message — user ID withheld — telling her that I knew she'd stolen the money, and that I'd be watching her carefully from now on.

"Of course, your reply was sent a long time after Laini's text was received on your phone," Ryan said.

"An hour and a half later," Capshaw confirmed.

"But that couldn't be helped. You could always say you'd

missed the message from her initially. Let's return to what happened at the top of the quarry," Ryan said.

"You argued with Laini," I told Bethany. "You tried to make her understand how you felt."

Bethany sighed, trailing her fingers across the blue silk of Laini's kimono.

"How did she react?" Ryan asked.

"She laughed. Laughed! But it wasn't funny. She was ruining my business, hurting Carl, breaking my heart," Bethany said, her voice catching in her throat.

And for the first time, I saw that Bethany truly believed she'd loved Laini. That maybe she'd even been *in love* with her, perhaps even obsessed with her. If I'd seen it sooner, I would have suspected her sooner; when woman kill, they usually kill an intimate partner and usually for reasons of love and hate.

"You pushed Laini over the edge," Ryan continued.

"Yes. I mean, I didn't intend to, I just saw red and it happened. It's not like it was premeditated."

"Yes, it was," I said. "The note, the bike, the texts — it was all planned."

Bethany sent me a look filled with deep hatred. I had the sense that if she could've moved, she would've beaten me over the head with her IV stand.

"You ran down to her car in the parking lot. You left the note in her purse after you'd rubbed it all over with a rag or a tissue or something, smudging any prints. Then you cycled back to your house," Ryan said.

"That woman in the police station?" I said to Capshaw. "The one complaining about cyclists not wearing the proper reflective gear? She's your witness. The cyclist was Bethany here."

"Oh?" said Capshaw, clearly surprised.

I was petty enough to take delight in getting one over on her, and because you can't have enough of a good thing, I added, "And somewhere at Bethany's house, you'll find a paper recycling pile which you should check, because you may just find a blue envelope, addressed to Bethany in Laini's handwriting. It will probably have traces of pollen on it from stargazer lilies. You may find those same pink lilies on the compost heap, and if you check with the florist in town, you'll probably discover that Laini purchased a bunch on the morning of Saturday, March tenth."

Three pairs of eyes stared at me, amazed. Then Ryan cleared his throat and said to Bethany, "Then you returned the bike to the sugar works and went home to wait."

"Was it you who threw all those flowers into the quarry a few days later?" I asked.

"Who else?" Bethany said. "I loved her best."

I shook my head. "That's not love — holding onto someone, keeping them nearby because it's what *you* want, because it serves your needs. That's possession. Love is wanting the best for the other person, even when it costs you, even if it means letting them go," I said, and blushed for my hypocrisy, because wasn't that exactly what I was doing with Colby?

Bethany closed her eyes as though to block me out, but didn't respond. In the silence that filled the room, the memory of Laini blossomed. Her beauty, her blithe indifference to the obsessions and ambitions of others, her kind heart and merry laugh. And even pragmatic, hard-headed, tough-minded Ronnie Capshaw seemed to feel it.

"How could you do it?" she asked in a low, gruff voice. "Just snuff out her life like that? Such a waste …"

"*Waste?*" Bethany snarled, snapping her eyes open and surprising me with the ferocity of her tone. "Don't talk to me about waste. Laini didn't need any help wasting her life — she did that all by herself! Over and over again, wasting whatever and whoever came her way. She had everything anybody could want — beauty, money, popularity, love. *Everything!* It all came so easily to her, and she let it go just as easily." Bethany held her hands out, spreading her fingers, as though letting treasures slip from her grasp into a flowing stream. "It was unbelievable how everyone fell under her spell. And she didn't need it, often didn't even notice it. And they wanted her all the more because of that."

"We always want most what we can't have," I said softly. "We only chase the ones who run."

"I could have accepted it if she used what she was given, but she just wasted it. In the pageants, she had enough beauty and charm to go to the very top, but she simply stopped competing," Bethany said, her voice harsh with resentment and envy. "She had intelligence but quit her degree. She had the love of a good man, a life in Colorado, with money and a shot at a family, and she waltzed away from it all. She had a vital role in the business I'd spent years and years building up, and all the opportunities that lay ahead, but she was perfectly happy to let that all slide. She had Carl, but she threw him away." Bethany stopped for a moment and swallowed hard before continuing in a low, throaty tone. "And me. She had me — my love, my friendship, my hope and happiness. But it all meant less to her than a new adventure. She wasted it all." Bethany's glance slid to the window, and her gaze took on a distant quality, as though she was seeing something very far away. "She wasted me."

Epilogue

I watched Kennick Carter scatter Laini's ashes via live streaming on Facebook. He did it in Santa Ana, not Spain — either the life insurance money hadn't come through yet, or the lure of the nearby Santa Anita racetrack was too strong — but at least there were olive trees and sunshine. And Kennick told me Laini had never been to California, so I reckoned she would have approved of being in a new place.

It would have been lovely if the four winds lifted her ashes up into the air, but it was a still day there, so the gray dust merely fell where it was strewn — on grass and earth and the reaching roots of gnarled tree trunks. The winds would come, though, sooner or later, and the rains. And then Laini would be everywhere and nowhere, as perhaps she'd always wanted.

Kennick had tears streaming down his face as he said goodbye to his sister. So did I. My mother, who'd watched with me, was surprisingly dry-eyed.

"Laini's in the arms of the Goddess, now," she said. "You did good, Garnet."

"I guess."

I'd helped to find a murderer, and I had to believe it mattered that justice would be served, but it didn't change the fact that the bright spot of beauty and color that was Laini was still gone from the world. And there was the undeniable fact that I'd also inadvertently done damage — to Ryan's reputation, Jim's bones and Bethany's neck. It wasn't clear what would happen to the Sweet 'n Smoky syrup business, though I guessed Bethany would try to sell it as a going concern — she could hardly run it from behind bars. I could only hope that the people who worked there would get to keep their jobs.

"You *did*," my mother insisted. "You cracked the case."

"I guess," I said again.

I thought I might, just might, have cracked something more personal, too. From the time I died, I'd been confused about who I was. The pendulum of my identity had swung from my old rational, logical self to this new intuitive, risky me, and I'd struggled to integrate the two sides. I still didn't know how to do that, or whether it was even possible, but maybe it was enough for now that the two sides coexisted within me. Like my eyes did. I had one brown and one blue eye — they didn't match, they shouldn't occur in the same face, but they did. And although they were unusual and freaked people out a little, they still worked.

I no longer wanted to be rid of my psychic abilities. There was no doubt that without them, I wouldn't have solved Laini's murder. Heck, I wouldn't even have suspected that it *was* a murder. My gift — as unpredictable and exasperating as it was — had value. If I could learn how to use it better, then I could, just maybe, use it to help people.

"What will you do now, dear?" Mom asked, brushing my fingers away from my mouth. Some aspects of me, unfortunately, hadn't changed.

"I'm back to Boston next week." I'd finally finished and submitted my thesis. "Any day now I should get feedback and suggestions back from Professor Perry, and then I'll get stuck into revisions."

"And after you graduate? What will you keep yourself busy with then?"

I tickled Lizzie's fuzzy stomach with my foot, thinking about my future. My phone pinged, and I checked to see who'd sent me a message. *Skeptical Singh. G-Man.*

"Buttons," I said, opening the text and reading it.

"What's that, dear?" my mother asked.

"Buttons. And button men."

Dear Reader,

I hope you enjoyed this novel! If you loved this book, I'd really appreciate it if you'd leave a review, no matter how short, wherever you bought it or on Goodreads. Every review is valuable in helping other readers discover the book.

Visit my website (www.joannemacgregor.com) to join my VIP Readers' Group and get my monthly newsletter, with advance notice of my latest releases, competitions, giveaways and offers for free review copies, as well as a behind-the-scenes peek at my writing process. I won't clutter your inbox or spam you, and I will never share your email address with anyone.

I'd love to hear from you! Come say hi on Facebook (@JoanneMacg), Twitter (@JoanneMacg) or Instagram (joannemacgregor_author), or reach out to me via my website (www.joannemacgregor.com/contact) and I'll do my best to get back to you.

– Jo Macgregor

Other books for adults by this author

The First Time I Died
Dark Whispers

Acknowledgements

My thanks to my editor, Chase Night, and to my fabulous beta readers, Emily Macgregor, Nicola Long, Edyth Bulbring and Heather Gordon for all their invaluable feedback — I'm so sorry you always get to read my books in their raw, unfinished state! I'm also grateful to my expert Vermont reader Cameron Garriepy and to Dr. Stephanie Erin Hart for helping me with the medical details. You all help improve my writing immeasurably, and I deeply appreciate each one of you!

Made in the USA
Columbia, SC
01 February 2021

32160533R00200